WHOSE BABY?

"When an infant is left on a particular gentleman's doorstep," her father said sternly, "it generally signifies one thing."

"Oh, Papa," Madeleine said, scandalized. "You can't think the child is *his.*"

"Have you looked at that infant? Really looked?"

"Many people have fair hair and blue eyes," she replied. "This is England, may I remind you, not Spain or China!"

"Don't try me, child," her father replied. "The moment I discover that infant is his, we are quit from here. I shall not allow my daughter to join with a man who would do such a thing. I had rather consign you to a convent!"

"A convent!" Madeleine cried. "But we're not even Catholic!"

Her father went on as if he had not heard her. "It seems senseless to remain here," he insisted, turning to his wife. "I suggest we leave today, before Madeleine's affections become engaged."

Madeleine's heart sank. "I'm afraid it's too late for that Papa."

Her father stared. "Oh, Madeleine," he said quietly.

"Oh, Madeleine!" exclaimed her mother, smiling and clapping her hands.

Books by Marcy Stewart

CHARITY'S GAMBIT
MY LORD FOOTMAN
LORD MERLYN'S MAGIC
DARBY'S ANGEL
THE VISCOUNT TAKES A WIFE
LADY SCANDAL

"An Indefinite Wedding" in
FLOWERS FOR THE BRIDE
"Lady Constance Wins" in LORDS AND LADIES
"A Halo for Mr. Devlin" in
SEDUCTIVE AND SCANDALOUS
"The Enchanted Bride" in MY DARLING BRIDE

Published by Zebra Books

THE BRIDEGROOM AND THE BABY

Marcy Stewart

Zebra Books
Kensington Publishing Corp.

http://www.zebrabooks.com

ZEBRA BOOKS are published by

Kensington Publishing Corp.
850 Third Avenue
New York, NY 10022

First Printing: June, 1999
10 9 8 7 6 5 4 3 2 1

Printed in the United States of America

For my editor,
Tracy Bernstein,
with appreciation

And special thanks to
Peggy Jocher

One

"Here's to marriage," said the viscount, Ethan Ambrose, and downed his brandy with a shudder. Slamming the glass to the bar, he signaled the tavern keeper with a scowl and a peremptory wave. "Another one, Jack, exactly like the last!"

"Hear, hear!" encouraged the shorter of the viscount's two companions, George Redding, who also raised his glass.

Moving slowly, the sad-eyed tavern keeper brought the required bottle and poured, serving milord first, then the stout fellow with the receding hairline to his left. When he reached the third gentleman, Scott Brandt, the young man shook his head.

"Someone's got to keep the horses on the road," he said, by way of explanation.

"Yes, and I'm the one to do it," declared Lord Ambrose.

"Not tonight, you're not," Brandt said darkly.

Golden eyebrows slanted downward as the viscount weaved closer to the speaker. He was not accustomed to drowning himself to such an extent, or hadn't been until recently. Of late he had discovered this path led to forgetfulness and the cessation of pain, at least for a time; and tonight, he needed to numb his memory more than ever. Therefore, he could not like the scolding tone in his friend's voice. Did he fancy himself to be his nursemaid?

"Are you implying that I'm *foxed*?"

"Did you hear me say so?" Brandt sent the tavern keeper a warning look, and the owner nodded slightly. "Jack's wanting to close, my lord."

"*Is* he?" Lord Ambrose turned unsteadily and examined the room in surprise. The whitewashed walls, stained with years of soot and grime, the crude supporting timbers, even the familiar cobwebs in the corners were shadowed in gloom. That, he thought sluggishly and with a sudden desire to laugh, was undoubtedly because none of the candles on the tables were lit. Aside from themselves, the room was empty. Perhaps he should think of going.

No.

"I'm getting married," he said, swinging back to the bar and jiggling his glass. "Calls for a celebration."

"There won't be any reason to celebrate if you don't please Miss Murrow's parents."

"What's not to please?" The viscount extended his arms expansively, a man waiting to be measured by his tailor. Feeling the room sway. he quickly clutched the bar.

"Ho, the vanities!" shouted George with a laugh.

"No vanity," Lord Ambrose said in injured tones, leaning against the scarred wooden surface of the bar. "I meant only that I walk, I talk, I breathe, I'm male. What else could Miss Madeleine Murrow require?"

"Don't forget the title," George added.

Brandt lowered a disapproving look. "This is no way to speak of the lady who may become the viscountess."

Knowing his friend was correct did nothing to ease the viscount's mood. After all, Scott had the advantage of freedom, unlike himself, who must stoop to marketing his title to the wealthiest heiress he could find for the sake of his ancestral home. How tasteless it all seemed; how diminished it made him feel—especially when he considered the kind of woman his potential wife must be to accept such a liaison. He had never believed himself to be a dewy-eyed romantic, nor had he given much thought to marriage in the past; yet it didn't seem too much to ask that he have at least a *fondness* for his betrothed. He had only met Miss Murrow briefly; he didn't know anything about her, excepting she was rich.

And that was all that mattered, in the end; he must keep his promise.

"What do you know of how I should speak?" he grumbled. "You've never set eyes on her."

"And you've only met her the one time. How clear an impression can be made during a weekend in the country?"

"Not much of one, apparently," Ethan answered, drawing watery circles with his glass on the wood. "I was impressed with her brownness. Brown hair, brown eyes, olive-brown skin that declares too much time outdoors." He swung his head in Scott's direction. "Just like you, old fellow."

George crowed. "Give over, Ethan! Tell me she don't look like Scotty, please!"

"Not that bad, perhaps, but then she doesn't have his sparkling personality, either."

"Scotty? Sparkling?" George slammed his fists on the bar, his round cheeks twisted in merriment. "What have you done, Ethan? If she's the antidote you say, why ever are you going through with it?"

The viscount became motionless. "Can it be you don't know?"

"He knows," Scott said in a quiet voice, and tugged at the viscount's arm. "Come, my lord. Let's be off, now."

Ethan shrugged away Brandt's hand and lifted his glass. "Another, Jack." In the doing, he caught sight of himself in the mirror behind the bar. Raw grief sliced through him, so hurtful he wanted to cry aloud.

Would the wound never heal?

When the tavern-keeper acceded to his demand, the viscount raised his glass to his image.

"To Lucan," he said.

His friends followed the line of his vision, their faces sobering. As one, they signaled for Jack to fill their glasses and joined the viscount in toasting the mirror, echoing solemnly, "To Lucan."

At that moment, Miss Madeleine Murrow was staring into the cold darkness through the windows of her father's coach-and-four with growing distress. Antonia Murrow, her mother, lay in a half-reclining position on the bench opposite herself and her father, Thomas; even with two pillows beneath her head and a blanket around her shoulders, she appeared dreadfully uncomfortable, and Madeleine could not bear to see her pale suffering any longer.

Her mother moved then, her skirts rustling as she searched for a better position. A soft, unwilling groan came from her throat. Madeleine's gaze swerved from her mother to her father.

"Papa, please, can we not stop?"

"What would you have us do, child? Sleep beneath a tree?"

She heard the impatience in his voice and knew it for what it was. He felt guilty for not stopping earlier as her mother had suggested. No, he had said, they were through Wilts; it was only a few miles more to Somersetshire, the village of Brillham, and Lord Ambrose's estate. Antonia would be much more comfortable there than in a flea-infested inn. But he had not taken into account the possibility they might throw a wheel, or that one of the horses could go lame. Or that their driver would fall ill, as was the case. Every mile or two Lindon would draw the horses to a halt and run for the woods. Something he ate, he'd explained after the first stop, his face pasty-looking as he called up to his master.

She had asked her father if he could not drive the coach. "We'd still have to stop for Lindon," he had said. "Unless you think we should leave him on the side of the road."

Her father had meant it for the best, extending their

journey. Sometimes she wished it wasn't so easy for her to understand how others felt and thought. She wished she could get angry occasionally and stamp her foot like headstrong heroines in novels.

Bettina, her sister and dearest friend, had been like that. She had had no difficulty becoming angry, because her decisions were made at the drop of an eyelash, and truly, she never understood anything. How her eyes would flash, her cheeks flush crimson, and the tart words fall off her tongue! The gentlemen had loved her for her fire and her spirit.

Poor Bettina.

Warm tears came to Madeleine's eyes. She blinked them away before either of her parents noticed.

"Let's see if I cannot help you rest more easy, my dear," Thomas said, addressing his wife. He slipped to the other seat, carefully pulling her into his lap. "Better?"

"Much," Antonia said with a weak smile.

In the darkness of the coach, Madeleine gazed at her parents, her eyes becoming moist again. She lifted her head and pretended to be fascinated by the carriage's satin ceiling. Her mother must not suspect her heart's heaviness—that she was dreading, rather than looking forward to, this sojourn at Lord Ambrose's estate.

Recalling their meeting two months ago at the Tates' red brick manse in Hampshire, she stifled a sigh. Lord Tate, during one of his many walks with her father, had happily supplied the history of the young viscount. Although not a man to invest overmuch importance to the peerage, her father had nevertheless been impressed with Ambrose's impeccable bloodlines. Her mother, soft-hearted lady that she was, thought the viscount handsome and interesting-looking.

Madeleine believed him to be the coldest creature she had ever met.

Perhaps he would prove to be otherwise, but she hardly cared one way or the other. She harbored no illusions that love and romance awaited her at Westhall, but she hoped

marriage did. It was the only gift she could offer her
mother, and offer it she would—before it was too late.

"Let go," said the viscount, and jerked free of Scott's
supporting arm. "D'you think I'm a child? I can very well
walk by myself."

His companion stood aside, bowed, and swept one arm
outward as if to say, *proceed.* Lord Ambrose nodded once
and straightened his waistcoat. The gesture was meant to
straighten his dignity as well, since Scott seemed to doubt
it so much.

Perhaps they had closed the doors of the Yellow Talon
two hours later than usual. And what if he did drink
deeper than normal. That didn't mean he couldn't handle his liquor. He had stayed on his horse, hadn't he, all
the way to George's house and now his own?

Ethan watched the groom lead their horses toward the
stable and felt a shiver of admiration for his black, Viking;
what a proud piece of horseflesh he was, dancing and tossing his mane like a debutante at her first ball. The Ambrose
stable once held many such fine beasts. He might have lost
all but the nags, but at least he'd kept Viking. Truth was,
he'd sooner sacrifice the house than lose him.

Scott was still bent in his bow, looking impatient. Ethan
stepped boldly toward the front doors of his home. After
three paces, he felt his knees buckle. Brandt, blast him,
had his arms out before total disaster occurred. The viscount glared at him. Scott glared back, his face only inches
away.

Ethan began to laugh.

He was still laughing when Burns opened the door,
shards of disapproval in his small, hard eyes. He continued to laugh as butler and friend dragged him up the
stairs. He tried to help, but his legs would not step high
enough, and that struck him as even more amusing.

When they reached the first-floor landing, his two assis-
tants propped him against the wall to catch their breath.

Ethan began to slide downward and gasped helplessly as they lunged to stop him. Gads, if Lucan could see him now—his legs were limp as cloth!

Quick as a lightning bolt, his merriment dissolved.

He lowered his eyes. From here he could see through the balustrade to the entrance hall. The front door stood open; Burns must have been too busy helping him to close it. With interest, he registered the sound of heavy wheels crunching on gravel.

Scott's expression sharpened like a hunter coming to point. "Is that a carriage?"

"So it would seem," Burns said in his death-toll's voice, each syllable dragging as if pulling a ball and chain.

They behaved so gravely. What could be serious about company arriving?

"Who—who's there?" Ethan sang the words, pretending to be frightened. Laughter sputtered back to life.

"Quickly!" Scott shouldered his weight, as did Burns, both of the men dragging him down the corridor to his bedchamber. Ethan couldn't help noticing his boots were making waves in the threadbare runner. That, too, was funny.

"Brutes," he said, when they pitched him onto his bed. A sack of potatoes would receive gentler treatment. He struggled upward. "Should greet my guests."

"You're not going anywhere." Scott turned to Burns. "Do what you must, man, to see to them. I'll take care of him."

One might think Brandt were the master and not himself, Ethan reflected as he watched the butler walk from the room. "I am the viscount," he declared. "I will . . ." He could not remember what he was going to say. Oh, yes. "I will see to my guests."

"Quiet, idiot." Brandt pulled at Ethan's coat, throwing it into a heap on the floor. When he began to unbutton his waistcoat, Lord Ambrose slapped his hands away and sat up.

"You . . . are being too familiar." How he could make himself laugh! "I will do this myself."

"Hurry up, then, and pray to God that's not your future wife and her family downstairs. If they see you like this . . . are you certain you can get yourself into bed and stay there?"

His friend looked worried enough for the two of them. Ethan waved him onward. "Make yourself easy. I'll be *perfectly* fine."

"I'd best go down and see how Burns is handling things, then. If it is the Murrow family, I'll tell them you're ill."

Scott closed the door when he left. Ethan felt suddenly cut off, and rebellion crossed his mind. He would go downstairs. It was his house, after all; at least for the present. He scowled; he plucked at his waistcoat for an indefinite length of time. He could not remember if he was supposed to button or unbutton.

A wave of dryness passed over him, and he began to perspire. Scott would not lie to the Murrows; he *was* ill. Ethan reached for the bedside table and the chamber pot hidden within. As he did, he lost his balance and tumbled to the floor, the empty vessel rolling madly to crash and shatter against the wall.

"What was that?" Madeleine asked.

Mr. Brandt sent her a gracious smile. "What was what, Miss Murrow?"

"That noise. It sounded like a thump, then glass breaking."

"A . . . thump?" His gaze drifted from one corner of the entrance hall to the other, as if expecting to find a noise in the massive, faded tapestry hanging from the gallery or perhaps in the suit of armor guarding the stairs.

"Yes. I believe it came from the first floor."

He appeared to be at a loss. There was no need to look to her parents for confirmation; the butler had already ushered them into the library, where he was hastily building a fire. Only she had lagged behind, awed by the proportions and austerity of this narrow but extraordinarily high hall. It arched all the way to the roofline and was crisscrossed with wooden beams, like a miniature cathedral.

The slender gentleman at her side had politely remained with her as she stared. Now, it was he who held her attention, and she gazed at him with undisguised curiosity. He could not have missed hearing that sound, unless he was deaf, which he certainly was not; he had introduced himself and conversed with them too prettily for that. Why did he pretend?

"I only mention it in case Lord Ambrose might have broken something or—need help," she said.

A guarded look came into his eyes. "How kind of you to worry so."

"You said he was ill," she reminded him.

"Yes, of course. If he needs anything, he will let us know."

Somewhat mystified, she gave him a small smile. There was no use discussing the sound further; it mattered little, anyway. Still, she studied him covertly as they walked to join her parents. He owned a compelling attractiveness, she thought; golden eyes, lean features, and brown hair too shaggy for fashion; she wondered if he'd allowed a Brutus cut to grow long. She liked his tan jacket in a soft wool that begged to be stroked, although she would never dare do such a thing.

Who was he? Why was he here? She could not wait to find out, although she must be discreet in her inquiries. Her father was forever saying her curiosity put others on the defensive, and she supposed he was right. If only she didn't find people so compelling.

Bettina had never understood this compulsion of hers, either, although even she would have been interested in Mr. Brandt. Handsome gentlemen never failed to interest her sister. What Bettina never fathomed, however, was how

Madeleine could experience an equal desire to know about the lives of the cook, the nursemaid, or the vicar's elderly father.

And now the butler was claiming her notice. In a voice as deep as faraway thunder, he apologized for the lack of a proper welcome and said he would fetch refreshment as soon as he awoke the chambermaid to lay fresh linens on the beds. She detected a veiled reproof in all of this, as did her father, for he immediately gestured dismissively.

"Never mind that," he said. "I'm at fault for arriving before you expected." Madeleine knew this to be a politeness, for whenever guests were scheduled to visit their home, preparations were completed far in advance; an early arrival was cause for further celebration, not excuses. "My wife is very tired. If her bed could be prepared at once, I would be grateful." He turned to Antonia, who was lying on the settee by the fire. "Or do I misspeak, my love? Do you require something to eat? Madeleine?"

Both ladies demurred, although Madeleine wished desperately for a cup of tea and warm bread, at least. She dared not delay the butler a moment longer than necessary, though, for apparently servants were at a premium at Westhall.

As Burns walked ponderously from the room to do her father's bidding and Mr. Brandt made polite conversation, she gazed about, finding confirmation of her observation everywhere she looked. Ashes lay thick on the hearth; the bookshelves, or what she could see of them, were dusty and the volumes in unattractive disarray; and the Jacobean furniture had gone too long without the benefits of polishing, the surfaces of tables scratched and dry.

Evidently household economy did not extend only to servants, for the furnishings themselves were out-of-date and faded. The crimson settee upon which her mother lay, for an example, looked as hard and uncomfortable as a bed of bricks; and the chair in which she herself sat possessed an alarming tendency to dip in the middle.

But none of this came as a surprise. She knew why Lord

Ambrose had extended his invitation—that it had nothing to do with her, but everything to do with her father's wealth.

The thought brought no bitterness, only resignation. If one must be married, and she had reason to believe she must, mutual convenience seemed as appropriate a reason as any. Lord Ambrose needed funds to keep his estate. He had made no secret of this; his solicitor had explained the situation to her father's solicitor. She rather admired him for his honesty; he could have tried to win her affection through flattery and a show of admiration at Lord Tate's, but he had shown the walls more attention than her.

This, she admitted to herself, did bring a *slight* touch of pique to her vanity.

Perhaps he found her unattractive. Well, many had not. She had had her share of proposals in her three-and-twenty years, and she believed some were spurred by genuine affection. It was difficult to know, however, when one was the sole heiress to an unencumbered fortune. And though that fortune had been made in business, their name was not tainted as some, for her father was regarded as a gentleman, not a businessman. Grandfather Murrow had been the one to dirty his hands in coal, while Papa expanded his earnings through wise investments.

Even so, not all of Society opened its doors to them. This bothered neither her mother nor herself, but she knew her father longed for ultimate respectability—the kind a connection to the peerage would bring. He tried to keep it hidden, but it was one of the things she understood about him. Her father may have attended Eton and Cambridge, but *his* father went to his grave illiterate and with the flavor of the London streets forever ingrained in his speech. She could only guess at how much this had affected her sire's life among his peers.

Although she sympathized with him, this alone would not be reason enough to sacrifice herself. There were others.

She gazed at her mother, who looked to be on the edge of total exhaustion. Fortunately, the butler returned at that moment to say the maid was turning out Mrs. Murrow's bedroom.

"Perhaps I could go upstairs now?" asked that lady. "If the bags have been brought up, I could . . ."

"Prepare yourself for bed, yes," finished her husband. "A capital idea. Will you allow us, Mr. Brandt?"

Madeleine saw worry flicker through the young man's eyes.

"Naturally, sir," he said, finally. "I only hope the servant is done." He motioned toward the door. "Please."

Burns stirred himself to lead the way. "If you will follow me."

Goodness, but things seemed formal here. Madeleine's father scooped her mother into his arms, carrying her as if she possessed the weight of a small child. She followed behind, and Mr. Brandt accompanied her.

Before she began to ascend the stairs, Madeleine noticed a short hall running to the left, at the end of which was an open door leading to a small room. From here she could see a fireplace and a large painting of two young men above it. The room had only the light from the hall for illumination, but she saw identical shocks of flaxen hair, blue eyes . . . the same face. She thought she recognized Lord Ambrose in the look of the youths. Was it possible he had a twin?

"Miss Murrow?"

She could not help feeling irritated at poor Mr. Brandt and his genteel look of disapproval. How she wanted to examine that beautiful portrait! But there was nothing to be done but walk docilely upward.

They found her mother's bedroom near the turning of the stairs. Inside, a young woman in a wrinkled uniform was floating a sheet over the bed, her wispy hair rising and falling with it.

"Woosh, and I'm not done yet," she said in an aggrieved voice as they entered.

"Quiet," Burns whispered heavily.

"You be quiet yourself," returned the maid. "Some of us have been working since dawn this morning and might only have just closed their eyes when *scoot!* they're told to get up again and earn their keep. Well, that's *all* I'm earning, I can tell you that much, and a fine keep it is, too, when the pigs at my uncle's farm has better to eat than such as I."

Mr. Brandt turned mortified eyes toward the Murrows. "I do beg your pardon for Betsy; she's been with the family a long—"

"Out, woman," Burns commanded. "I shall finish the bed myself."

"No, you won't," Betsy said. "Can't any man make a bed better than meself, and look at that poor lady there, ready to sink." She smoothed a coverlet over the sheets. "There now. All done."

"Is there no one to attend my wife other than this overworked young woman?" asked Thomas.

"We are expecting help on the morrow, sir, from the village," Mr. Brandt said.

"Had I known, I would have brought my wife's maid. Never mind; Burns, inform my driver that he is needed to fetch Zinnia straightaway. He'll know whom you mean."

Antonia slid from her husband's arms to stand beside the bed. "No, let Lindon sleep tonight; he's not feeling well. Tomorrow will be soon enough."

When Madeleine said she would help her mother dress for bed, the men moved from the room, following the maid like ducks as she announced her intention to prepare the adjoining chamber for Mr. Murrow, then the young lady's. Madeleine found their valises stacked against the wall, and she opened the one reserved for Antonia's nightrail. Some time later, she tucked her mother in for the night and entered the hall.

To her consternation, everyone seemed to have gone to bed, and she hadn't the foggiest notion which chamber was hers. She could, however, see that one door remained opened halfway down the corridor. Treading softly, she headed toward it.

As she moved to enter what she supposed must be her room, for the bed had been turned down and a fire lit in the grate, she heard a sound at the end of the hall. She paused and watched as the door to the furthermost chamber swung open. A hand grasped the frame, and then, as if he'd found it necessary to pull himself through, Lord Ambrose appeared. He leaned weakly into the corridor, unaware of her at first. When his eyes finally met hers, he reeled slightly, then straightened. She had the sense of one ready to challenge.

Unmindful of what he might think, she regarded him intently. He certainly did look ill. In the two months since she had met him, he'd lost weight, and the shadows beneath his eyes matched the aching blue in them. Golden hair fell across his forehead; he wore neither boots, jacket, cravat, or waistcoat, and his shirt and pantaloons looked as if he had slept in them.

She could not help noting that a hole had worn through his left stocking at the biggest toe.

Disheveled though he might be, he truly was quite striking.

She felt a strange sensation inside, as if her heart were turning inside out.

He moved slightly closer, although he did not leave the support of the doorway. "How good to meet you again, Miss Murrow," he said with a mocking little bow, "even if it is before I expected. Are you pleased with what you see?"

She almost stopped breathing. "I beg your pardon?"

"You were gawking at me as though I were an insect beneath a entomologist's glass."

"Oh." Her cheeks burning, she added, "I'm sorry if I seemed to—if you thought I—" Oh, bother it; how dare he be so rude? "I was not *gawking*. You look ill, and naturally I was concerned."

"You are . . . most considerate."

By the cynical expression on his face, she could see he did not believe her. Was he so conceited he thought she had stared because he was pleasant to look upon? Surely be did not imagine she had never seen attractive men before, not to mention enjoyed their attentions!

"Thank you." She drew out the words, imbuing them with a sincerity too strong for belief. "Would that my consideration matched your gracious hospitality."

His eyes sparkled; she could almost think in appreciation if her opinion of him had not sunk so low. Suddenly, he clutched the doorknob, his pallor increasing.

"Lord Ambrose!" Remembering her father and mother and perhaps Mr. Brandt were trying to sleep on this floor, she stepped a few paces closer to him and stopped beneath one of the wall sconces. In a softer voice she continued, "Are you all right? Shall I send for someone?"

He ran his free hand—the one not holding onto the brass knob—across his face and the back of his neck and made a wan attempt at a smile. "I thought to go outside for a while, but I believe I must lie down again. Forgive me; I've been ill."

Indeed, he was. She now stood closely enough to scent the origin of his sickness. He was . . . he was *inebriated*.

Why, on the eve of the day he expected her, did he find it necessary to drown himself in drink? There could be no good reason; certainly not a flattering one.

Making no attempt to hide her shock, she stepped backward. He saw her distaste and disillusionment, and worry crept into his eyes.

And well it might, she thought.

Fool. Idiot!

Too much planning had gone into this betrothal-to-be for him to blast his chances at the first draw.

With his back pressed to the closed bedroom door, Ethan gathered strength to return to bed. His chamber

pot lay where it had shattered; fortunately another was
hidden in the wardrobe. The two wide windows in his
bedroom had been painted shut long ago. He wished he
could have escaped the house for that breath of outside
air, but so be it. Small enough punishment for the manner
in which he had treated Miss Murrow.

He might be soused, but the velvet haze that had sent
him into hilarity earlier that evening had dissipated before
be spoke so rashly to the young woman. Although he had
little respect for a chit willing to sign away her life to a
stranger for the privilege of being called viscountess, he
could not imagine why he'd felt driven to lessen his prospects by embarrassing her.

The effect of long habits, perhaps, he thought, remembering his brother's reproaches. Or his disgust at selling
himself to the highest bidder. No, he modified with a
mirthless laugh. The *only* bidder.

He had better cover his disgust, and quickly. Otherwise,
the paralyzing weekend he'd spent at the Tates (and others like it) had been for nought if he frightened away the
first heiress willing to have him. He could not delude himself into thinking more would be forthcoming. Even this
one would not have been possible had Lord Tate not as-
sisted him. He recalled how Tate had chafed at his petition to keep quiet the darker aspects of his history; he
could not rely on him to do so again.

He moved toward the bed. Tomorrow was another day.
He would make a better accounting of himself then.

*Far into the night, when she was certain the house lay sleeping,
the woman crept up the stairs with a basket clutched in her hands.
When she arrived at the first-floor balcony, she stopped, trans-
ferred her burden to one hand, and removed her slippers with the
other. Padding down the hall, she walked to the final door and
paused, cradling the basket in the crook of one arm. The note,
she saw, was still attached to the handle. Tenderly she parted the*

blanket, gazed at the face of the sleeping infant nestled there, and wished to die. She pressed a kiss to each cheek, lightly so as not to wake the baby, and slowly, soundlessly, turned the knob.

Two

Had his skull been caught between a pair of grinding rocks, it could not feel worse, Ethan decided the next morning.

It's what you deserve. Don't give in to it.

He rose, stumbled to the mirror above his dresser, and groaned at the wretched-looking man staring back.

"I see you less and less often, Lucan," he mumbled to his image.

Bad as he appeared, he smelled worse. He must have a bath and shave before presenting himself at the breakfast table. The sun had only just cleared the horizon; mayhap he had a hope of service before the guests arose. Grateful for whatever had awakened him so early, he pulled the cord.

He stretched and forced himself to the window. The untamed garden abutting the side of the house looked dismal on this cool morning; even the weeds appeared lifeless. The greenery, such as it was, melded to a barren field that stretched into the distance until meeting the wood that bordered their land and the Redding estate.

As always, the thought of the owner of that estate, William Leed Redding, brought a flare of anger. Fortunately, Redding's daughter, Alice, and son, George, brought more pleasant feelings. The two younger Reddings, Lucan, and himself had been friends forever, and nothing the father did or ever could do would change that.

A sudden, high-pitched noise put a rude end to his

reflections, and Ethan grabbed his head in agony and swerved. He had no difficulty locating the direction of the sound; a basket in the corner. Where the devil had that come from? He crossed the room instantly, yanked the container from the floor, and looked inside.

An *infant*?

A very angry infant, who met his eyes in full-blown rage, mouth open to emit cries that curdled the blood in his veins.

Deuce take it, what was this thing doing here?

Cursing descriptively, he went to the door, basket in hand, recalled the Murrows sleeping down the hall, and stopped. With a look of horror for the squalling baby, he put the basket down, covered his ears, circled the room, and returned.

"Quiet!" he demanded.

If anything, the babe redoubled its efforts.

"God help me!" he cried, and knelt beside the child. "Please, *please* stop crying."

It was then he saw a note attached to the handle with string. With fingers that trembled, he opened it.

There was only one line, printed in ink and written very plainly, without a distinctive style; he did not recognize the handwriting. He read it once, twice, a third time, and could make no sense of the words. Refused to do so.

Please take care of our little one, for I cannot.

Our little one?

Had he spawned this atrocious brat?

In spite of the cacophony, he threw his mind backward over the last nine or ten months. Naturally he'd had encounters, but he prided himself on careful selection, confining himself to bored widows and expensive cyprians. Surely none of them had been so careless. And after Lucan's death, no one had interested him. He had to admit the possibility of fatherhood, though, and he could almost hear his brother's warnings and disapproval.

But just as likely, some hapless female ruined herself

with a blacksmith or a peddler and decided a viscount's house was her orphanage of choice.

The more he thought, the more it made sense. What wench wouldn't prefer to have it put about that her off-spring possessed noble blood? It would not be the first time such a thing happened. And, given his reputation, none of the inhabitants of Brillham would doubt the story.

While he tried to think, the baby continued to howl. He would admit to siring the entire village if only this child would stop screaming.

His eyes wandered to the door. He could not under-stand why people were not flooding his room to investi-gate, although he was thankful they were not. Maybe the cries were not so loud as he first thought. Every sound did tend to magnify with his head in its present state, and this wriggling, thrashing pestilence was quite small. He had no experience in judging the age of infants, but he didn't think it possible for a human being to be much tinier than this; its arms were no thicker than his thumbs.

No, blast it! Diminutive it might be, but those cries could wake the dead. Where was Betsy when she was needed? Why had no one answered his summons?

He gazed wildly at the baby, tapping his chin with his fist. In swift decision, he loosened his fingers, flexed them fastidiously, and settled his hand over the infant's mouth. Although this muffled the sound slightly, the feel of tiny lips moving beneath his skin appalled. He snatched his hand away and wiped vile wetness on his sleeve.

In nearly the same motion, he pulled the edges of the blanket higher and covered the baby's face. The resulting quiet was so immediate and profound he almost wept.

Nothing could contain its rage *that* quickly, though, he thought in sudden unease. Had he suffocated it? He flung back the blanket in time to see and hear a bellow of out-rage; the monster had quietened only to draw breath for its loudest protest yet.

In a frenzy, he seized the basket, strode to his wardrobe, opened the doors, stuffed babe and basket within, and slammed it closed. Feeling near death, he stumbled to his bed and sprawled facedown.

No one is coming. Go find Betsy or Burns! He would in a minute, as soon as his brain stopped rolling like a runaway coach.

God help him, he could still hear it. Without moving his head, he patted the bed until his fingers found a pillow. He clutched it over his ears. Still the sound seeped through. The cries were diminishing, though, the voice weakening. He fancied he could hear heaving breaths in between the wails. The edge of anger had left its tone to be replaced by pathetic, mewling sobs.

The pillow grew loose over his head. He nudged it aside. His fingers clawed the counterpane for an instant, and then he pushed himself upward.

When he opened the wardrobe and removed the basket, the babe did not heave a renewed assault on his ears as he'd feared. Crying softly around its fist, it had closed its eyes against him, as if abandoning all hope.

Where in the name of thunder was the maid?

Ethan laid the basket on the bed. He had seen babes and their mothers in cottages. If he could jump hedges on Viking, surely he was able to make his unwelcome guest more comfortable and thus render it quiet.

First he had to wipe the disgusting moisture from its eyes and nose. He poured water from his bedside pitcher into the washbasin, then moistened a towel. The water was very cold; it probably wouldn't like it. Cringing in anticipation of howls, he dabbed the face. Eyes opened in surprise and worry, but soon closed again. The hopeless whining continued.

Gingerly, he slipped his fingers beneath the child and lifted. When the head bobbled back, he cupped it with one hand and held the baby at arm's length. The child wore a white dress, the embroidered cloth of good quality although not expensive, and a matching bonnet. Beneath the garment he could feel the babe's damp napkin, but there were limits to his hospitality.

"Who are you?" he asked the infant, who opened blue eyes to give him a wobbling squint, then shuttered lashes almost as long as the wisps of hair escaping the bonnet. Its mouth curved downward into a perfect little pout.

He gave a cynical laugh. "If you're not female, I'll eat this basket."

Ethan lowered his gaze to the rough willow container, his eyes lingering at the finely stitched pink ruffles lining the interior. By its thickness he knew padding lay beneath; a soft bed for his guest. A miniature pillow, edged in lace with a single word embroidered upon it, lay at one end. *Dearest,* read the curling script. His brows knit together.

With a gasping series of soft cries, the baby recalled his attention to herself. Reluctantly, chewing his lip, he cradled the child closely to his chest. As soon as he did, she turned her head to him, searching.

"Hold, brat," he said, pulling away. "I may or may not be your father, but as sure as there's a hell, I am *not* your mother."

The babe's entire face crinkled in disappointment. Bracing himself for another session of yells, he lay her head against his shoulder and began to pace. She didn't scream, but in a way, her soft moans were worse. Surely they would wrench the heart of a murderer.

A tap sounded and, before he could blink, the door opened. Recognizing the maid, be felt his stomach settle back into place. "At last! Where have you been?"

Betsy took one glance and turned to stone. Her lips moved soundlessly for a moment.

"Is that a baby?"

"No, Betsy, it's a squirrel." He bounced the infant slightly; she sighed and shuddered against his shoulder. Looking sharply at the silent maid, he saw she appeared ready to believe him. "Of *course* it's a baby!" he said in exasperation. "Do you know anything about it? Someone brought her into my room last night in that basket while I was asleep."

"Well, I'm sure *I* don't know nothing." Having regained

control of herself, she flounced to the basket and fingered the note. "It's *yours*, milord?" Her eyes rounded, and her lips climbed upward. "Oooh . . ."

"Hold! You are not to say anything to anyone about this, do you understand? It's worth your position, Betsy; I mean it."

"My position," she mimicked, wrinkling her nose and rocking her head from side to side. "Who gives a cow's tongue for that? I could find better positions at the poorhouse, and kinder employers, too."

"You could not; no one else would endure your insolent tongue. Now stop rattling and listen to me. If the Murrows get wind of this, my plans are destroyed, do you understand? *Finis.* No marriage to Miss Murrow, no saving Westhall, and no increase in household help and wages."

"No increase? Why should I fret o'er an increase when I already haven't been paid since last Christmas?"

"Stop griping. You have a roof over your head, which is more than I can say any of us will have if this marriage doesn't take place. Am I making myself clear?"

"Yes," she said sullenly. "My lips is sealed like a tomb."

"That should bring me more comfort than it does." By the quietness of the being on his shoulder, he thought she might have fallen asleep. He was afraid to disturb her by looking. "She's hungry. What do you have for her to eat?"

"What do I have for *her* to eat? I hadn't even got enough for meself. Cook parceled out the bacon this morning like it was gold. 'We have to save the most for the guests,' says she. And never mind the one and only maid, who has to do all the work in this house with nothing to strengthen her."

He grimaced. "Have the Murrows breakfasted already? It's so early!"

"You don't have to tell *me* it's early. I'm the one what had to go and fetch water for baths and brush out their clothes. And after *they* went outside to walk, *I* had to make beds and unpack valises, then go down to the kitchen and help Cook slice apples for tarts, of which I doubt there will be enough for *me* to have any—"

"They're walking? I can't imagine that Mrs. Murrow has the strength. She was nothing more than an invalid at Lord Tate's."

"Mr. Murrow and Miss Murrow is walking. The poor wife's sitting on the bench out front 'taking the air,' as she calls it. She's all wrapped up tight and snug, but I still don't think brisk air is good for someone so sick-acting. Mr. Brandt's cooling his heels beside her. I reckon he's trying to be a good host, unlike some I could mention."

He ignored this dig. "That explains why no one heard the infant." He had been pacing, and now he swerved to a stop. "Betsy. We have to hide this child before they come back."

She stared at him. "Don't look at me; I don't know about any secret hidey places. If I took her upstairs to my room, they'd be bound to hear her sooner or later. You know how this place echoes. And besides, a babe needs somebody every minute. Are you expecting me to look after her and do my duties as well? Because, I'm letting you know that I draw the line at—"

"Be still, woman. It's obvious the child will have to go to someone in the village; preferably a recent mother who can nurse this one as well as her own."

"Oh, that's a good plan, that is, with you trying to keep it quiet and all. That sure ought to do it. Won't nobody think a thing of you bringing an infant for somebody to nurse."

"I wasn't planning on taking the child."

The maid stepped back a pace. "You're not expecting *me* to do it, surely?"

"I am."

"Well, if that ain't the most—I quit!"

Her indignant expression seemed far out of proportion to the task at hand. "Betsy, you've been here so long, you wouldn't leave if I gave you the sack. What's wrong with finding someone to care for this child?"

"Because if I do it, people is going to think it's mine! You want me to ruin meself?"

He couldn't help chuckling at this, adding coal to the flames.

"Oh, you may laugh, but you don't know how people are." Her hazel eyes sparked as she set her fists on her hips. "And maybe you don't think that just because I ain't married, I'm not going to be. Well, here is some news for you: I'm young, I got prospects. Or do you think I'm so plain I should give o'er my future happiness to take care of *your* problem?"

He had seldom thought about Betsy's looks one way or the other. She had a frowsy head of blond hair; her features were average, he supposed, and she was plump, well-rounded in the ways a man liked. He could understand that she would have admirers.

"Betsy, no one could believe this child is yours. *Think* for once, will you? You go into the village two or three times a week. How was it you hid your . . . ah . . . delicate condition? When did you give birth and recover? If you'd been away for a while, that would be different."

"Don't dream it's never happened. Me mum told me of a girl she knew back when she was young who dropped a child that way. Kept it secret the whole time, she did. Never got a belly so big she couldn't hide it behind her clothes. Never missed a day of work. Nobody would of ever known if they didn't find her babe when the trash pail tipped over."

"Blast you, Betsy; what an image!"

"Well, the babe lived, didn't it? Anyways, I can't take that little 'un nowhere, not if I want to hold up my head."

He suddenly realized how quiet the room had grown. By angling his neck and cutting his eyes downward, he could see the infant had indeed fallen asleep. The pink cheek turned toward him was round as a peach. He sighed. "Do you have any other ideas, then?"

"Who, me? One thing you can count on is that I've

always got an *idea*. What if you was to take it back to its mother?"

"I don't know who the mother is. I don't even know if I'm the father!"

She huffed. "Well, that's what comes of living like you do, ain't it? You can't expect nothing different. Your seeds is coming home to roost, and about time, too."

He sent her a quelling glare, then returned to his pacing. There had to be a solution; there *must* be one. As he turned to the window, he heard a muffled sound. After a lifetime of Westhall's creaks and groans, all of them magnified by its cavernous hall, he recognized the significance of the noise. Someone had entered the house. The Murrows had returned.

Betsy's eyes met his. Ethan didn't waver. "I think I have it," he said.

Three

What an odd place, Madeleine thought as she followed her parents into the house, the butler holding the door for them. The grounds were as plain as any she had seen. The walk had been refreshing, but to imagine a lifetime of exercising amid such surroundings daunted her spirits. Hardly a tree to break the landscape, and merely a scraggly hedge as ornamentation; and the only flowers visible were the ones nature saw fit to raise.

And the house! Mr. Brandt had told them it was slightly more than a century old, but it looked more like *six* centuries to her. A curious hybrid of castle and cathedral, its dimensions were more deep than wide—rather like an abbey she had visited once. With all that stone and with so many cracked, mullioned windows, she halfway expected it to crumble around her ears at any moment.

But her dowry could rectify many of the lacks at Westhall, she supposed, *if* she decided to go through with it. She had tossed and turned last night thinking of the viscount and his sour words, his drunkenness, and his beautiful, troubled face. She would give a great deal to make her mother happy, but she was not a martyr, nor was she foolish. After a night of little sleep, she could not deny she found Lord Ambrose intensely attractive. She also recognized what she'd refused to acknowledge after their first meeting at Lord Tate's—that she had felt that same tugging appeal then. However, a strong marriage could not be built on physical admiration alone, and she would *not* wed anyone she did not respect.

He was probably not even awake yet, she thought, and wrinkled her nose with disdain. Her parents were early risers and had raised her to be. Only the idle and slothful lay abed in the daylight hours, she had been taught to believe.

Her mother and father were turning to enter the library when Lord Ambrose dispelled her suspicions by appearing at the top of the stairs. With him was the maid, Betsy. Beside Madeleine, Mr. Brandt draw in a quick breath. She could understand his surprise. Was Lord Ambrose holding a *baby?*

"Good morning," the viscount said in an unusually cheerful voice and began to descend the stairs—*still in his stockinged feet,* she noted. "Forgive my appearance," he added with a laugh, his gaze bouncing from one to the other of them. "We had unexpected visitors last evening after everyone went to bed, and I've not had the chance to dress yet—I shall in a moment—but I'm certain you know the cause—you *did* tell them, didn't you, Burns? About my cousin?"

"Your cousin, milord?" Burns intoned.

The viscount's eyebrows lowered. "You remember. Connie. And her husband, James. They were tearing off for London to see his mother, who is near death." He moved his gaze from the butler to scan their eyes again. "Poor soul, it will be a blessing when she goes. As it happened, James realized too late that an infant might disturb his mother; the town house is quite small, he said. Therefore, they stopped here to beg refuge for their little one, and I could hardly refuse."

"Of course you couldn't refuse," Antonia cried, edging closer to the stairs with gleaming eyes. Her mother always had a weakness for babies, Madeleine recalled.

"Certainly not," Mr. Brandt echoed in faint tones. "How could anyone?"

He was holding the infant, Madeleine kept thinking.

Lord Ambrose, not the maid. She found this difficult to reconcile with what she knew of him. If this meant he was of a gentler nature than suspected, the knowledge was welcome.

"This cousin of yours—James, did you say?" began her father.

Lord Ambrose paused for the merest fraction of an instant. "My cousin's husband is James; she is"—he stifled a yawn—"Clarice."

"Connie," Mr. Brandt said sharply. "He meant Connie," he added to the others.

The viscount leveled him a look. "Connie Clarice, yes. You're such a stickler for entire names, Scott." He had reached the foot of the stairs, and now he handed the child to Antonia, there being little else he could do with her arms outstretched so appealingly. The babe did not awaken during this exchange, and Madeleine thought she had never seen anyone look so relieved as Lord Ambrose. "Did you want to ask me something, Mr. Murrow?"

"Whatever your cousin's name is," Thomas continued, "I'm wondering why they didn't leave a wet nurse. Or is she sleeping?"

The viscount gave an awkward laugh. "Actually, that is a bit of a problem. Connie hadn't secured a maid yet, being so set on tending the child herself; she never would have left the child had their situation not been desperate. Fortunately I was able to assure her we'd find someone."

"Women is *forever* giving birth in Brillham," added Betsy, who had accompanied Lord Ambrose down the stairs and now stood among them like a guest. The viscount slid her a dampening look. "Well, it's God's own truth," she said defensively. "I meself can think of two new mothers within a stone's throw of here. I'm reckoning either one will have more than enough milk for two, because they're real hefty girls, both of them; built like cows, they are."

Burns coughed into his fist. "Be about your work, girl."

The maid's eyes flared. "Who are *you* to tell *me* to work, you overfed, stuffy old—"

"Betsy." The viscount stepped between the servants. "Why didn't you tell me about the mothers earlier?"

"That was because you wanted me to go"—she stopped, tossed a fretful glance at her spectators—"you know. Before you told me to say—"

"Yes, yes, that's of no consequence now. Do be off to see about it straightaway. The babe is hungry."

"You want me to take it?" she asked.

The viscount's gaze darted to the child. "No. Bring someone here. Oh, and clothing as well. Undergarments and that sort of thing."

Was that a protective look she saw in his eyes? Madeleine wondered. He kept watching the child in Antonia's arms as if guarding it.

As Betsy hurried off, Thomas said, "Do you mean to say your cousin left the infant without so much as a change of clothing?"

Lord Ambrose stared at him. For once he did not seem to have an easy answer. And then, just as he drew breath to speak, Mr. Brandt surged into the breach.

"Naturally she would know old clothing is stored in the attic. Everyone keeps baby clothes for sentiment's sake. My own grandmother, for an example, has my entire layette preserved as if for a museum. She would show it to you if you hinted at the slightest interest."

"May fortune preserve us from such a fate." Lord Ambrose crossed his arms and leaned against the newel post.

"Only trying to explain your cousin's behavior," Mr. Brandt said resentfully.

Thomas paid no attention to their quarreling. "Still seems odd to me."

Madeleine was beginning to think so, too; not from the viscount's words so much as his strained attitude. The tense undercurrents running among him and his friend and servants could not be missed, either.

"Oh, how can you gentlemen grumble so about details

when there is this beautiful child to admire? Look how tiny she is! She cannot be more than a few days old, if that. I wonder that your cousin felt well enough to travel."

Antonia had cradled the infant so that its face was evident to them all. Madeleine moved closer, as did the others excepting the butler, who appeared to disapprove of the entire business. The child truly possessed great beauty with its perfectly shaped mouth, upturned nose, and curling blond lashes, but it was her own mother's expression that brought joy to Madeleine's heart. She had seldom looked so alive in the past few years.

"She *is* exquisite." Madeleine turned to the viscount and found his gaze resting on the infant. "What is her name?"

For the length of several heartbeats, she thought Lord Ambrose had not heard her. Finally, he brought his eyes to hers, and she could almost hear them ripping from the child, so reluctantly did he turn. His gaze moved on, wandering restlessly as the company waited. One would almost think he couldn't remember her name, Madeleine reflected with growing disillusionment. Perhaps after last evening's debauchery, he could not.

"Door," he said suddenly.

"Door?" exploded Thomas. "Someone named this poor mite *Door*?"

"Rie," the viscount declared. "Dorrie . . . Hall . . . Burns—" the butler, who had gone to guard the front door, turned suddenly in shock "—side. Burnside."

"Dorrie Hall Burnside," Antonia repeated. "Lovely name." She looked so doubtful that Madeleine bit her tongue to prevent herself giggling. "Unusual, too."

"That's my cousin in a word," Lord Ambrose said, and gestured toward the library, indicating they were to proceed within. "Highly unusual."

"A family trait," Mr. Brandt said beneath his breath. Walking obediently toward the library, Madeleine found herself agreeing, but thought him extremely disloyal to say so.

* * *

The next few hours passed at a hectic pace, but that was fortunate to Ethan's way of thinking. It gave him less time to dwell on the mystery of the child's parentage, a subject that threatened to consume him, when he should be centering his effort on making amends to Miss Murrow.

After leaving the babe in Mrs. Murrow's eager care, he ordered Burns to bring his bathwater, then bathed, and dressed in a white shirt and cravat, tan pantaloons, his favorite waistcoat with the vertical blue stripes, and an azure jacket that wanted replacing but was in as good a condition as any he had. When he had almost finished with his toilette, Scott came to learn the true story of the baby's arrival. Ethan told him as succinctly as possible.

"You mean to say the child is yours?" Brandt's face was a portrait of disbelief and shock.

"Why not speak a trifle louder, Scott? There's a chance the Murrows didn't hear you."

"How—" He lowered his voice "How will you keep up this charade? The Murrows will wonder why your fictitious cousin never comes back to claim her child."

"I'll think of something when the time comes. The first order of business is to find the identity of the infant's mother."

"This could ruin everything. Miss Murrow is charming, utterly charming—"

"It's not necessary to tell me that," he said, resentfully. Closer acquaintance had already begun to mend his first impression of her, and now he found himself looking forward to knowing her better.

"But her father is old-fashioned and as protective as a bear. If he discovers you've fathered a bastard, your last best hope will be gone. What do you plan? How will you proceed?"

"We continue as best we can—what else? Now leave me. Your hand-wringing is making me jumpy; I expect next you will be frothing at the mouth."

By the time Lord Ambrose had tied his cravat into a semblance of neatness—how he missed his valet, long lost as a measure of economy—Betsy had returned with Janice Marshall, a young mother of a five-month-old boy. As her husband had left home to seek work in London, she agreed to stay on the premises provided she could care for her babe as well. The viscount saw to it that she and her boy, Clyde, were tucked safely away in the attic nursery with Dorrie, who was crying to be suckled as he hastily left.

Dorrie Hall Burnside. Not a bad nomenclature for a second's notice, be told himself as he walked downstairs for luncheon, even if he did have to use a few visual helps. He had never in his life claimed to be creative.

As he descended, he could hear the Murrows conversing in the library. Were they early for everything? If so, *that* could prove deuced annoying. But then he detected Scott's voice as well. What a good friend he was, always there to assist; as watchful of the diminishing Ambrose fortune as Ethan himself. Although that was not total altruism on his part; Brandt's livelihood was pinned to his own.

But if Scott didn't take care, he would harm more than help by making Ethan appear bad by comparison. Scott was such a *good* man; always first with the soothing word, the correct gesture, the gallant response. He was almost as perfect as Lucan; mayhap that explained why he had been more Lucan's friend than Ethan's.

At the bottom of the stairs, the viscount's hand tightened on the newel post. He closed his eyes. No one was as perfect as his brother. No one.

He forced his lids to open. Time to be charming, he counseled himself, and wondered if that was possible.

It had better be possible. Contrary to his first thoughts, Madeleine Murrow would have to be courted to be won. She was not the insipid female he remembered from the weekend at Lord Tate's. In truth, be began to doubt all his initial impressions of her. He had been drinking deep that weekend, as he recalled—not the best method for making good judgments. Thus, last evening he had been surprised to scent a whiff of humor from his future intended; today he'd seen unmistakable signs of intelligence in her eyes as she tried—yes, he was sure of it—*tried* to swallow his unlikely tale of Dorrie's arrival. But what else could she do, she or her skeptical father? The truth was unbelievable. Unimaginable. And worst of all, if he truly was the father, unforgivable.

He pasted a smile on his face, tugged his waistcoat straight, and entered. Scott was seated on the settee beside Mrs. Murrow, who had occupied her hands with needlepoint; and Mr. Murrow stood with one leg propped on the hearth, prodding the flames with a poker. Miss Murrow sat next to the fire, an open book in her lap. He thought he spied a spark of admiration in her eyes when she looked at him, but it disappeared so quickly be could not be certain. He decided to take encouragement from the possibility.

"How fares little Dorrie?" Mrs. Murrow asked after greetings were renewed.

"Happy to be fed," he answered. "As I'm sure we'll all be in a moment." He certainly would be, having had no time for breakfast. He rang for the butler, who responded promptly, and asked if luncheon was ready.

Burns bowed. "I've only now returned from the kitchen, milord. The meal will be delayed for about a half hour."

Ethan's smile became strained. "Thank you, Burns." When the butler reversed direction, the viscount walked to the threshold with him, saying under his breath, "What's wrong now?"

"The maid bought a spoiled chicken and had to get another," the butler returned in a rumbly whisper.

"Betsy again." When Burns nodded, the viscount added, "I thought we had another pair of hands coming from the village today."

"Yes, milord, the greengrocer's daughter, but she took ill yesterday."

The viscount glanced at the company in the library. Scott was conversing with the Murrows, but Miss Murrow wasn't attending very well; she was watching Burns and himself. Caught, she moved her eyes away, her cheeks pinkening. Feeling a hint of amusement, he moved closer to the butler and softened his voice further.

"You did tell her we'd pay."

"Yes, milord. She was willing, but her illness came on suddenly. According to her father, she wishes to work— *very much* wishes to work he said—and will come as soon as she recovers her strength."

"Let's hope that happens quickly." Lord Ambrose moved as if to return to his guests, then pivoted back to Burns. "This greengrocer's daughter; is she the plump young one with yellow hair?"

"Annie Farlanger's not so young anymore, milord. Thirty if she's a day."

Young enough, "Does she have beaux?"

The butler straightened, giving him a severe look. What had he done this time—did Burns think he was interested in the chit? "I wouldn't know, milord. I do not indulge in village gossip."

For a moment Ethan felt himself back in the nursery, the formidable servant's disapproval slitting through him like splinters of glass. Shaking himself mentally, he met the man's eyes. He was the master of the house now, whether he wanted to be or not, and no mere servant could intimidate him.

"Did you have enough interest to ascertain the nature of her illness?" He invested as much contempt as he could into his whisper.

"Her father didn't say, and I did not ask."

"I'd like you to find out what's wrong with her."

Doubt entered the butler's expression. "Farlanger did mention she wasn't contagious, if you're worried about your guests."

It had not occurred to Ethan to concern himself with contagion, but he seized upon the opportunity. "Yes, I am. Mrs. Murrow is not strong, and we can't risk bringing a disease on the premises. Yes, tell Farlanger that and bring me his answer."

After an instant's hesitation, the servant said, "Is this falsehood, milord? I don't like being caught as I was this morning in the matter of your"—he cleared his throat—"cousin."

The viscount felt himself grow warm. "You see that lady over there? Half the time she's so weak she cannot walk. Now do as I say, Burns, as soon as you've finished helping in the kitchen. I'm famished."

The butler stared resentfully beneath bushy eyebrows, then bowed and walked from the room. Ethan forced brightness into his face and returned to his guests.

Mrs. Murrow smiled at him and set her needlepoint aside. "Lord Ambrose, I was just remarking to Mr. Brandt about how attractive are the tapestries in the hall. Did members of your family make them?"

"My grandmother, yes; a lifetime's work. There are more in the withdrawing room; would you care to see? We could tour the downstairs rooms while we wait for luncheon if you like."

Such a perfect host he was, he thought as the Murrows moved to their feet, Scott hurrying to assist the older lady. The strain of maintaining civility for the next two weeks loomed before him, like the entire range of the Alps waiting to be crossed. He could not deny feeling a touch of interest when Miss Murrow passed beneath his eyes, however. She looked more attractive than he remembered. Perhaps it was the pink of her gown that softened her.

Ordinarily, he preferred fair-skinned women with rosy cheeks, but Miss Murrow's Mediterranean coloring suited her well, especially as her skin was as smooth as porcelain. He began to think she possessed the kind of beauty that grew on one rather than dazzled at first sight. Had her hair been black, *then* she would have caused every eye in a room to fasten upon her entrance; her features were excellent enough. It was the brown hair that, while clean and pretty enough in its own right, saved her from that fate. Judging from the vain and shallow beauties he had known, Ethan thought her fortunate.

At that moment, Miss Murrow was feeling considerably less than fortunate. As she trooped from withdrawing room to music room to dining room, she wondered what the architect of the manse had been thinking. Surely the ceilings were at least fifteen feet tall, a thing that might be elegant in vast rooms. However, Westhall's chambers, although proportioned comfortably, were none of them large.

She felt like a toy moving inside a box. A gray, drafty box filled with old furniture and worn cloth. This house could not begin to compare with their comfortable manse in Kent with its flower-filled gardens, rose trellis, white latticework pavilion; and inside, tastefully furnished and proportioned rooms with the charming servants' stair leading to an attic filled with mysterious shadows, dusty corners, and treasure trunks where two sisters had whiled away their childhood. Only a few days had passed since she last saw it, but how she missed that home and its low ceilings.

On the other hand, there were no memories of Bettina tied to Westhall to haunt her. This place had that at least in its favor.

While they explored, Lord Ambrose kept up a running commentary about the history of this, the legacy of that; Chinese vases, fan collections, and a hideous old pot reputed to be from ancient Rome. She could not help thinking it was no wonder they buried it in the dirt.

Sometimes Mr. Brandt would add a sentence or two, all of it favorable to the Ambrose history. When he did, the viscount attended him with a display of politeness she saw through like glass. Mr. Brandt taxed his patience for some reason; why, she could not tell, for the gentleman seemed all that was proper to her.

As for Lord Ambrose himself, she sensed he tried very hard to be pleasant as he guided them through the rooms. She liked listening to his raspy voice; it compelled attention. His behavior made a nice change from last night, but she remembered well the scent of liquor on his breath and would not soon forget it.

One of her friends from school had married a man too fond of his drink. He gambled and drank away her entire fortune in the space of a year. No one had heard from her in a long time, although there were rumors the couple had moved to Ireland and become potato farmers.

She knew enough to be cautious when choosing a mate; yet studying Lord Ambrose as one would consider making a purchase—*this* quality goes into the *in favor of* column; *that* behavior belongs in the *against*—made her uncomfortable. She had not expected her visit to be easy, but that was when she didn't think of him as a living, breathing person with a character and history all his own. Now that she was beginning to, it was worse; much worse.

After viewing the last ground-floor chamber, the morning room—a room that managed to depress despite its yellow-and-white color scheme—the group filed past the stairs and seemed destined to return to the library.

"Won't you show us your study?" Madeleine asked impulsively, when it became apparent he was going to neglect what she most wanted to see.

A silence fell. The animation on the viscount's face smoothed over, as though a hand had wiped it away.

"There's nothing of interest in there," he said.

He sounded harsh enough to draw a sharp look from Madeleine's father. Her expression, too, must have reflected how taken aback she was, for Mr. Brandt gave her arm a soothing squeeze.

"Ethan's study is not the place to visit before a meal," he said in jesting tones. "He gets so angry when a piece of paper is moved that the servants dare not clean anything. You can imagine what a rubbish trap it is."

"Come, my dear," said Antonia. "We don't want to intrude on our host's privacy, and to say truth, I had best sit down awhile." Thomas immediately offered his arm, and her parents turned to enter the library. "It's been a long time since I've been on my feet this much, hasn't it, Thomas? Perhaps I grow stronger."

"I am certain of it," Thomas said in a solicitous voice.

Instead of following her parents' lead, Madeleine kept her eyes upon the viscount willing him to change his mind. She didn't care a fig for the room's tidiness, but was dying to get a closer look at the portrait.

Slowly, the viscount moved his gaze from Mr. Brandt to her. After a moment, he shrugged slightly and gestured for her to proceed toward his study. She walked eagerly forward, the two gentlemen following.

She allowed herself a quick glance at the portrait above the fireplace and then, so as not to seem too taken with it, moved on to examine the rest of the room. The study was small and lined with bookshelves on two walls. A massive desk sat before the window; it struck her as odd until she realized it was designed for two, one person to each side. She saw only one leather chair placed with its back to the window. A glance at the titles on the nearest shelf revealed a taste for horse breeding, astronomy, theology, and philosophy. My goodness, what an eclectic collection, she thought, then dismissed the books for her true objective.

Standing beneath the painting, she saw that the two young men appeared to be on the verge of adulthood, yet there was enough boyishness in their faces to make her uncertain if one of them could be Lord Ambrose. One stood, the other sat. The standing boy rested his hand on the back of the chair; she could not determine if the gesture was proprietary, protective, or simply the command of the artist. Both boys looked outward.

Now that she had a moment to study their faces, she began to note subtle differences. Although both subjects looked pleasant, the sitting boy's expression was slightly more serious, his cheeks fuller and his eyes more round.

She had the impression of an inner gravity, or perhaps a placidity that bespoke knowing one's place in the world. The second fellow looked . . . innocent, she thought; but in a strange way, for the spark in his eye promised devilment.

With an enthusiasm that could not be restrained, she whirled on the viscount, who had come to stand at her left elbow. "Is that you in the portrait?"

"Which?" he asked, his gaze nailed to hers.

From his expression, she had the sense that her answer was inordinately important to him. For an instant she was afraid to answer but then thought, *how absurd.*

"The one standing, of course."

From the smile in his eyes, she guessed she had chosen rightly.

"Are you *certain?*" he quizzed, confusing her for a moment.

"I can only be certain if *you* tell *me.*"

"Alas, I cannot. My brother and I promised never to disclose the secret."

Mr. Brandt stepped into her line of vision, startling her; she had forgotten he was here. "My guess is you're correct. Normally, the elder would stand, taking the preeminent position, but the twins liked to twist minds by changing places. You cannot imagine the disasters they caused."

Lord Ambrose smiled at him. "Scott, would you be so good as to see to the status of our meal? Perhaps you could light a fire beneath Burns."

"Start a fire beneath Burns, Ethan? You always did have a knack with words." If Mr. Brandt took offense at being ordered from the room, he gave no sign as he disappeared into the hall.

"I didn't realize you have a twin," she said.

"Had, Miss Murrow. My brother died six months ago."

"Oh. I am *truly* sorry!"

"I believe you are. When I visited Lord Tate, your father

told me your family had experienced a similar tragedy in the death of your sister."

She nodded, instantly flooding with the old sorrow. "But you did not mention your own loss to him."

"I hope you'll forgive me for that. The injury was too fresh. Even now I find it difficult to speak about it."

"I understand." She wanted to ask him a thousand questions but dared not. "My sister died nearly four years ago. She . . . drowned. Did my father tell you?"

"Yes. It must have been terrible for all of you."

"Terrible does not begin to describe it, Lord Ambrose. She died in a pond on our property. It *was* on our property, that is; Papa had it filled in." More than that she could not tell him; a family must be permitted its secrets. "My mother's decline began at that time. Sometimes I fear the grief will never lessen for any of us." She dashed a look at him. His eyes rested softly on her, and she felt her heart turn over. "My sister and I were very close, but a twin . . . I have heard there is a special bond."

"What you've heard is true." His gaze drifted to the portrait, and she felt him drawing inward. His pain was so tangible she wanted to weep. "A very special bond." His jaw tightened. "We'd better join your parents, Miss Murrow."

Reluctantly, she moved to follow him, but her eyes lingered on the painting. She felt as if she could study it forever. She sensed there was much to be learned here about the viscount and his brother, but she feared she would not be granted the opportunity. Lord Ambrose seemed strangely possessive of the portrait, else he would surely display it in a more public place.

"How did your brother die?" she asked, then could have bitten her tongue for its impulsiveness. "I'm sorry; I shouldn't have asked that. I'm too inquisitive; Papa is always telling me so."

"Lucan was shot."

The words came so swiftly and with such hostility that she recoiled. "Shot?"

"A hunting accident."

"How awful!"

He leaned against the door frame. A casual pose, but the flames in his eyes belied it. Like the force of a strong wind, his anger swept around her. Here lay the viscount's true personality, she was certain; gone was the smiling, tightly controlled man of the morning. She recalled his display of temper the night before. Yes, this was the real Lord Ambrose, and she could hardly contain her disappointment.

"Allow me to satisfy your curiosity by explaining all of it, and then we'll be quit of the subject, shall we?" His tone was acidic. "Imagine if you will, a field of men and dogs hunting grouse; a stray bullet is fired, and my brother falls. After several hours of struggling for life, he succumbs. Does that satisfy you, Miss Murrow?"

Indignation rose, but she struggled to keep it from her voice. "I grieve for your loss, Lord Ambrose, and I'm sorry if I seemed intrusive in my questions. I would not have you relive hurtful memories for the world."

That should make him see how a well-behaved adult acted. But truth was, her tongue longed to form a vicious retort. He was not the only person to be victimized by the brutal, careless acts of others.

Rather than soothe, her words apparently served to enflame him.

"No? Then you would be the first." He strode to the center of the room and glared at the portrait. "Neither on that day nor in all the time afterward has anyone stepped forth to say, 'I think I did it; I was firing in his direction,' or, 'I stumbled and my weapon discharged.' How does that strike you as to reliving painful memories? Every time I look into the faces of the men who were present at the shoot. I relive that day, and they are my neighbors; they dwell all around me, do you understand? I cannot see any of them without thinking, *Are you the one who took my brother from me?*"

He was not enraged with her, she realized then; he was

simply *angry*, and she could understand why. Her own ire dissolving, she said gently, "But . . . you would not seek revenge, surely; not for an accident . . ."

He shot her a look of disbelief. "Do you think no penalty should be extracted for a criminal act of this magnitude?"

"I only meant that it would be difficult for anyone to confess to such a deed. He would lose the respect of everyone, and to what end?"

"A man of honor would do so."

"Yes, but perhaps no one believes he is guilty. My father has spoken of such shoots; after attending one he refused to go to another. He calls them 'madness in the guise of games,' with everyone firing at once."

"Not if they are well run. Westhall's were."

The edge in his tone had eased, and she imagined a beast returning to its lair. His rage might be hidden, but it was still present.

"Lord Ambrose . . . knowing the identity of your brother's killer . . . would that make his death easier?"

He whirled upon her. "No, but at least it would silence the tongues of those who whisper it abroad that *I* murdered him to gain the blasted title!"

Her hand flew to her cheek in horror. "No, my lord! Surely no one says so horrendous a thing!"

"Oh, do they not? Don't be naive, Miss Murrow. Open your eyes and learn the hearts of men."

Hot tears rose to her eyes. "But . . . *can they not see how well you loved him?*"

His gaze flew to hers. So much tearing sorrow in his expression, and something that made her heart beat faster. His lips parted as if he meant to speak but could not find the words. At that moment Mr. Brandt entered the room, and she felt strangely let down at his timing.

"Burns says luncheon is prepared," he said in a cheerful voice, and then, glancing from one to the other, looked hesitant. "Ethan?"

Four

Several evenings after the Murrows' arrival, Lord Ambrose was dressing for dinner when he heard a knock at his door. It was Burns with a message from the vicar's family; they would be a few moments late and begged that he proceed without them.

The viscount had invited Reverend Abbott and his family to dinner, as well as the Reddings, to meet the Murrows. He was dreading it, for he and William Redding wasted no love on each other. However, he could hardly invite the children without the parent, and the children were his best friends and neighbors.

Thanking Burns for the message, Ethan closed the door and returned to the task of buttoning his waistcoat.

During the past days, he had had no opportunity to explore the parentage of his small charge. Of a necessity, entertaining the Murrows became his primary occupation, and it was an increasingly pleasant one, especially when he had the opportunity to speak with Miss Murrow alone—an opportunity that came all too rarely thanks to the vigilance of her father. As Scott had said, the man was protective.

The possibility of a wedding began to seem less and less a sacrifice, and more an event to anticipate. A tenuous relationship was flowering between Miss Murrow and himself, spawned, he believed, from their moments together in the study. Since then, they had not spoken so deeply to one another, but the experience forged a bridge between them, or so he believed. The way she had looked

and talked with him, the understanding in her eyes, sur-
passed that of many of his closest friends. Perhaps only
those who shared the kind of losses they had could truly
feel empathy for each other.

Staring at his reflection in the mirror, he dared to ask:
Was it possible he could find peace? He did not request
happiness in this life; that begged too much for a man
severed in half. But peace? Could he not find it with the
tranquil, understated beauty visiting beneath his roof?

Only one thing struck him as a potential obstacle; no,
two. First and foremost, Thomas Murrow, who was no
one's fool. He might have been as pliable in Lord Tate's
matchmaking hands as Lord Ambrose himself, but he was
not precisely salivating to be rid of his daughter. He was
a careful man, and the questions he asked about the baby
were increasing daily. His favorite theme seemed to be:
Had he heard from his cousin yet?

Naturally, it did not help that Mrs. Murrow was so struck
with the child that she must hold it for what seemed hours
at a time, thereby bringing Dorrie to her husband's constant attention. Since the lady could not easily venture
back and forth from the nursery, the babe must be
brought down to her, which in turn meant Miss Murrow
had to pet and play with it as well—and *she* had become
quite the imp about involving *him*—teasingly taking the
child, then saying she must leave the room for only a
moment and would Lord Ambrose hold Dorrie until she
returned? She had done this on at least three occasions,
so he knew it was purposeful. He could not imagine what
her intent was in this, unless she enjoyed seeing the startled look he never seemed able to hide.

As he brushed his hair, his lips curved upward. It
seemed to him—and he didn't believe it was imagination—that the baby preferred him above all others. However, this might not be an advantage, given the
circumstances. His smile faded.

The second obstacle was Madeleine's curiosity. He knew
it signaled an intelligent, active mind. That was a trait he

sought in a wife. But not if it led her to discover the truth—or what *might* be the truth—about the child. She threw almost as many questions at him as did her father, only her inquiries were for details about his cousin and her husband and their mutual history. *What was his cousin like? Had they played together as children? How did she meet her husband, and did Lord Ambrose find him amiable?* He found himself sinking deeper and deeper into lies, and more than once she caught him contradicting himself.

Dorrie Hall Burnside could not have arrived at a less opportune time. Especially since everyone seemed obsessed with her.

He glanced at the clock on the mantel. Twenty minutes before his guests were due to arrive. Time enough to interview the greengrocer's daughter, who had finally made her appearance that morning. Burns had discovered little about her illness; only that her sickness had been quick. No other family members had succumbed to it. The viscount's suspicions were fully aroused.

Pulling on his father's heavy garnet ring, he paused. This did not belong on his finger. Not his.

He felt the draw of the mirror and, without wishing to, raised his eyes. What hell was this, to see his brother's face every time he looked at his reflection?

He placed his palm on the glass. *Here we are, Lucan. Hand touching hand, and yours as cold as death.*

His gaze slid toward the decanter on his bureau. He moistened his lips.

No. Busy yourself. No oblivion tonight.

Without looking into the mirror again, he walked swiftly from the room.

Madeleine was scratching through her jewelry case looking for her favorite emerald necklace when she heard a knock at the door, then her father's voice. She bid him enter.

"Well, aren't you the lovely one?" he remarked.

"Thank you, Papa," she answered a trifle wearily. He always said that, so a compliment from him bore little meaning. "Am I late?"

"No, we have ample time. I only this moment saw the viscount on his way down the servants' stair." He brought a side chair closer to the vanity and sat. "For what are you looking? May I help?"

"I can't find my emerald."

"Oh-oh. Your mother has borrowed it. Did Zinnia not ask you first?"

Madeleine abandoned her search and plucked a sapphire pin from its velvet case. "No, but that's all right; I was probably in the library. This butterfly brooch will look just as well on cream, don't you think?"

"Anything looks well on you, child."

She forced a smile. He could not know how she disliked his perfunctory encouragements. From her childhood, he had seemed to think it his duty to make her feel beautiful. It was compensation for the birth of Bettina, she knew. Her younger sister's striking coloring and vibrant personality had won instant admiration wherever she went, even as a small girl. Papa seemed to think Madeleine would suffer jealousy or hurt by the inevitable comparisons, but she never had. She was as much an admirer of Bettina as anyone, and had loved her fiercely.

That did not hide her sister's faults from her eyes, however. She had tried to counsel Bettina when no one else would, and to little effect. Madeleine believed her father interpreted her frustrations with her sister as envy. Thus, she viewed his compliments as meaningless.

"Are you looking forward to meeting the viscount's friends tonight?" she asked, hoping to stop further flatteries.

"Very much. I trust the dinner will give us a wider perspective on our host's character."

Madeleine's fingers stilled for an instant, then she calmly finished pinning the brooch to her gown. "Do you have doubts in that regard?"

"Well, young lady, that's why I came to see you alone, without your mother, for I know you hope to please her above all things. Have you formed an initial impression about Lord Ambrose?"

Had she formed an initial impression? Ethan Ambrose was the most enigmatic man she had ever met. He changed from one moment to the next. He could be arrogant and condescending with the butler, and sometimes Mr. Brandt. (She had yet to discover why that gentleman lived here; at times he seemed to be a servant, at others, a guest.) He spoke familiarly to the maid, as if she were an old dog to be kicked about, although it must be admitted Betsy appeared to bring this treatment upon herself as well as enjoy it. To Madeleine and her family, he occasionally seemed too eager to please; and it was that Lord Ambrose she felt the most disillusioned with, for she knew the reason smacked of desperation, not affection.

And of course, there was the stinging memory of his behavior on that first night.

Overshadowing all of these was the grieving twin she had found beneath the portrait.

She felt as if she had not discovered the true man yet. But she was intrigued. More than intrigued.

Since her feelings involved doubts, she dared not share them with her father. He would order the horses and coach before she had spoken the last word.

"I think it is too early to say."

"You always were careful with your thoughts."

He eased back and crossed one leg over the other. As she wound a lace-edged ribbon through her curls, she slid a curious glance at him. His familiar features, plain but beloved to her, looked worried. His nose was redder than usual; a sure indication of concern.

"What's wrong, Papa?"

Running fingers through his gray-streaked hair, he breathed in deeply, then exhaled. "The viscount troubles me."

Her heart began to pound. "In what way?"

"I begin to wonder if be's a proper choice for you."

"But I thought—"

"I know what you thought, child. You want to please both your parents, because that's the kind of daughter you are. I've always known it, and you have always made me proud."

She allowed the tip of the ribbon to slip from her fingers and faced him. *This* was not the sort of thing he usually said, and she feared the softness in his voice would make her misty if he did not stop.

"Papa, you—"

"Hush, child; allow me to finish. I know you fear for your mother's health, as do I. We have both watched her pining away for Bettina these past years until her strength is little more than a bird's. And, as you well know, she has lately voiced a desire for grandchildren before she dies. She is not a manipulative woman, Madeleine; you realize she is too kind for that. But Antonia *does* want you settled before . . ."

She had seldom seen tears in her father's eyes. Groaning inside, she reached for his hand and clasped it between both of her own.

With his unfettered hand, Thomas pulled a handkerchief from his pocket and swiped his eyes. "Sorry, child. All that aside, you cannot sacrifice your future happiness simply to soothe your mother. She would not wish it. Therefore, you must form your judgment without consideration of what you do to fulfill her dreams. Do you understand?"

"I do, but what has happened to change your opinion of Lord Ambrose?"

"No one thing stands out; only a compilation of discrepancies."

"Such as . . . ?"

"That baby, for an example—"

"Oh, but I think it is famous of him to care for his cousin's child. How many bachelors would do so?"

"Precisely."

"But . . . his action speaks in his favor, does it not? He behaves wonderfully with the infant."

"Yes, but does it not seem unusual to you that he would take in a child when his house is filled with guests who may or may not become his family? This is not the time to invite upset."

She felt her lips move into a stubborn line. "Even more to his advantage, Papa. That proves his kindness, surely."

"Yes, but this relative of his. What woman would abandon her newborn to a cousin she barely knows? For that must be the case; you asked him if they had spent time together as children and he said no."

"Well . . . perhaps they wrote one another . . ."

"You are running after windmills, child. Why did the woman not stay at home with her infant? That would have been the best solution by far. And most telling of all . . . *why* have we heard no word from her? Any normal mother would be frantic to know how her babe fares!"

Madeleine stared at him for several seconds before saying, "Do you believe the viscount is lying?"

Her father held her eyes and shrugged deeply. "What do you think?"

"If he is . . . to what purpose?"

"Ah, my dear. There's the rub."

Slowly, Madeleine turned back to the mirror. Perhaps with a well-placed question or two, she would be able to discover the truth. But not tonight. Tonight, she would discover what kind of friends the viscount had. One could often learn much about a person from the company he kept.

"You like infants, Annie?" Lord Ambrose asked.

"Oh, yes, milord, do I ever!"

Ethan smiled. After a brief trip to the kitchen, he had discovered the greengrocer's daughter in the attic, taking a turn at rocking the babe while Janice nursed her son in the adjoining bedroom. He could not imagine a more appropriate place to find Annie Farlanger than in the nursery, holding her daughter.

She gazed down at the child, her grin making red balls of her cheeks. Like the infant, her eyes were blue, her hair light—more yellow than the child's, but those things could happen. Ethan set his own chair rocking and tried to control his excitement.

"Dorrie seems to have taken a special liking to you."

She blushed furiously. "Oh, no, milord. She likes everyone. She's a pleasant child, she is."

"She is indeed. Her mother must be very proud."

The girl gave him an uncomfortable look. "I guess you would know more about that than such as I."

"What do you mean by that?" he asked sharply.

"Nothing!" Her skin blotched. "Only as she's your cousin, not mine, milord!"

"Oh." He laughed lightly. "Of course. I beg your pardon."

"That's all right, I guess."

She glanced at the door with longing in her eyes. He supposed he was making her nervous. She *should* be nervous and more, abandoning her own child and naming him the father. A person like that was capable of anything. He stilled his chair, ready to catch her should she bolt.

"Do you ever wish you had your own baby, Annie?"

This surprised a giggle from her, and the blush returned. "Sure, but only if I was wed. Every girl I ever knowed wants a baby."

His gaze narrowed. "But what if you weren't wed?"

"What?"

"What if you had a baby without marriage. What would you do then?"

The color completely drained from her face. "But that wouldn't happen. I'm a good Christian girl. I go to chapel every week. And Da would flay me alive!"

"Come now, Annie. This happens in the best of families. You meet someone who attracts you. He tells you how pretty you are—"

"Nobody tells me I'm pretty," she said in a whisper. "People's always saying I'm fat."

"Many men prefer women with flesh on their bones. And you *are* an attractive woman."

"I am?" She began to tremble. Dorrie whimpered in response.

"Of course," he said heartily. "And after hearing this man's sweet words, you find yourself falling in love—"

"Aye." Her eyes were very wide and frightened.

"—and the next thing you know . . ." Lord Ambrose nodded significantly toward Dorrie, never taking his gaze from Annie's.

Slowly, she looked at the child. When she returned her eyes to his, they were awash in tears. He felt a stab of triumph, until she began to shake her head.

"No, no, no, no!" Rising, she handed Dorrie to him, her face contorted. "I heard about you and your womanizing ways, but I ain't going to be one of your conquistadors. You may be a lord and fine-looking as well, but it ain't worth burning for!" She backed from the room as she talked. "I—I do thankee for the offer, though, but . . . get thee behind me, Satan!"

With that, she dashed away.

Lord Ambrose stared after her, his mind a jumbled mass of dashed hopes. As if sensing Annie's rejection, Dorrie began to wail. He looked at her in bewilderment, stared hopefully at the bedroom door, and prayed the wet nurse behind it would come to his rescue, but no one did. Helplessly, he stood and began to pace, patting the orphan's back.

"Never mind," he told Dorrie. "We'll find your mother yet."

A few minutes later, Betsy huffed into the room. "What in blazes have ye done now, milord? Annie's gone and quit, and right before dinner's to be served!"

Five

In the moments before Lord Ambrose joined them in the library, Madeleine and her parents were introduced to the Reddings by Mr. Brandt. The older Mr. Redding reminded Madeleine of a stern ancient who attended their chapel in Kent. Everything about him seemed fierce: even his profile, which resembled a bird of prey—all downturned, sharp angles. But while Mr. Heilig had been soft as goose feathers on the inside, Mr. Redding did not give that impression.

His son George stood a trifle less than average height, like his father; but there the physical similarity ended. His figure was . . . cuddly, to give it the kindest name. To her delight, he possessed the rollicking laugh of other such cuddly persons of her acquaintance. She found his blatant flattery to herself and her mother endearing rather than offensive, since he offered it in such good spirit.

But of the three Reddings, it was Alice who commanded one's attention. She embodied that paradoxical exception that sometimes happened in families—rather like a flowering tree among a petrified forest, Madeleine fancied. Miss Redding possessed beautiful features, made the more so by her expression of friendliness. In height, she almost matched her brother and father; yet she did not seem gangly or ashamed of her stature as some women might; therefore, one did not think of her as tall, but striking. Her figure was lean, but suitably proportioned for her frame. When she sat beside Madeleine on the settee, Madeleine felt insignificant in comparison.

Alice did not allow her to feel so for long. Her eyes sparkled; her voice resonated low and vibrated with enthusiasm; her laughter rang sincere and often. While she and Madeleine conversed, Madeleine became the center of Miss Redding's universe. Suddenly, she felt witty beyond all nature; her remarks compelled the deepest interest; she was a creature to be cherished. She suspected she was being charmed, but Alice was so guileless, she could only respond in kind. In the space of minutes, Madeleine and Alice were on a first-name basis, and the young woman seemed to fill a void Madeleine never knew was there.

That Miss Redding would treat others with the same generosity of spirit could not be doubted. Therefore, when Lord Ambrose entered and Alice trilled his name while lifting her hand to be kissed, Madeleine shivered at her sense of abandonment. Such a small, mean spirit she had, to feel a pang that the viscount's eyes brightened in a way they never had for her! Naturally he was happy to see his friend; they shared a lifetime of experiences between them. How petty she was to feel threatened.

The older Mr. Redding broke off his conversation with her father to greet the viscount with a brief bow. "Just looked out your window a few moments ago. Thought I saw Farlanger's daughter running across the garden."

Madeleine felt surprised to see the viscount blush; she hadn't guessed he could. "Yes," he replied, "she had to return home unexpectedly. I trust her leaving won't delay dinner overmuch."

"Won't be unusual if it does. I ate before I came, thank the gods. I've learned to do so when invited here."

Alice's laugh was tinged with embarrassment. "Father, you are so droll. Whatever will the Murrows think of you, criticizing our host for the crime of inviting us to dinner?"

"Hear, hear," George exclaimed. "We've been rescued from Magdala's cooking for one night—what does it matter when we're served, so long as we don't have to eat curry!"

Mr. Redding bristled. "A well-ordered house runs on time."

"Ordinarily, I would agree," said Mrs. Murrow from the chaise lounge which had been brought downstairs for her. "But here the food is worth the wait; the viscount's cook is marvelous. And personally, I find the spontaneity of this household refreshing, Mr. Redding."

The older gentleman's eyes softened as he looked at Madeleine's mother. "No doubt you are right, madam. You may call me William if you wish."

"And you may call *her* Mrs. Murrow," Madeleine's father said, knotting his fists on his hips and glowering in an extravagant display of jealousy. Although this act brought the desired chuckles, Madeleine knew her father had conveyed his point. He still felt toward her mother as he had when they were young, and it made the possibility of losing her even more poignant.

Surely her mother would rally from what the physician believed to be her final decline. She had more color in her cheeks since coming to the viscount's home and appeared to possess greater energy. Of course, those improvements could be attributed to the prospect of seeing her daughter betrothed. Madeleine moved uncomfortably. The days were flying past; a decision must be made soon.

Mr. Redding meandered to her parents' side of the room and began to talk about the cook he had brought from India. Lord Ambrose took that opportunity to move his chair closer to the young ladies and George. He was followed by Mr. Brandt, who had seemed strangely invisible since the arrival of the Reddings.

"Do you like to ride, Madeleine?" Alice asked, moving aside her white-silvered skirts to allow the viscount more leg room. "Has Ethan shown you the countryside?"

Madeleine admitted she did enjoy riding but no, they had not yet had such an excursion. *And why not?* she wondered with an abrupt sense of neglect. The only outing she'd had since coming here was a trip by coach to the village, and that was with her parents.

"I cannot believe it." Alice glared playfully at the viscount. "Whatever can you be thinking, Ethan? You haven't shown her Viking?"

"We've not had time," he said, sending her a telling look.

"Since when do you need time to show off your black? Madeleine, he is quite mad about his horse, not that I blame him for that. Viking is stunning! But do not allow him to start talking about him, for he's worse than a schoolmaster."

"Worse than MacAllister!" laughed George.

"MacAllister?" Madeleine asked, smiling vicariously.

Alice touched her knee briefly, instantly including her. "He was our tutor years ago, and Father brought him back last spring to help us learn the latest waltzes and improve our Italian and French for our grand tour next year. The trip will be our way of celebrating the end of the war." She turned her large, lapis lazuli eyes upon the viscount. "None of this explains why you haven't taken Madeleine for a ride."

"There is the matter of a suitable mount for Miss Murrow," he said reluctantly, obviously pained at the lack in his stable.

"Oh, nonsense. We can supply her a beast. Madeleine, why don't we plan something for this week—shall we say Friday? We could all go—you and Ethan, George and I."

"And Mr. Brandt," Madeleine prompted, certain that Alice meant to include him but had only forgotten.

"Oh, of course," she said quickly. "Scott, you're welcome to join us as well."

His smile was thin. "Thank you, but I'm afraid I cannot."

Lord Ambrose tilted his head. "Come on, old man. What else do you have to do?"

"Oh, many things—the accounts for one, and the agricultural expert might come by that day—"

"Put them off," said the viscount. "You need to lighten—"

"The Abbotts have arrived," Burns announced at the doorway.

A middle-aged man and woman entered, followed by a young lady Madeleine soon learned was their daughter. A flurry of introductions gave her to know that the Rev. Joseph Abbott was Brillham's only vicar. He was a lightweight man who moved with the hidden strength of a caged lion. His thick, dark skin made her wonder at an Italian ancestry, and it was repeated in his daughter, Leah. Her poreless complexion stretched over pleasant but for the most part unremarkable features, excepting a pair of small, beautifully shaped eyes with large brown irises. These she kept well hidden, being either too shy or naturally reticent to look up often. Her mother, Elizabeth, was gray-haired, stout, and had the demeanor of a woman accustomed to voicing her demands and having them obeyed.

By the time greetings were exchanged, dinner was announced, and the company retired to the viscount's cavernous dining room. Madeleine had not yet become accustomed to this chamber. Its high, narrow dimensions and lack of carpet or tapestry caused resounding echoes. Tonight, the eeriness of sound and stone threw her imagination into furious activity. She could easily visualize a second set of phantom diners sitting between each guest. Even worse: as in the grand hall, a suit of armor rested here; this one leaned against the wall next to the butler's pantry. She halfway expected it to creak into motion while moaning some cryptic warning.

The diners took their places, and Madeleine was delighted to find herself seated close to Alice. While conversations murmured around the table and the first course began, that young lady leaned past her brother to speak to Madeleine.

"Are you cold?" she asked. "I thought I saw you shiver a moment ago. Shall we send for your wrap?"

"A wrap will do little for me," Madeleine responded. She hushed her voice, conspirator-like, her eyebrows lowering dramatically. "I'm experiencing a coldness of spirit, not flesh."

"Ooh, you frighten me!" laughed George, who was caught in the middle and had little choice but to listen.

Alice pulled a face. "Oh, I do understand what you mean. The dining room is quite medieval, isn't it? My father says this table and chairs have been here since he was a boy, and who knows how long before that! I can almost see King Arthur at it, can't you?"

"Except the table's rectangular, not round," George reminded.

"Don't be so literal, George. Oh, but Madeleine, does the atmosphere not make you fear the Ambrose curse could be true?"

"The Ambrose curse—what is that?"

As it happened, Madeleine's question, spoken in a more shrill tone than she normally used, fell loudly into a conversational lull. The silence that followed her words was so profound her ears began to burn.

"Curse?" Thomas echoed after a moment. "What curse?"

Madeleine looked to Lord Ambrose's place at the head of the table. His face had gone as white as the cloth, and she felt his anger whipping past her like a lash.

"I'm sorry," Alice said in bewildered tones. "Did you not"—she looked at Madeleine, then her parents. "Has no one told you?" Her worried gaze returned to Ethan. "I should *not* have brought it up! Only . . . I thought you or one of the servants would have spoken of it by now . . ."

"Why would we?" he asked curtly.

"I apologize, Ethan." She looked crushed,

"No need to beg pardon, my girl," Mr. Redding said between slurps of soup. "Someone would have mentioned it sooner or later."

"What's this about?" Thomas asked again.

"Nothing but foolishness." The viscount's gaze continued to rest resentfully on Alice. "The kind of story old women whisper to their grandchildren at night."

"Is it, indeed? I'd like to hear it."

Antonia placed her hand over her husband's. "Dear, if he doesn't want to speak of it, then he shouldn't."

Reverend Abbott waved a piece of bread, drawing the attention of everyone. "I'll tell it if you like, lad. Telling stories is part of my vocation, just as it was my Master's."

"No. I'll do it." Ethan slowly set down his fork. When he raised his eyes, Madeleine had the ridiculous conviction he was no longer behind them.

"Three-and-thirty years ago, a band of gypsies came to the door of Westhall requesting a place to stay for a few days. My father was a young man—a rash young man, or so I've been informed. He wanted nothing to do with ne'er-do-wells who hadn't the strength of character to earn an honest wage and their own place to live, and that's what he told them.

"Unfortunately, it had rained for several days straight, and the river that bisects the back acreage of our property was swollen. Since the gypsies couldn't stay, they attempted to cross the river as a short route to the village. Several of them drowned, including two children, the matriarch of the tribe, and her adult son."

Antonia breathed in sharply, and Madeleine clenched her hands together at the needlessness of those deaths.

The viscount's mouth twisted ironically. "The matriarch survived long enough to pronounce a curse on the Ambrose family. 'No male in the family shall live past three decades of life,' she decreed. Why she chose that number, I don't know, unless her own son was thirty. Or perhaps she guessed my father to be that age. In fact, he was twenty-seven, and by an unfortunate coincidence, he lived only three more years before losing his life." His gaze flickered from Madeleine to her parents. "I will tell you before you hear it somewhere else, and probably exaggerated for its drama. My father died while overseeing his attempt to build a bridge across the river. The structure collapsed while he stood upon it, crushing him."

"Oh, my dear," said Antonia, her eyes glistening. "To have lost your father so young . . ."

He sent her a gentle smile. "The tragedy happened a few months before we—my brother and I—were born. Although we grew up wishing for a father, we did not have to recover from the sorrow of losing one, for that was the only way of life we knew."

Madeleine believed him to be softening his loss for her mother's sake, and his compassion moved her. His speaking of his brother as if they were of one mind—*the only way of life* we *knew*—folded her heart. She also felt intrigued by his sire's actions.

"We haven't seen all of your property yet, Lord Ambrose," she said. "Was the bridge ever completed?"

"Never. My mother had the pilings torn down and every stick of wood burned. She forbade my brother and me ever to go near the river."

George, his mouth stuffed with bread, laughed. "Which made it into the forbidden fruit, naturally."

"Yes, it did," Alice said, smiling tenuously in the viscount's direction. "We spent much of our adolescence there fishing and floating boats and learning to swim. I'm afraid I was a nuisance much of that time, being so much younger and a female. I am happy to say the boys were tolerant of me; at least, reasonably so."

She was attempting to restore herself in Lord Ambrose's eyes, Madeleine saw. When he responded with a faint smile of recollection, she felt relieved. If he were so vindictive he couldn't forgive his lifelong friend a simple slip of the tongue, she would have been disappointed in him.

"Do you know your father's intention in building the bridge?" she asked Lord Ambrose. "Do you think he had a change of heart?"

"Was he sorry for his part in the gypsies' deaths, you

mean? My mother never spoke of his motivation or any-thing to do with the accident, but it's a compelling notion."

His gaze lingered on hers, warm and lively with interest. She found herself returning his look, her pulse quicken-ing. From the corner of her eye, she saw her mother ob-serving them with pleasure. This made her self-conscious, and she resolved to concentrate on her meal instead of asking so many questions.

Mr. Redding clattered his spoon into his empty soup bowl. "Knowing your father as I did, he might have thought building a bridge would dissolve the curse."

"Are you implying my sire was a superstitious man?" Lord Ambrose asked.

"Hard not to be when the proof lay before his eyes," Redding said.

"Father," Alice reproved quietly.

At that moment, Betsy entered the dining room carry-ing an enormous tray of creamed pork and vegetables. Blowing the hair from her forehead and sighing deeply, she set the tray on the sideboard.

"Burns could help, but thinks he's above it," she said under her breath, but Madeleine heard her plainly, as did the viscount, from his irritated expression. "He ain't above a worm's droppings, should anyone ask me."

Madeleine placed her hand in front of her lips to hide her smile. When Lord Ambrose flashed a look of fury at the maid, and Betsy returned it with a fierce scowl, she had to laugh. The maid gave her a grudging grin and began to serve the meat. Feeling the viscount's glance return to herself, Madeleine spotted a twinkle in his eye that shot delight down to her toes.

Redding eyed the platter hungrily. "Seems obvious to me. When he lost his firstborn, how could he not think of it? He thought the sun rose on that boy. Either he meant to protect himself, his future offspring, or both. He'd have been a fool not to take all precautions."

"Now who is sounding superstitious?" Reverend Abbott said in a playful voice, shaking his finger at the older man.

"Curses and the occult world have no place in a good Christian's home *or* his conversation."

"You don't know, Joseph," said his wife, who looked mightily intrigued by this topic. "Everything in the world is not in the Bible. *Phaetons* are not in the Bible, are they? Yet they *do* exist. Maybe not in our household, but for some people. Or do you think *phaetons* have no place in a Christian's conversation?"

Reverend Abbott bowed his head and smiled the smile of the long-suffering. "Now, my dear, this obsession you have with phaetons—"

"Did your father lose *another* son?" Madeleine burst, not able to stand the suspense an instant longer. Her amusement had faded into tension. She felt as if she were watching the approach of a runaway carriage and had no place to hide.

The viscount, his eyes narrowed upon Mr. Redding, did not answer immediately. Betsy had at that moment arrived at the older gentleman's plate, and she slapped down his serving of pork with such force that the cream sauce splattered across his cravat.

"Idiot!" Redding exclaimed, slicing an irate look upwards. With jerky motions, he dabbed at his neckcloth with his napkin.

"So sorry, I'm sure," Betsy said loudly, the expression on her face belying the words. "Here, let me help you, sir." She placed the platter on the table, dipped her serving cloth in Mr. Redding's glass of water, and made swipes at his cravat until he batted her hands away in irritation. George snorted, then began to cough into his napkin when his father glared at him.

Apparently cheered by these acts of insubordination, the viscount returned his gaze to Madeleine. "To answer your question, Miss Murrow: Yes, we had an older brother, Jonathan. Unfortunately, he died two years before we were born. He was only five. It was a fever that took him, as it does many small children. You should not read any dire meanings into his death."

Without awareness, Madeleine leaned back as Betsy very carefully laid a slice of pork onto her plate.

His father, she was thinking.

His brother.

His twin.

How far could one carry coincidence?

That was one question she dared not ask. But her eyes were solemn as she looked at him, her heart heavy as lead as she made calculations based on what the viscount had said. The curse was pronounced thirty-three years ago. Three years later, his father died and the twins were born. Depending upon the months involved, Lord Ambrose had to be twenty-nine or thirty years old.

By the time Betsy staggered dramatically into the dining room with the plum pudding, Ethan was convinced his chances with Miss Murrow were gravely compromised. After Alice betrayed him by resurrecting a subject he hoped to avoid, Madeleine had scarcely spoken.

In retrospect, he should have cautioned Alice and George to monitor their conversation. But then, someone else would have mentioned the curse, and warning everyone was preposterous. Perhaps it was for the best. He could not in good conscience enter into a betrothal with Madeleine without telling her the truth. He would have liked to postpone it a little longer, that was all.

And now, apparently, Madeleine could think of little else. More than once he caught her watching him, her expression morbid. Probably wondering how long he had.

Not long, he wanted to say to her, then laugh to show how little he believed in the ravings of an old woman who had died decades ago.

Lucan had given no credence to the curse, either, an insidious voice reminded him. He swallowed the thought with his pudding.

He wished he could banish his fears concerning Madeleine so easily. Almost as daunting were the wary glances her father kept sending. He, too, seemed unnaturally quiet at table, and Ethan imagined a world of thoughts passing behind his intelligent eyes. The viscount felt certain he was not gullible to the point of believing in witchcraft, but something had dampened his enthusiasm.

With a sense of things falling apart, he had to admit he'd noticed Mr. Murrow's hesitancy before tonight. Where was he going amiss? The question desperately needed answering, and not only to keep Westhall alive. Somehow in the last few days, the estate had ceased to be his primary concern. Madeleine Murrow was.

She enchanted him. She seemed easily the most caring person he'd ever known. Her conversation, even her questions, illustrated depths of thought unusual in anyone, male or female. Her quiet beauty had seeped through his pores and into his heart and mind. Had he ever considered her ordinary in looks? How blind he had been.

At least he had an ally in her mother, he believed. She would make an excellent mother-in-law, if given the chance; her generous spirit was a striking contrast to that of his own mother, who had died an angry woman six years before.

In all fairness, most of his mother's anger had been directed at herself, not only at him and the fate that took her husband. It had been her idea to use modern farming techniques, but she had little useful knowledge. Thanks to faulty advice and a run of foul weather for several seasons, she had taken the estate to the verge of ruin. Lucan and he had done their best to redeem the damage, but their resources were too small to make much difference.

Lucan. Sorrow swept over him.

The taste of plum soured in his mouth. He lowered his spoon. The place inside him, that secure place where Lucan had once dwelled—*I am not alone: my brother is with me*—welled upward into his chest, his throat. His heart seemed a silent tomb now, hard as iron; heavy and deadening as chains pulling a drowning man to the bottom of the sea.

Alone. So alone.

Stop. He had to stop thinking of him, or he would become ill, as he had so many times before.

Oh, God, why Lucan and not me? Was your need of him so much greater than my own?

Perspiration began to bead at his temples, his upper lip. He dashed it away with shaking fingers.

Feeling someone watching him, he looked up. It was Alice, her eyes as filled with sadness as his own heart. She knew the depth of his sorrow, because she endured it as well.

Beyond Alice and George, Miss Murrow leaned forward to look slowly from him to Alice, then back again. The tiniest of frowns marred her brow.

In spite of his distress, Ethan felt a wisp of good humor. Was it possible Miss Murrow was misreading matters; could she be feeling the slightest bit jealous? What a favorable sign.

Perhaps this dinner had not been a total waste. The thought restored him to a measure of normal feeling.

Afterward, when the gentlemen joined the ladies in the library, Mrs. Abbott boldly caught his eye. "Lord Ambrose, what of that baby I've been hearing so much about? Might we see it?"

He immediately went on guard. "Have people been talking about my cousin's child? I'm surprised at their interest."

"Why should you be?" Redding lowered himself into the viscount's favorite leather chair. "There's little enough to gossip about in a village this size, especially as none of us can recall this cousin you keep mentioning. Your father and I were boys together, and I never knew of her family. Must be on your mother's side, as he was an only son, and his sister never married."

"My mother's side, yes," Ethan said rapidly. "And a distant cousin at that. I'll have Burns fetch the babe if she's awake."

The butler did not appear overjoyed at this assignment, but within minutes he returned with Dorrie held stiffly in his arms. With a cry, Mrs. Abbott rushed forward and took the child. As Burns retreated, she started murmuring endearments in childish syllables bearing little resemblance to the English language, Ethan thought with increasing nausea. Still, he could not fault her assessment that Dorrie was the prettiest child ever to breathe. Dorrie, however, apparently disagreed and began to fret.

"Oh, does dee leedle one not like Elizabuth?" Mrs. Abbott cooed to the child over a cacophony of suggestions from all sides. "Is her scaring dee pretty leedle babee?"

Ethan could bear no more. He shot from his seat on the hearth and scooped Dorrie into his arms. "She likes to be walked," he told Mrs. Abbott. Within seconds, the infant fell silent, her cheek pressed trustingly to his breast pocket.

"Well, she likes *you*," the vicar's wife said in offended tones.

He could not prevent feeling a ridiculous swell of pride. When he glanced up and saw the interest he was attracting, he quickly turned to Madeleine and spotted a pleasant warmth in her eyes.

"Would you like to walk Dorrie?" he asked her.

"I could, I suppose," she said, lifting her arms for the babe. "But when she is with me, I've found she likes to lie on her back." She smiled as she laid the child lengthwise on her lap. With her hand cushioning Dorrie's head, she gently swayed her legs from side to side. Wide-eyed, Dorrie peered upward at her face.

Madeleine will make an excellent mother, Ethan thought. It was not a stretch to imagine her cuddling a child of their own. Although this might be a child of *his* own. How would that news settle with her? He could not believe any woman would like it, and his muscles tightened at the possibility that the adorable, helpless bundle on her lap might spell the ruin of their relationship.

"I think the baby just smiled at you!" said Alice, who was again sitting beside Madeleine on the settee. "Oh, may I hold her when you are done? How I love infants, and she is so delightful!"

And so it went for the space of the next quarter-hour; while conversations bubbled among small groups, every woman in the room had a turn nesting the baby—with one exception. Only Leah Abbott appeared uninterested in holding the infant. Even stranger, when Mrs. Abbott, who was sitting next to her on the loveseat, made a second, more successful attempt at cradling the babe, Leah actually shrank away from the child.

Odd behavior for a female, Lord Ambrose thought.

Before long, Dorrie tired of being passed around like a box of truffles and started fussing again. Intent on consigning her to the nursery via Burns, the viscount lifted her from Mrs. Murrow's arms. A sudden impulse led him to Leah's side.

"This is your last opportunity, Leah," he said.

She dashed him a look of dread, then turned her eyes downward and shook her dark cap of curls. "No, my lord, I don't care to."

Her voice was so soft he had to stoop to discern it from the murmur of several conversations; and when he understood her words, he could not believe them. Crass though it might be, he could not help asking, "Why not?"

"I just . . . don't like babies."

Mrs. Abbott poked her in the ribs, hard. "Don't go around saying so, girl. *That* kind of word gets out, you won't have a chance of marriage."

"I'll never get married."

The vicar's wife cast her eyes heavenward. "Stop being melodramatic or you truly *won't.*" She gave the viscount a long-suffering look. "She's back less than a week, and already her mood is as sullen as it was before we sent her off. What's a mother to do?"

"I'm sure I have no idea, ma'am. Have you been away a long time, Leah?"

The young woman glanced at him resentfully and said nothing. Her mother moved into the breach. "She's spent the last three months visiting her aunt in Wales. We hoped she would snap from this gloom, but you see how successful we were. Some young women are just that way, though. Melancholy. What she needs is a good husband and a family."

Mrs. Abbott continued to rattle on in the same vein. Ethan could barely contain his excitement. *Go easy. Don't repeat the Annie Farlanger disaster.* As unobtrusively as possible, he glanced from Dorrie to Leah. Yes, there was a resemblance. The coloring did not match, of course, but the father could have been blond.

Like himself. He was blond. But there were some things a man didn't forget, and an illicit tryst with the vicar's daughter topped the list.

"Lucan would have noticed I had gone," Leah said when her mother ran out of words. "He didn't miss things like that. People were important to him."

"Leah!" Mrs. Abbott cried.

Lord Ambrose straightened. "No, she's right." He smiled briefly. "People *were* important to him."

In that instant he decided to return Dorrie to the nursery himself. Banishing his suspicions of Miss Abbott for another day, he fled the room.

Six

Long after the guests departed and everyone had gone to bed, Madeleine lay in her four-poster, propped upright with both pillows, reading by candlelight. She longed to sleep, but felt horrendously alert; too alert to read, certainly; but perhaps that was the fault of her novel, which had a heroine so virtuous she simply wanted to shake her. What she needed was a grand adventure; maybe a rousing tale of the sea and buried treasure. Anything to stop thinking about the Ambrose curse; anything to put her wildly growing attraction to the viscount into a more sensible frame. She feared she would soon be beyond logical thinking where he was concerned, and that could prove disastrous for her future. She *must* remain detached and make this most vital decision with her head, not her heart.

Placing the despised novel on the bedside table, she stepped from bed, swirled her wrapper around her shoulders, slid her feet into her slippers, and lifted the candle. Shielding the flickering brightness with one hand, she walked downstairs to the library. Thanks to the flames of a dying fire in the grate, she found greater light here.

She lifted the candle to eye level and began to run one finger along the spines. There seemed to be a preponderance of histories and biographies. Perhaps she should take one of these; surely that would make her sleepy.

"My kingdom for Sir Walter Scott," she murmured.

"You will find him on the opposite side of the room,

first row of shelves, somewhere near the middle," said the viscount from the doorway.

She nearly shrieked. "Oh, Lord Ambrose! I didn't know you were here!"

"I was in my study and saw your light moving down the stairs." He moved forward a trifle unsteadily. She lowered her eyes to the glass of scarlet liquid in his hand. Her disillusionment was so extreme she dared not look at him but returned to the books, pretending to scan titles.

In the meantime, he crossed the room. Long seconds later, he returned with a novel which he placed in her hands.

"Rob Roy." She smiled faintly. "Thank you. I—I'm sure I'll enjoy it. Good night, Lord Ambrose."

"I wish you would stay."

She looked pointedly at his wineglass. "I fear that would be an intrusion; you already appear to have a companion."

"What, this?" He held up his glass. "Sometimes wine helps me to sleep, but it's not helping tonight. Please don't go. We have so little opportunity to speak with each other alone."

Lowering her lashes, she debated. He looked wretched. He looked as if he could use a friend. But if her father found her alone with the viscount in her night attire, he would explode.

"Of course, if you're too tired . . ."

She came to her decision suddenly. "I'm not tired at all, Lord Ambrose."

"Please call me Ethan. Seems ludicrous to be formal when in this kind of situation."

"And what situation is that?"

"Don't be coy; I don't like it. You know I'm referring to our two-week trial period."

"I was not being coy," she said, miffed. "I wasn't sure whether you meant *that* or *this.*" Demonstratively, she plucked at the skirt of her wrapper.

"I see. My apologies, then, and my compliments. You

look well in blue." He gestured toward the fireplace and Madeleine, mollified, went to the settee. To her discomfort, he sat beside her. "Well?"

"Well?" she echoed, mystified.

"May I call you Madeleine?"

"Oh, certainly. Although you may not wish to do so in front of my father."

"Well said. He is rather formal, I've noticed; a stickler for propriety."

Her chin rose. "Is something wrong with that?"

"No," he said softly, giving her a half-smile that failed to reach his eyes. "I'm certain everything is *right* with that."

"Some people would do well to emulate his example."

"Ah. You would not by any chance, be referring to me?"

She chose not to answer, but instead gazed into the fire.

"It's merely a glass of wine," he said, shaking it slightly to make his point.

"You had more than a glass on our first night here."

"Yes, and I do apologize for that. It's not a regular occurrence, I assure you. You have seen me take wine with meals since then, and I've not repeated that episode."

She looked him squarely in the eyes. "This is important for me to know . . . Ethan." How odd it seemed to say his given name. "Do you"—she tilted her head toward the wineglass—"depend upon that overmuch?"

He stared into the mellow liquid. "If I did, would I tell you?"

Madeleine studied his profile. "Yes, I believe you would say truth."

"Do you?" His smile was sweet but incredulous. "Then I say to you truthfully: I do not have a problem with drink."

"That first evening . . . why did you do it *then?* Was it because of me?"

"I tried to convince myself it was." This cut her to the bone, and she moved responsively. "Madeleine," he said swiftly, placing his hand around her wrist for an instant.

"That didn't come out well. I didn't know you then, and you were an easy excuse for my gloom."

She digested this for a moment. "Do you often have such moods?"

"Not often." He looked away from her, took a sip of wine, and set his glass on the table.

Very softly, she ventured, "Have these periods of gloom increased since your brother's death?"

Anger flew into his face, then quickly died. "You have named when they began."

"I suspected as much. Grief affects everyone differently, I believe. It was that way in our family when Bettina died. Papa preferred to be alone; my mother deteriorated physically, and I wept myself to sleep every night for ages." She called her mind to the present and leaned toward him earnestly. "The grief never goes away, but it becomes less sharp in time. Perhaps I shouldn't say this; I don't have the right, but as someone who cares about you . . . *Ethan,* your drinking is not a difficulty *yet,* but may very well become so if you do not stop."

His gaze moved over her face, filling her with odd, pleasurable sensations. *"Do* you care for me, Madeleine?"

She straightened. "How vexing that you hear only what you want to hear and leave out the important parts."

"That *was* the important part to me." A gleam lit in his eyes when she frowned. "All right I'll tell you another important point: drink soothes the pain."

"How you frighten me! That is precisely the kind of thinking you should avoid."

"It is?" His eyes were smoldering into hers now. Nervously, she moved backward a fraction of an inch and felt the settee's wood arm at her spine. "What would you recommend I think about instead?"

"I . . . I believe . . . probably that you should—"

His lips quietened hers. Shocked, she made a feeble effort to pull away. Instantly, his arms slid around her. She could feel every movement of his fingers through the thin layers of cloth at her back. She melted toward him, her flesh singing at his touch.

I have been kissed before, she thought, the sensations flowing through her body making her mad with pleasure, but never like this.

After a dizzying interval, she pulled away from him, gasping. "Ethan—"

"Madeleine," he whispered, his voice husky as he moved to bring her into his arms again. His eyes were unknowable, saturated with desire.

She fought her true wishes and turned from him, straightening her wrap primly. "That is quite enough, my lord. If you do not stop, I shall have to leave."

Slowly, he withdrew his arms. "Have I offended you?"

"Oh, no," she said immediately, and touched his hand briefly to show how much she meant it. Had he offended her? She had just experienced the best few minutes of her life! "No, you have not."

"You must forgive me. I suppose I *have* had too much to drink. Makes a fellow forget his inhibitions."

She gave him a sharp look. "I see. I'm grateful you told me the true reason you felt moved to kiss me."

A slow smile lit his face. "The true reason is that I find you irresistible. I didn't lie to you; I've only had the one glass. I only said so to see what you would say."

"Are you playing with me, my lord?" she asked indignantly.

"Not half as much as I'd like," he replied, his eyes on her lips.

Heart thundering in her ears, she ripped herself from the settee to stand several feet away. "You . . . overwhelm me. Our acquaintance is not long enough for this sort of intimacy."

"Unfortunately, we don't have much time to improve that acquaintance, Madeleine. There is scarcely more than a week before you leave."

"Is that why you made the most of this opportunity?"

she cried, her spirit wilting. "Did you make love to me in order to sway my opinion—to win my affection?"

"Yes, I did," he said, his eyes solemn.

"You admit it?" she gasped, wanting to burst into tears.

"If you must have everything analyzed, Madeleine, the main reason I kissed you was because I could not prevent myself from touching you. But yes, I had ulterior motives as well. What man, finding himself falling in love with a beautiful woman, would not hope to encourage an equal sentiment in his lady?"

How beautiful his words sounded to her ears! But did he mean them? She longed to believe he was beginning to love her.

The irony of her thoughts suddenly struck. For long and long, she had felt nothing, as though her heart had been buried with Bettina. Therefore, she had approached the possibility of marriage with no more emotion than a statesman negotiating a treaty. Now that it appeared there were no obstacles in the way of that marriage, she did not want to go through with it unless love was involved. No, not *involved*. It must be the primary reason.

Had she lost all good sense?

If the viscount had been a boring, pleasant gentleman who did not enlist her affection to any degree, she would have had no qualms in marrying *him*. Or at least, she did not think she would. But since he frightened her with his frailties, tore at her emotions with his grief, and, worst of all, set her heart and body on fire with desire, she was afraid to commit to him.

She had not lost her mind, she realized with sudden insight. She was terrified of being vulnerable to this man. He held the power to hurt her.

"How can I know if your affection is genuine and not caused by your need for my father's wealth?" she asked, the words spilling from the depths of her soul.

He sprang from his seat and walked to her. Alarmed he would try to kiss her, she turned her back to him. He moved very close, so close she could feel his breath on her cheek. When his hands slid down her arms and linked at her waist, her skin pebbled, making her shiver; she did not have the strength to resist, but leaned against him and closed her eyes.

"You know that need is there," he whispered. "I've made no secret of it."

"I know," she admitted.

"It was a promise I made to my brother."

Her lashes raised. "Was it?"

She sensed him gathering his thoughts. "The day Lucan . . . was shot. He didn't die immediately." He was silent a moment, and she laid her fingers over his hands as he struggled. "I was with him in the field. He knew he didn't have long. Lucan understood me better than anyone. I had never taken the estate seriously; in my mind, it was his responsibility as the older brother." He gave a humorless laugh. "Ten minutes my elder, and a world of difference in accountability. As he lay dying, he charged me with maintaining our inheritance. He said he trusted me to keep the line going. I was not to give in to my own desires, or my sorrow. There was nothing I could do for him. Nothing except give my word to carry out his wishes."

"Which you did," she said softly.

"I did." He inhaled deeply. "Therefore, I determined to find a way to finance the renewal of this pile of stones."

"Enter Madeleine Murrow, stage right," she said with some bitterness.

"But how delightful an entrance. I had not counted on finding love as well as everything else."

"You have not known me long enough to be certain of your feelings."

"Ah, Madeleine, you torture me. How long must I wait? I would visit your father in the morning were it up to me."

She tilted her head backward in annoyance. "Is that supposed to be a proposal?"

"If you're ready to hear it, I'm prepared to give you my best effort."

"I think I shall collapse with the romance of it," she said, hardly knowing whether to be amused or angry.

"I'll go down on one knee if you like," he said lightly.

"No." He was very quiet behind her, and she felt his frustration. "Too fast, my lord. Too fast by far."

After a brief hesitation, he said, "I bow to your wishes."

She could no longer hide her greatest fear, and turned within his arms to face him. Ethan . . . this curse. You don't—"

"Is that what's troubling you? How I wish Alice hadn't brought up *that* subject." His hands loosened from her waist, and he moved to the fireplace, sat on the edge of the hearth, and crossed his arms over one knee. "There's nothing to it, Madeleine. Only an unfortunate series of coincidences."

She wished she could believe him. "It doesn't worry you?"

He sighed explosively. "I blame Alice for this. She knows the whole thing is meaningless."

Madeleine fought a desire to call him back to her. Instead, she followed him to the fireplace. "Alice didn't know we were ignorant of the curse. Please don't blame her; she meant nothing by it."

"Oh, didn't she? You're already caught in her web, I see. You don't understand the relationships here, so you shouldn't try to speak with an authority you can't support."

"I'm sure you're correct," she said, fighting to keep her voice reasonable, remembering his grief. "But how can I learn if you won't tell me?"

How can I learn if you won't tell me?

She could not know how her words disturbed him. After the past few days, and especially after the blood-boiling intensity of the past few moments, he wanted to pour his entire life into her ears. It was the first time he'd felt this way since Lucan left him; but there were things no gentleman could say, especially not to a woman he hoped to marry. How could he explain Alice's motivations when they so closely involved himself?

Well. Not precisely *himself.*

"I don't know how to make you understand a lifetime in only a few words." He stood, lifted the poker, and nudged the ashes, then started piling on pieces of wood. "I suppose I should begin by telling you that everyone loved Lucan."

"If that is true, then everyone loves you as well. You were twins."

He smiled at the loyalty he heard in her voice. "No, you don't understand. We were like two sides of a coin. He was all goodness and light. I was darkness."

"Oh, pooh. No one is totally good or bad."

He stared at her. Almost, almost she could make him laugh about his deepest-felt inadequacies, but the scars ran too deep. He turned back to the fire.

"In this case it's true. You'll understand in a moment. One of the reasons I left the running of the estate entirely to Lucan was because he was so competent at everything he touched. I took no responsibility for anything except my own pleasure. The only occupation of remote worth that caught my interest was breeding horses, but we didn't have the funds to pursue it. Therefore, I played. I brought him . . . great sadness."

He stabbed at the wood, wishing for the moment it was himself.

"Lucan often told me I was wasting my life and potential. I never listened to his counsel; instead, I resented it. How I worried him with my mistresses and gambling." When her eyes widened, he nodded. "Oh, yes. I suppose I should have told you about those vices as well, although I promise you, that sort of thing is in the past. Still, there are more sins. Would you like to hear the list? Do you have all night?"

He closed his mouth abruptly. Next he would be explaining about the baby upstairs. Did he want to send her packing?

"Was he as brutally honest as you?" she asked after a moment.

He laughed. "Honest, yes. Brutal, no. Had you met Lucan, you wouldn't have given me a second thought. It was impossible not to love him. You could not have helped preferring him over me. Everyone did."

"Oh, Ethan, not *everyone,* surely."

"Yes, everyone, my mother included. I think it galled her that Lucan and I looked so much alike, yet acted so differently. She and I didn't get on at all well, and as I grew older, I spent much of my time in London to escape her sharp tongue."

"If your perception of things is true, how difficult that must have been for you."

"I would have hated him if I could, but that was impossible. He had my best interest at heart. He had *everyone's* best interest at heart. It didn't matter whether the person was the village baker or the marquess in the next county. And his was not an idle concern, either; his caring activated him. For an example: a few years ago, there was an outbreak of fever among our laborers. Lucan not only saw to it that everyone had food, blankets, and medicine, but he visited them. Do you know what it means for a commoner to have a lord serve him? I declare to you, my brother came close to being worshipped."

She folded her hands at her waist, paced a few feet, and turned with a serious, scowling look. It was a masculine gesture to see in so feminine a creature—made the more compelling by the way her garments draped over her graceful curves—and he didn't know whether to smile or to clutch her in his arms again. Discretion being the better part of valor, he did nothing.

"Sometimes, Ethan, memory softens the true character of a loved one. I've seen it happen with my mother and Bettina. She doesn't seem to recall the times my sister made her weep with frustration."

"I understand that, but in this case it doesn't apply. Lucan was a religious man. If he had been the younger of us, I think he would have become a clergyman; maybe even a missionary. His caring knew no bounds; he lived to give to others."

Her frown deepened. He saw her struggling to believe. He could not blame her. Who would think a young man— a *peer*—with every advantage, could be so willing to sacrifice all? Had he not lived nearly every day of his life beside Lucan, he would not have believed it, either.

"Have you ever seen the copies young artists make of paintings by great masters?" he asked. "I'm like that. An inferior copy. I've lived with that knowledge all my life. You have only to ask to find it's true. Notice sometimes the way Burns looks at me; he hates me for surviving my brother. He prefers I had died rather than Lucan. He's not alone."

"You should give him the sack, then," she pronounced.

"I can't do that."

"And why not?"

He shrugged. "What would he do? He's not a young man anymore, and positions aren't that easy to find."

"Are you telling me you feel an obligation to the butler? A certain loyalty because of his years of service?"

"I . . ." He saw her trap and stopped.

"Such a dark man you are, Ethan Ambrose. How you frighten me."

Despite an elevation in his spirits, he felt bound she should know the truth as completely as he could tell it, for to remain silent could bring her hurt. "Alice loved my brother. Since we were children, she built her world around him, but Lucan dwelled on another level than the rest of us. He treated her well, but no differently than anyone else. This went on for years. Alice could have wed many times over; you see how attractive and charming she is—"

"I had noticed, but thank you for reminding me."

He grinned briefly. "At any rate, Lucan's life was full without a wife; but I suppose a sense of obligation to the future led him to finally propose—"

"They were *betrothed?*" Madeleine said in agonized tones, her hands flying to her cheeks.

"Yes, I think he'd given up on me as a candidate to fulfill that duty with someone. He asked her to marry him a couple of months before the accident. They were to have wed last fall."

"Oh, how horrible for her!" She began to pace. "But—but she has recovered so well!" Her eyes flew to his. "That didn't sound—I mean, she seemed so happy tonight that I never would have suspected—if she loved him for so long, I can't understand—"

"Never mind, I know what you're trying to say. Alice is capable of hiding her feelings."

"I don't know how she does it. Of course, she has her family. And—"

Again she gazed at him, this time with dawning horror. He watched her calmly, willing her to guess what he could not say.

"And you," she said, her voice trembling. "She has you."

"No, Madeleine, she does not have me."

He would never speak of the scene three months ago when Alice had begged him with tears raining down her cheeks to take Lucan's place. He was not his brother, he'd told her, and never could be. Her love was for Lucan, not him. He could not fulfill the role of a substitute, nor would he try.

"But she's not given up on the possibility, has she?"

"I shall always love Alice," he said carefully. "She is like a sister to me."

Madeleine nodded thoughtfully. "I see. Therefore, when she so casually mentioned the curse, she was hoping to discourage me."

He could not answer this, and he turned his gaze aside.

"Thank you for letting me know," she said softly, and, giving him a swift kiss on the cheek, hurried from the room.

Seven

Madeleine descended the stairs late the next morning, having overslept after a restless night. Everyone else had long since breakfasted, and she ate cold toast alone in the dining room. When she joined her family in the library, she found her father reading the newspaper and her mother working on a needlepoint project which would recover a pair of footstools in their morning room at home. Mr. Brandt, her father told her, had gone to visit the cottages to determine what needed to be repaired that spring. The viscount was riding.

"Have you noted how he rides every morning, no matter what the weather?" Antonia said to her daughter. "I find such energy remarkable."

Thomas rattled the pages of the newspaper without looking up "There's nothing remarkable about it at all, dearest. He's a young man. All young men have energy."

That is certainly true, Madeleine thought, remembering last evening with a mixture of pleasure and sadness.

Had the viscount been sincere when he declared his affections were engaged? Every instinct said he was, yet she was a practical woman. She would like to believe she was irresistible as Ethan had said, but sensibility decreed her wealth must have something to do with her attractiveness.

Yet he had told her many things he need not, such as his gentle warning about Alice. How *that* knowledge had hurt! She had looked forward to forming a close relation-

ship with Miss Redding, but such appeared impossible
now. She could forgive many things in a friendship, but
deception was not one of them. How she dreaded their
outing on Friday.

She had brought *Rob Roy* downstairs with her, and now
she sat in the chair with the drooping seat and prepared
to read. After a moment, her father folded his newspaper,
set it on the floor beside him, and went to close the double doors to the library. This last was so unusual that both
women looked up from their occupations.

Returning to his chair, he glanced from one to the
other of them. "We're so rarely alone together at Westhall,
I thought we should take advantage of this opportunity.
Antonia, I spoke with Madeleine for a few moments last
night about her impressions of the viscount. What
thoughts have you to share?"

"I? What matters most to me is Madeleine's happiness,
although I do find Lord Ambrose delightful. He has such
a manner with little Dorrie. I declare I have never seen
the like in a man—excepting you, of course, Thomas; you
were all that could be wished for with our daughters. How
do *you* feel about him, Madeleine?"

The young woman was opening her mouth to speak
when her father said, "She's not firmed her opinion yet.
She is more giving than I. Each day that passes, I find
more to doubt in his character."

"*Do* you?" Antonia said, her expression surprised.
"What have you seen that I have not?"

He gave her a fond look. "Many things, I'm certain,
since your sweetness does not allow you to think ill of
others. I find the situation of the baby to be suspicious. I
have trouble believing in this cousin of his whom no one
has ever seen. After last night, I'm experiencing more
doubts. Did you note Mr. Redding's questions about her?
He was skeptical, too."

Antonia pulled herself to a more upright position in
the chaise lounge. "Dear, Mr. Redding appeared suspicious and cross about the viscount in every little matter."

"True. Redding had little patience for him. That's another blot against Lord Ambrose."

"Or a blot against Mr. Redding," Madeleine said.

Thomas studied her. "In all the years he's lived next to the viscount and his father before him, Redding had not heard of this relative. That's very odd."

"What do you think it means?" Antonia leaned her head against her pillow and watched him beneath drooping lashes.

"When an infant is left on a particular gentleman's doorstep, it generally signifies one thing."

"Oh, Papa," Madeleine said, scandalized. "You can't think the child is *his.*"

"Surely not, Thomas!"

He stood abruptly and went to the window, clasping his hands behind his back as he stared outward. "Have you looked at that infant? Really *looked?*"

Madeleine recalled the child's blond beauty and felt a knot of dread tighten in her throat. She had to admit finding a resemblance did not stretch her imagination too far, but . . . no. Her father was spotting enemies when none was there.

"It seems to me you have Lord Ambrose accused and condemned in one stroke," she said. "Have you also determined the identity of Dorrie's heartless mother?"

"Mayhap I have." Thomas turned, his eyes narrowing in curiosity upon his daughter, and she suspected he was wondering why she defended the viscount so strongly. "Do you recall last night that Mr. Abbott saw the maid running across the garden? I saw her, too. She also had the same coloring as the child. Why do you suppose she left so abruptly? Could it not be that she and Ambrose had a lover's tiff? Or perhaps seeing her babe set feelings of guilt into motion."

Madeleine stifled an impulse to run screaming from the room. After last evening's meeting with the viscount, she had felt her doubts turning to trust, her attraction deepening to something more serious, perhaps love. To hear her father's suspicions now was like being splashed with freezing, briny water.

"It's not like you to be so unfair," she said. "There are a thousand possible reasons why the girl had to leave; and as to the baby's resemblance to her or Lord Ambrose—many people have fair hair and blue eyes. This is England, may I remind you, not Spain or China!"

"Don't try me, child. The moment I discover that infant is his, we are quit from here. My daughter will not be subjected to the shame and grief of raising an illegitimate child, nor shall I allow her to join with a man who would do such a thing. I had rather consign you to a convent!"

"A convent!" Madeleine cried, and, hoping to restore her father to his senses, added, "We're not even Catholic!"

"Thomas," Antonia protested, her voice growing reedy, "you're only speculating. Are you certain the thought of losing your daughter has finally become real to you, and you will grasp at anything to prevent it?"

"Antonia, there is nothing I want more than to see our daughter settled and happy." He sighed deeply and stared at the ceiling. "There is also the matter of the curse."

"Oh, yes, the curse," Antonia reflected slowly. "That *did* frighten me a little. You don't think there's anything in it, do you?"

Madeleine tried to rein in her fear. "Surely you don't. A curse doesn't hold power; that would mean magic is real."

"Did you hear yourselves just now? Both of you are intelligent ladies not given to fancies, yet I heard the tremble of fright in your voices. To answer you: No, I don't believe in curses. But I believe the viscount does, else why did he not share it with us before he was forced to do so last night?"

"Perhaps he didn't want to worry us," Madeleine suggested, "in case one of *us* believed in such things." She looked from one parent to the other. "Which we don't, of course," she added firmly.

Thomas shook his head. "Where there is belief, there is power. If Lord Ambrose believes he will die at thirty or before, he very well may do so. I've seen it occur on the battlefield. Men will awaken one morning convinced that is their day to be shot and it will happen. I have no desire to see Madeleine widowed within a year's time."

"I think Lord Ambrose can be counted upon to have more strength of will than that." Madeleine invested her words with a conviction she did not entirely feel.

Her father went on as if he had not heard her. "Now that we've shared our misgivings, I have a proposal to make. It seems senseless to remain for the second week. I suggest we leave now, today, before Madeleine's affections become engaged."

Madeleine's heart sank. She cleared her throat. "I'm afraid it's too late for that Papa"

Her father stared. "Oh, Madeleine," he said quietly.

"Oh, Madeleine!" exclaimed her mother, and clapped her hands.

It had become her mother's habit to send for the baby between luncheon and her afternoon nap. Today, in light of the questions Thomas had caused to enter their minds, Madeleine wondered if that invitation would be extended. She need not have doubted; Antonia made her request of the viscount as always. He gladly complied, going to fetch the child himself as he sometimes did.

When he entered the library with the baby, Madeleine could not help thinking how possessively he held Dorrie. He beamed as he handed her to Antonia, commenting on how mature the babe was growing, saying she hardly cried anymore.

Reluctantly, Madeleine succumbed to the pull of Thomas's eyes. He gave her an expressive look that plainly conveyed his thoughts: The viscount sounded proud of Dorrie.

As proud as a father.

Oh, how she detested thinking such things about Ethan. She blamed her own sire. How could someone that dear be so annoying?

She was enjoying her turn with the baby—Dorrie kept trying to pull Madeleine's fingers into her mouth—when she heard the front door open. Seconds later, Burns announced their visitors: Miss Redding, George, and a gentleman named Jarrod MacAllister—the tutor, Madeleine recalled, thinking she'd never seen anyone who looked less like one. He appeared to be in his mid-thirties and had thick, waving hair, one lock of which lay across his forehead in romantic disarray. His nose was too large for handsomeness, but the warmth in his eyes and his air of friendly intelligence made him highly appealing. He wore an odd, black velvet jacket over his pantaloons.

Alice and George were dressed in riding clothes. Alice's crimson velvet habit set off her golden brown hair beautifully. That much Madeleine would give her, but no more.

She feared she would not be able to converse with the young woman to any degree of civility, but her gentle raising rescued her. When Miss Redding came to sit at the end of the settee nearest her chair, Madeleine even summoned a smile.

"Oh, there is that delightful baby again," Alice said. "When you are done, I should like to hold her. I almost never get to see any children; only our youngest uncle's brood, and his last is five and not at all amusing."

"Guess you're surprised to see us so soon after last night," George said. "We rode as far as Cotter's Cottage, and Alice decided at the last minute to stop on our way home."

"I wanted Master Jarrod to meet Madeleine," Alice added. "And now he's to see the infant, too. What a fortunate day for you, Jarrod."

"I feel fortunate," he replied. He came to stand beside Madeleine, then crouched at her chair. "May I? No, I don't want to take her; she might break. I simply want to look." Madeleine raised Dorrie a little higher for inspection. "What a lovely child," he said after a moment. "May she grow as wise as she is beautiful."

"Jarrod, are you blessing babies now?" Alice said with a laugh. "I vow there's no end to your accomplishments."

"I thought it a pretty one," Antonia remarked in a tired voice. Madeleine felt a familiar pang as she studied her mother's face for signs of exhaustion. Not far to go before she must rest, she thought, then caught Ethan's gaze on her. He smiled, then turned his eyes to Antonia. She watched his expression narrow to one of concern.

Gradually she became aware that Alice was tapping her knee. "Gracious, Madeleine, where were you? Is it my turn now?" She laughed as Madeleine placed Dorrie in her arms, then began to make comical faces at the baby. After a moment Madeleine was laughing, too, albeit grudgingly. Alice drew one in, that was certain; and she lacked pretension—an unusual quality in a beauty. She did not mind looking foolish.

"Ethan, when your cousin returns for Dorrie, you must make her promise to bring her child back every few months so that we can watch her grow." Alice clapped the baby's hands together in a playful rhythm. "You will, won't you?"

"What? Oh. Yes, certainly."

"Have you heard from her yet?" Thomas asked. Madeleine directed an irate look at him.

"No." The viscount sounded distracted. Exactly as she might expect him to sound, Madeleine ruminated, if he were lying. Immediately, she felt guilty for thinking such a thing. Her father was not correct; he could not be. "No, not yet. I'm sure I will soon."

Alice slanted mischievous eyes at him. "Do you remember when we were young and used to play orphanage?"

"*You* used to play it," George said. "I don't think you enlisted us more than once, and, as I remember, it was your birthday."

"Oh, more than once, I'm certain. Am I not right, Ethan?"

"I don't recall."

"Of course you do! You would play the director and I the nursemaid. George, Scott, and your brother were the orphans we rescued from the shipwreck. Oh, what terrible children the orphans were! Madeleine, we had to lock them in a closet until they promised to be good."

"Lucan was the director," the viscount said quietly.

Alice looked bewildered. *"Was* he? Are you certain?"

Master Jarrod said, "What does it matter, after all these years?"

"I suppose it doesn't, except I was so sure . . ."

"Mayhap they switched places that day," George said. "The twins were always doing that," he added, looking at Madeleine, "especially when they were younger."

Alice scooped the baby higher in her arms and rose. "Really, George, as if any of us would have been fooled by that." She came to stand beside Mr. Murrow's chair and, much to his surprise, deposited the infant in his arms. Returning to her seat, she continued, addressing her remarks to the Murrows: "They were more unalike than alike, especially if you knew them as well as we did. The twins never deceived us—"

"Or so we think!" George interrupted with a laugh.

"—because their interests were very different."

"Not about horseflesh, they weren't," George said.

Alice smoothed the folds of her skirt where the baby had rested. "That's true. From childhood they rode together every day, always the same route around the estate."

"Not always," Ethan said.

"Well, almost. Lucan once told me your mother said a master should make his presence known." Again, she turned to Madeleine. "She encouraged them to ride the grounds when they were small, and it became a habit, I believe." Her gaze returned to the viscount. "Ethan continues to make that circuit. Sometimes, if I awake early enough, I spot him from my window."

No wonder he has not asked me to ride with him,

Madeleine thought. This ritual is a link with his brother. She was not certain such a thing was healthy. He had dwelled alone far too long.

With her eyes still fastened on Ethan, Alice continued, "At that distance, I can almost imagine it's Lucan I see."

"Come, Miss Redding," said Master Jarrod, shifting forward in his chair. "You'll have everyone thinking you're of a gloomy frame of mind." He scanned the Murrows with an apologetic look. "She's not usually like this. I think she's tired."

Alice gave an exasperated laugh. "Really, Jarrod, you overstep yourself." The tutor flinched and fell silent as she began to speak of their planned excursion on Friday.

Evidently Alice's graciousness did not extend to the hired help, Madeleine thought with a twinge of sympathy for the man. And then, her attention caught by a movement, she turned to watch Thomas shift the baby to her mother's arms. His face was impassive, but she recognized the distaste in his eyes.

Ethan is not the father of that child, she wanted to say. But if he was, could she bear it?

After Bettina, she didn't know if she could.

The arrival of Scott Brandt pushed aside her dismal thoughts. He looked windblown and tired after his day outside. Madeleine noticed a smear of dirt on the sleeve of his jacket. He stood tenuously at the threshold, as if he didn't know whether to enter or not.

"I hope I'm not interrupting," he said.

"How could you interrupt?" Ethan replied, sounding cross. "You live here."

"Yes, I know, but—" He seemed to realize the futility of explanations and gave that sad smile Madeleine was coming to know. "I've visited the cottages." Walking forward, he took a seat on a footstool near the fire. "All but two need rethatching. Mrs. O'Tooley appears to be in her final decline and has requested the vicar—"

"Excuse me, Scott, but all those repairs and things; it sounds as if you have business to discuss, and we were just leaving." Alice stood, and Master Jarrod immediately sprang to his feet, followed by a more reluctant George. "Please don't be offended, but Father expects me to read to him this afternoon. His eyes are not what they used to be. No, don't get up, gentlemen. Burns will see us out."

Madeleine struggled to keep her expression even as she bid the Redding party farewell. When the front door closed behind them, Ethan turned to Mr. Brandt.

"Well, Scott, should I ever need a room cleared, I know whom to call." Madeleine was struggling with her indignation at Ethan's unkindness when his face suddenly cleared. "Did you say Mrs. O'Tooley wants the vicar? I'll go fetch him."

Surprised, Mr. Brandt said, "Had you not rather send the groom?"

"No, this needs the personal touch. I've known Mrs. O'Tooley forever."

"Then I could go. It's not necessary for you—"

But Ethan was already walking from the room.

"I should like to go as well," Madeleine declared after him.

The viscount's steps slowed, and he turned. "That's very kind of you, but this is likely to be a dull errand."

"It doesn't sound dull to me," she said, giving him a reproachful but twinkling smile. "I'm beginning to feel quite housebound."

"Madeleine," Thomas said uneasily, "why don't we take a walk? That should cure your restlessness."

"It might, but I'd like to speak with Miss Abbott again, and her mother," she said, and prayed God would forgive her the lie.

"She needs company, Thomas," Antonia said.

"Did we not just say goodbye to company?" he asked, sounding irritated.

"My stable is sadly lacking, I'm afraid," Ethan added. "The horses—"

"If you have a light carriage, we could put one of our

beasts in the traces if you like. Otherwise, I could ride our Legacy; she's broken to the saddle."

Madeleine looked at him hopefully. She didn't know why he didn't want her along, but she was determined to go if she had to run alongside his Viking. More than a few questions needed answering.

To give him his due, he capitulated graciously. "Miss Murrow, it would be my pleasure. We'll take the gig; be sure to fetch your wrap." He made as if to move on, then stopped. "And we may as well bring the infant, too. I'll get her blanket."

It was Madeleine's turn to be surprised. She gazed at her parents in bafflement and received equally mystified looks in return.

Eight

Traveling with a baby was not quite so simple as bringing along a blanket, Ethan discovered. The wet nurse insisted on feeding Dorrie before they left, as if the child would starve in the hour or two they would be gone. Then Betsy packed a basket with napkins, pins, a change of clothing, and other items he could not imagine them using. After that, in case she might take a chill, the babe was wrapped in enough layers to restrict the movements of a buffalo.

Life would be much simpler if he were in charge of the nursery, he was certain. Since he did not aspire to such an assignment, he let the women bustle and order him about while declaring him mad to take a newborn outside in the chilly air. He did not bother to remind them that it was a beautiful spring afternoon or argue in any way. Such would have only prolonged the agony of waiting, since the maids were enjoying their roles as authorities far too much.

When he handed the babe up to Madeleine in the gig, he saw similar doubts mirrored in her eyes. She did not wait long to express them.

"Why did you decide to bring Dorrie?" she asked, as he snapped the reins over Legacy, the gentlest of her father's bays. She looked down at the small head bundled within the blanket. "Not that I mind, of course."

"Did you notice how much Mrs. Abbott enjoyed her last night?"

"Yes, and how her daughter did not."

"Shyness, I'm sure." And guilt. "I'm hoping to bring a little joy into their lives." Among other things.

"I'm certain the ladies will appreciate seeing her, if they're at home."

They had better be there. He noted her eyes flickering over the worn fittings of his old black gig, then moving outward to scan the countryside. At least bluebells were blooming in the meadows. Even so, she must think the rolling, marshy landscape with its occasional cottage and sheep pen to be dull as ditchwater. Westhall was not far from the sea; he should take her there. Surely that would perk her eyes. But she had probably been to the shore a thousand times. He was a drowning man grasping for sunbeams to float him.

Kent, her homeplace, claimed many gracious houses and gardens. According to Lord Tate, Mr. Murrow's home was a jewelbox of treasures and good taste. What did he have to offer her? Nothing, really. Instead of searching for the identity of Dorrie's mother in order to protect his name, the best thing he could do for Madeleine would be to declare paternity and frighten her away.

Unfortunately for her, he was not that unselfish.

They passed a farmer driving an empty wagon in the opposite direction. The old man tipped his hat and looked with open curiosity at Madeleine and the baby. Yet another person he did not know, Ethan thought. No doubt Lucan had brought him venison and hare to eat when he was down with rheumatism.

How he made himself ill with his envy. Even in the midst of mourning, he still felt the old pangs.

The baby began to make disgruntled sounds. These did not appear to bother Madeleine in the slightest, as she merely rocked the child without even looking at it. How he detested hearing a baby cry. He would rather listen to Reverend Abbott deliver a three-hour sermon.

"What's wrong with her?" he asked after a moment.

"I'm sure I don't know. Babies make all kinds of noises, I believe."

"When she does that, it usually means she's only getting started." As if to prove him right, the sounds increased to little cries. "You should hold her close to you."

She cast him a tolerant look and did as she was told. Dorrie responded by wailing. Madeleine patted her back and jostled her, which only made the infant's temper worse.

Almost frenzied, Ethan stopped the gig in the middle of the road, threw the reins aside, and lifted the baby from Madeleine's arms. Dorrie's screams increased. Used to a more complimentary reaction, he became quite perturbed.

"Do you suppose she's ill? Maybe we should go fetch the surgeon."

"I don't know how sick she could be and still scream with such force," Madeleine said sensibly. "Give her to me and I'll examine her clothing. Perhaps she needs changing."

"If so, she's deuced demanding about her requests and needs to be taught some manners." He handed her back, and within seconds Madeleine discovered the culprit: a loose pin. The damage appeared to be only a slight prick in the thigh, and once the babe was rewrapped and soothed, she gradually quietened.

"Thank God," he said, and took the reins once more. "I believe between the two of us, we make one fairly efficient caretaker."

"I have almost no experience with babies," Madeleine said, sounding ashamed. Perhaps she thought he was criticizing her.

"At least you had the foresight to think of her clothes. I find it hard to remember how important details are to that little dictator. Things that would fail to bother the most contrary person alive take on mammoth proportions in her mind, yet she seems to be of a sweet temperament at other times. I don't understand her at all."

She smiled. "Yet you're very fond of her."

"As who could not be?" he said quickly, hoping to deflect her from an uncomfortable subject. "I saw your face before you discovered what was wrong. Your eyes were wet."

"She was in pain. I suppose babies can enlist your emotions, even when they're not your own." She averted her eyes for a moment, then looked directly at him, her tension evident. "Imagine how much greater that empathy would be if the baby were yours."

For one terrible moment, time slowed to a stop. He looked away from her to the road ahead.

"I'm not sure I take your meaning," he said.

She hesitated. "Were my words confusing? I simply meant what I said. A child's mother . . . or father . . . would be bound to feel their own baby's hurts more deeply than they would someone else's offspring. It seems natural, do you not agree?"

"Certainly," he said vaguely, his mind churning. Was it possible? Could this be a confession?

Please take care of our little one, for I cannot, the note had read.

The evening the Murrows descended upon his doorstep, he was . . . incapacitated. He had spoken to Madeleine in the hall, then retired. Sometime during that first night, the babe was delivered to his room.

Quite a coincidence, that. The Murrows arrived, then the baby, all in the same evening.

He almost laughed at himself. And yet, the timing of the infant's arrival and the Murrows' was too remarkable to dismiss. He wondered that it hadn't occurred to him before.

If Madeleine had given birth prior to her trip, it would be possible. Yet hiding the baby from her parents within the confines of a coach would have been difficult, to say the least.

Unless Mr. and Mrs. Murrow were a part of the scheme as well.

The viscount cast his mind back to the weekend at Lord Tate's. Mr. Murrow had been uncommonly eager to accept his suit, it seemed now. With Madeleine's obvious attractions, why should that be, unless he knew his daughter to be ruined? No other wealthy fathers had been willing to take a chance on him.

The deviousness of the scheme almost took his breath. He looked at Madeleine as if seeing her for the first time. She seemed uncommonly content cradling the infant, tucking the ends of the blanket around Dorrie's face so she would not become cold.

Was the woman he believed himself to be in love with false? What if all her sweetness, her affection and charm, were simply a ruse to snare a gullible husband?

There could be no more perfect a means to trap him, keep her baby, and save herself from scandal than make him think the child was his.

"Is there something you want to tell me?" he asked, his tone harsh.

"I beg your pardon?"

Gads, how innocent she looked. What an actress she was, if his suspicions proved true. He must step carefully, so as not to offend her if he was wrong. And how he prayed he *was* wrong!

"The baby," he said, forcing a smile. "Is there something you want me to know about her?"

She studied him, looking prettily confused. "I was thinking *you* might have something to tell about her."

"What?"

"I think you know what I mean, Lord—Ethan."

"I assure you, I do not."

She gnawed at her lower lip. "Honesty means the world to me."

This sounded promising. "As it does to me."

He suddenly wondered if he spoke truth. If she pronounced herself the mother of the child in her arms, he would be devastated. He didn't know if he could forgive a mistake of that kind. It would depend on the circumstances, he supposed.

One thing was certain. He would kill the man responsible.

Ahead, a lad waved protectively as his sheep crossed the road. Ethan slowed the gig to a stop. Except for the bleating of the animals, the quiet inside the gig became profound. He shifted to face her, and the tears standing in her eyes caused his heart to drop.

She blinked, obviously struggling to put together her thoughts. "Sometimes the best of people make mistakes," she began.

Dear God, she was going to confess, and how she suffered as she tried to frame the words. Although the knowledge crushed him, he could only try to make it less difficult for her.

"How well I know," he said. "I've made many." He gave a brief laugh. "Not that I am the *best* of people."

"Oh, I think you are, Ethan, in spite of everything."

His smile became strained. "In spite of everything?" Instead of replying, she dashed the tears from her eyes with her fingertips. "Oh, you mean the drinking," he said. "I've explained why I behaved as I did the first night you were here. That was an exception for me."

"And I believe you. That's not what I was referring to; please don't pretend to misunderstand any longer."

"I, pretend? What about *you?*"

"What about *me?*" she asked slowly. Suddenly, her brow smoothed. "Oh, I see. You want me to be totally honest before you speak. Very well, then. I agree there should be no secrets between us. Not after last night; not when we are considering so important a decision in our lives. And may I add that *whatever* you say will not"—fresh tears sprang into her eyes—"not necessarily spell the end. I'm certain"—here she lowered her gaze to Dorrie—"there must be some good reason why you . . . well. I shall let you speak in your own words in a moment." She drew a deep breath. "There *is* something I haven't told you."

Having understood nothing except her last sentence, the viscount thought, *Here it comes*.

"I know I don't have to ask for your absolute discretion in this matter."

"Madeleine, you may trust me."

Dorrie made a fussing noise, and Madeleine lifted her to her shoulder, rubbing the infant's back. "I know I can," she said after a moment. "This is difficult."

Ethan placed his arm across the back of the bench and squeezed her shoulder. "I understand." The lad and his sheep had long since crossed the road, but there were more important things than driving.

"I don't see how you can. When shame and love are mixed together . . ." The tears began to spill. Ethan searched his pockets for a handkerchief and handed it to her. "But then, I guess you do understand after . . . what has happened to you."

He thought this a little strong for his past, but he said nothing, only nodded encouragingly.

"When Bettina was born, she was like a shaft of sunlight on a gloomy day."

"Bettina," he said.

"Yes, my sister. You remember."

"Oh, of course." He felt lost.

"Not that we were *dispirited* in our family; just ordinary, I suppose. Three reasonably placid people living what might seem a dull existence to others. We were happy, but Bettina increased that happiness to joy. Sometimes, she plunged us into grief. But that is the way of strong personalities, have you not noticed?"

"What? Oh, certainly." He recalled once walking into the wrong lecture hall at Oxford. He felt much the same now.

"As she grew, she had many, many admirers. She was not wise, but tended to live for the moment. There is a kind of beauty in those who do that, as flames are beautiful. Yet one fears the fire is fragile, that it can quickly turn to smoke and ashes. We warned her, Papa and I, and sometimes my mother, although she loved Bettina so fiercely she thought her incapable of any wrong."

She paused to wipe her eyes, an awkward move with the babe in her arms. Silence pulsed between them, an incomprehensible silence to Ethan, who finally broke it by offering to hold the child. Madeleine passed Dorrie to him with a murmur of thanks.

"Only you cannot drive with her in your arms," she said.

"It's not impossible, but I'll give her back to you in a moment. We're not more than a mile from the vicar's, and I want you to finish before we go on." *Please,* he added silently. Once she quit reminiscing, he would press her to confess.

"As I mentioned, she had many admirers, but it was Lieutenant Arling who caught her heart. She could not have resisted him; he was handsome in his red uniform and had such a pleasing manner. I believe he would have married her, had he known . . ."

"Known what?" Ethan asked quietly, dreading the answer.

"That Bettina was . . . with child," she whispered.

Dear God! Did wantonness grow wild in families like weeds?

"But he didn't know." He struggled to keep judgment from his voice.

"He died before Bettina could tell him. Before even she knew, I think."

"Oh, I am sorry. The war took many good men."

"Yes, although he never went to battle; he was killed in a duel."

He paused. "I see. Over Bettina, I suppose?"

She moved uncomfortably. "No, actually, it concerned another female; someone's wife, I believe."

"What a cad," he couldn't help saying.

"Yes, I think so, too!" she said, and burst into tears. "Only—only, it is not good to speak ill of the dead. And

I do not like to think my sister drowned herself because of a worthless creature, but she did, she did!"

Stunned, he pulled her into his arms, managing to shift Dorrie so she wouldn't be squeezed overmuch. The baby apparently found this togetherness to her liking, for she made no sound.

Through her sobs, Madeleine continued to speak over his shoulder. "We never suspected she was *enciente;* we only found out through the note she left. She wrote that her shame and sorrow were more than she could bear to bring on our family. Oh, if only she had waited. She was so young, so rash. We would have forgiven her anything to have her with us!"

"Of course you would," he soothed. "I'm so sorry, Madeleine."

She moved slowly from his embrace and dabbed at her eyes. "Thank you, Ethan. Now you know everything."

"Everything?" The world turned dark around the edges.

"Could there be anything worse than what I've just told you? I hope it doesn't affect your opinion of us—of me. Papa has been afraid that if anyone knew, it would ruin my chances for a good marriage. I've always said that anyone who lays blame for Bettina's pathetic act is not someone I'd want to wed anyway."

She looked at him, and belatedly he realized she was waiting.

"Oh, I agree with you. You can be sure *I* don't feel that way. Your sister's death was a tragedy, but if any blame is to be laid, it lies at the lieutenant's door."

"Thank you for saying that, Ethan. Feeling as you do, I think—I think you can understand why we are so concerned about the circumstances of . . ." Her gaze dropped to Dorrie. "But you were going to explain."

Ethan's heart buckled as he, too, looked down at the child. Unless she was the most diabolical liar who ever lived, Madeleine was innocent. He had misread all her comments. *She* suspected *him,* a thing that made much more sense.

If he told her he was accused of being the father but had no inkling who the mother might be, what could she (and worse, her sire, who showed no signs of loving him) think? They would be bound to see Bettina's lieutenant as less evil.

His only hope lay in finding the child's true parents, and pray God he was not one of them.

Dorrie yawned and looked up at him trustingly. A butterfly winged between them, and her face creased in wonder, her hands drawing upward in response. Finding her fingers equally amazing, she stared at them, her eyes crossing. He chuckled, then felt suddenly bereft.

"Ethan?"

He dragged his gaze from the baby. "I'm sorry, Madeleine; I still don't understand what you want from me."

Her eyes clouded with disappointment. "Then allow me to make myself very clear. My family and I have been wondering why you've heard nothing from your cousin. In point of fact, we're beginning to wonder if there *is* a cousin."

"And well you might!" he declared. "I've been doing some wondering of my own. Connie and James were always flighty. I'm beginning to think they found an infant limited their travels." He moistened his lips; his mouth was dry with the taste of falsehoods. "It would be typical for them to have made up the story about James's mother. I can imagine them sailing off to Italy or somewhere, knowing I would take good care of Dorrie while they were gone."

She stared at him until he felt his face go hot. He saw little belief in her eyes.

"Here," he said, handing Dorrie over to her. "Mrs. O'Tooley lies ill, and we must be on our way." Quickly, he urged Legacy into motion.

* * *

The vicarage sat among a grove of ancient trees on the edge of the village. Hardly bigger than a cottage, the whitewashed house with its arching windows and thatched roof charmed Madeleine, reminding her of fairy-tale dwellings. She almost expected three sisters to dwell within, or three brothers, all of whom would set off on quests which only the youngest and most comely would accomplish.

She wished such things were possible, for then perhaps someone would wave a magical wand and make her doubts about Ethan go away.

When an astonished but delighted Mrs. Abbott led them inside, the low ceilings and simple, clean furnishings continued her illusion. The arrival of the saturnine Miss Abbott did not. Summoned loudly by her mother, she descended the narrow stairs, saw her visitors, and looked as if she wanted to retreat. Under the circumstances, however, she had little choice but to follow her mother's lead into the parlor.

"This is such a pleasant surprise!" Mrs. Abbott repeated. "Oh, will you allow me to take that darling baby, Miss Murrow? Surely I'll have better fortune today with her." Madeleine complied, and the vicar's wife settled into a wooden rocking chair set near the fire. "Oh, her is the sweetest leedle thing, isn't her?" She beamed at Lord Ambrose. "See, she does like me! I do believe she smiled!"

"I wouldn't doubt it a moment," he said. "Now, the vicar—"

"Oh, yes, pardon me for forgetting." She returned to Dorrie, shaking her head rapidly at the baby, her jowls jiggling. "Her took my mind off everything but her leedle self, didn't her?" A glance at the viscount. "He's gone to fetch some fish or veal for our supper tonight, whichever he can find. I expect him back at any instant."

She craned her neck to view her daughter, who had chosen to sit in a chair by the window, an isolated place intended to lend privacy for reading, Madeleine guessed. "Why are you over there, girl? I can scarcely see you! Go fetch some refreshments for our visitors, will you? Make yourself useful!"

Although Ethan and Madeleine protested that they wanted nothing, Leah rushed from the room as if given a reprieve.

"It's no trouble at all," the older woman said. "I'm forever trying to get that girl to learn hostessing skills. She needs to come out of herself more. She's always been too glum by half, my Leah. Don't know where she gets it." Again, she turned to Dorrie. "But her won't have dose problems, will her? Look at dose pretty, pretty eyes. Oh, dee gentlemen will flock around you like honey, won't dey?"

The viscount scooted forward in his chair. Madeleine sensed how annoyed the vicar's wife made him and would have been amused if she were not so distressed.

"At dinner you mentioned she was unusually despondent a few months ago," he said.

Mrs. Abbott's face seemed to close. Dorrie made an annoyed sound, and the lady shifted her position absently. "Yes, though I probably shouldn't have. For some reason, she doesn't like me to talk about her trip to her aunt's."

"I wonder why," Ethan said.

And I wonder why you're so curious, Madeleine thought. She had believed she understood him, especially after last night. Now she realized she knew nothing. He was as inscrutable as a book written in Italian or German.

Of one thing she *was* certain: He had yet to tell her the truth about Dorrie. After she divulged her most painful secret to him, he had responded with fabrication. She felt so angry and ashamed, she could scarcely look at him.

Of a sudden, Mrs. Abbott also seemed unable to meet the viscount's eyes. She appeared to have forgotten the baby as well, although she rocked her steadily.

"It's hard to say why," she replied finally, "Leah is so closemouthed. But I have my suspicions. Probably shouldn't put them to voice, though."

Ethan became the portrait of sympathy. "Sometimes it's

better to talk about problems. You may rely completely on our discretion."

Hearing this familiar strain, Madeleine's eyes narrowed. "I'm certain Mrs. Abbott knows what's best." She felt very uncomfortable discussing the state of Leah's emotions when she was not present to defend herself.

Hardly missing a beat, Ethan said, "Did something happen to upset her? A disappointment in love, perhaps?"

Madeleine could scarcely believe her ears. "That's a rather personal question, my lord," she said, forcing a laugh to reduce her tension.

Mrs. Abbott did not appear to take offense, although she stared at him intently. "It's strange you should say that, because—" Her eyes lifted to the doorway. Leah stood at the threshold holding a tray of strawberries, tea, cups, saucers, and plates. "Come in, dear girl. We've been wondering what kept you."

Madeleine's heart beat sympathetically for the young woman. By the deadening look Leah slanted in her mother's direction, she must have heard at least a portion of their conversation. She made no comment, however, but went about serving them with grim efficiency.

Accepting his cup of tea with impatience, the viscount studied Leah for a moment. "Perhaps when your mother is finished, you'd like to take Dorrie for a while."

She bowed her head and muttered, "I don't know why you're always trying to get me to hold her. I told you I don't like babies."

Mrs. Abbott looked shocked. "Leah, mind your tongue! The viscount is only trying to be kind to you."

"Let him be kind to someone else." She stood in a rush, moving toward the center of the room and making Madeleine think of an animal cornered by dogs. "He doesn't know what kindness is."

"Leah!" Mrs. Abbott's voice throbbed as if she had gone beyond embarrassment into a darker realm. "I apologize for her, Lord Ambrose. I don't know what's wrong."

"Wrong?" Leah cried. "I'll tell you what's wrong! He—he comes here with that face"—she jabbed her forefinger in the air, pointing at him—"and it is like a terrible, sick mockery! You speak of kindness! The true Lord Ambrose was kind; he was gentle. But instead of him, that—that person has taken his place! He is worse than an impostor!"

Even Mrs. Abbott was too astonished to answer this, and the three of them regarded the girl in stunned silence.

With a grunt, Leah turned and ran from the room. At the same moment, the front door opened and Reverend Abbott, a package in his hands, entered to stand at the opening which led into the parlor. His normally pleasant look faded to bewilderment as Leah paused, then lowered her head and fled up the stairs. He stumbled toward the parlor, his face creasing and uncreasing as he tried to fathom the situation.

"Well, I—I don't know," he said, finally. "That is, I'm very glad to see you, Lord Ambrose, Miss Murrow." He walked toward them with more confidence. "I seem to have interrupted something—"

Mrs. Abbott grabbed her nose. "Ooh, dear, I believe you found fish at market today. If you would be so kind to take it to the kitchen before it smells up the parlor, I'm sure Addie will take it from there."

"Of course, of course," he said humbly, and retreated.

"And then come back immediately," his wife called after him. "Lord Ambrose has something to ask of you." Lowering her voice, she looked from Ethan to Madeleine with a worried air. "I didn't like to say, because Leah is so secretive, and I'm not certain of this. But rather than have you thinking she's loose in the attic, I'll tell you what I think."

She centered her eyes on Ethan. "Your brother spent much time encouraging my Joseph in recent years. Lately, I mean, not too long before . . . well, he took to speaking with our Leah, sometimes walking with her outside. I think she mistook his interest, if you understand me. She felt his passing terribly hard." The older woman shook her head sadly. "A terrible thing, that—what happened to your brother. Leah's not been the same since."

Madeleine felt a throb of sympathy, although she could not quite forgive Leah for speaking so to Ethan. *She* might be angry with him, but that did not give the vicar's daughter license to strike upon his greatest insecurity: the unfavorable comparison of himself to his brother. That was beyond his helping (whereas lying was not, nor was fathering illegitimate babies, although *surely* he was innocent of that; he must be)!

Feeling softer toward him than she had in the past half hour, she glanced across the room, then felt her stomach clench. All color had drained from Ethan's face; he looked utterly shattered. When the vicar returned, Ethan mumbled instructions concerning Mrs. O'Tooley, then took his leave of the Abbotts with a minimum of words. Had Madeleine not grabbed Dorrie and hurried after him, she believed he would have forgotten them both.

Nine

Not long after the sun topped the trees the next morning, Ethan and Viking broke into a gallop across the rose-tipped grounds of Westhall. With his uncanny ability to read his master's moods, Viking flew like a windstorm, his hooves clipping the hard earth, his breaths pumping hard and steady. They were one being, a man-beast, without past or future, without confusion, distress, or bitter loss.

Or so Ethan wished. If only the rhythm of Viking's stride could banish the persistence of his thoughts. He longed for blankness, for the peacefulness of a newborn's mind. How well it must be for Dorrie, who anticipated each new experience and found fault only with physical discomfort.

His spirits had not sunk so low since his brother's death. He felt as if he'd lost Lucan all over again.

Yesterday, unable to endure Madeleine's fiery, curious glances any longer, incapable of carrying on the pretense of interested host, he had gone to bed by nightfall. He didn't want to speak to Madeleine. He didn't want to speak with anyone.

Well. He could not deny it would be good to converse with his twin. "Lucan," he would say. "Was your saintly life a lie? Were you as deceptive—no, worse—than myself? Did you seduce the vicar's daughter with your golden words, and leave yourself a hero in her eyes because of your untimely death?"

Please take care of our little one, for I cannot. Our little one.

Lucan's and Leah's? It could not be true; it simply could not! His fingers flexed into fists on the reins.

No, it did not bear thinking of, that his brother would violate the trust of a sheltered innocent. If that could happen, everything Ethan believed in was suspect.

Yet how overwrought the girl had been. Sorrow for a mere friendship could not explain such a display.

When he reached the wooded border that defined the boundary between the Redding estate and his, Ethan slowed Viking, guiding him among the trees as a respite. As he always did, he gazed upward at the thick stand of oak and ash leaves and listened for the sounds of birds and the rustle of undergrowth hinting at hare and squirrel. He gained none of his usual sense of peace, no feeling of the old connection with Lucan. He could not count how many times they had ridden this route together. Now he longed to be through. He should have gone somewhere else, broken the pattern.

Near the end of the wood, the path widened, and he urged Viking into a canter. Gray daylight shone ahead, and the beast gathered speed, his muscles bunching for a renewed sprint.

Lucan. All the times you reproved my behavior, claiming concern. Did you hide your own darker side? Why did you pretend?

Seconds before they would have cleared the last of the trees, Viking stumbled, whinnying sharply. Ethan had time for only a brief awareness that they were falling together when his world exploded into pain, and everything became dark.

"We may get rain today," Thomas commented, scanning the sky as he and his daughter strolled down the lane which passed by the viscount's house.

"Um," Madeleine answered. In only a couple of hours, it would be time for luncheon. She expected Ethan to appear from his ride any moment; he was, in fact, late. She didn't know what to say to him when he arrived.

Thomas gazed down at her. "We'd best turn around; your mother won't like us being out of her sight for so long with these clouds. She worries too much."

"All right."

Madeleine walked on. Mr. Murrow gently took her arm and guided her in the opposite direction. She did not appear to notice. Her father pursed his lips.

"I saw an elf in my bedroom this morning," he said. "He stood no higher than my knee and was dressed all in green with pointed red shoes. After playing several melodies on his pipe, he granted me one wish."

There was a pause. "How nice," Madeleine said.

"Do you know what I wished for?"

"What?" Madeleine said absently, staring at the viscount's home, studying its odd angles and profile. From here she could see her mother sitting on the bench in the side garden—if one could compliment it with such a title—with Mr. Brandt.

"I requested a daughter who would converse with me as my own used to do."

"Hm?" She gave him a vacant look, then came sharply to the present. "I'm sorry, Papa." Her eyes darkened with memory. "Did you say something about an *elf*?"

"So you *were* listening. I thought someone had taken my child and put a wraith in her place."

"I was woolgathering. I'll try to do better."

"Thinking about the viscount, I imagine. Did something happen yesterday? He seemed uncommonly quiet last night—as did you, I recall."

She turned solemn eyes upon him. "If you don't mind, Papa, I'd rather not speak of Lord Ambrose just now."

"I see." He clasped his hands behind his back. "He didn't become forward with you on the way to the vicar's, I hope."

"Pardon?" Her cheeks suddenly flushed. "Oh, goodness, no! You have nothing to worry about in that regard." Immediately, memories of their exquisite time together in the library flooded her, and her blush deepened.

His posture relaxed slightly. "Then you are experiencing doubts."

It seemed her father was determined to talk about him anyway. She wanted to let down her guard and tell him everything; it would be a relief to seek his advice. But his growing prejudice against Ethan precluded her voicing too many suspicions.

How the viscount's behavior on the previous day plagued her! Much of last night and all morning long, she'd reviewed his strange actions in her mind. He had questioned her about secrets . . . hadn't he? She struggled to remember their conversation word for word, but remembered only impressions.

"I told Lord Ambrose the truth about Bettina's death," she said, feeling her way, trying to recapture the gist of those moments.

Her father looked shocked. "Do you think that was wise?"

"He won't tell anyone," she said, and watched a meadow pipit wing skyward from a tangle of gorse. For a moment she wished she could fly away with it and leave her confusion behind. "Why should he? It would mean scandal for himself as well."

"If you marry him, you mean. That's not written in stone yet."

"He won't tell," she repeated firmly.

"But something is troubling you about it."

"Yes." They had reached the bottom of the viscount's drive, and she paused, not wanting to stop now that she had begun and knowing if they ascended the path, she could say nothing in front of Mr. Brandt. "When I spoke of Bettina, he seemed . . . let down. Oddly so. Not scandalized as I had feared, but . . . I don't know. Deflated, perhaps. As if he'd expected to hear something else entirely."

"Maybe our history disturbed him more than you thought."

"I don't believe so. And then there was his strange behavior with Leah Abbott."

"With whom? Oh, the vicar's daughter."

"Yes." She pivoted toward her father, clutching her hands behind her back in unconscious imitation of him. "Do you recall at dinner how he urged her to take Dorrie, and she wouldn't?" When Thomas nodded, she went on, "Well, he did it again! In fact he went so far out of his way to suggest it that I almost believe that was why he brought the baby with us yesterday. And the questions he asked about Leah when she was out of the room—how odd they were!"

"What kind of questions?"

"Well . . . . he asked Mrs. Abbott about Leah's mood before she left for her aunt's. And he wanted to know if she had been . . ."

Disappointed in love. That was the question he had asked.

She could not go on. Suddenly, the pieces of the puzzle were beginning to fall into place. If she said more, her father might guess the horrible conclusion she was drawing.

Ethan's bizzare interest in Leah's personal life . . . his prodding her to hold the child and her strange refusal to do so . . . As sure as she breathed, he suspected Leah Abbott of being Dorrie's mother.

There was no cousin; there never had been. But she'd known that for a long time, hadn't she? Even before his extravagant explanation yesterday about their whereabouts.

Italy, indeed.

And if he suspected Leah was the mother, what did that make him? Had he been so low as to father a child without knowing who its mother was? Perhaps his problem with drink was much, much greater than he let on. She had heard of such addictions that led people to forget entire episodes in their lives.

Her father gestured expectantly, prompting, "If she had been . . ."

She was not ready to voice her suspicions yet. She could be wrong; she prayed she was wrong. But let her father grasp a corner of her fears, and Westhall would soon be a dot on the horizon.

"Been? Oh, if she had been to Italy." She winced at the untruth. She did not lie to her parents, not since Bettina was alive, anyway, when she and her sister had tried to wriggle from their childish scrapes.

Her father appeared befuddled. "To Italy?"

Something moved at the corner of her vision, and she turned with feigned interest. A woman was approaching down the lane, seemingly headed in their direction. "Now who is this, I wonder."

They waited, both of them drawn by the sight of the forlorn woman in the frayed blue dress. She wore a ragged straw bonnet over pale hair that fell in strands across her shoulders. A large, disreputable reticule dangled from one arm. As she drew closer, Madeleine estimated her age as being eight to ten years older than herself. She was a pretty woman marred by deep shadows beneath her eyes and a body too thin for health, let alone beauty.

When she reached where they stood, the woman curtseyed and bid them good morning in genteel tones. "My name is Rose McDaniel, and I am looking for employment," she explained. "Someone in the village told me the master here—Lord Ambrose, is it?—might be looking for someone."

"I couldn't speak for him, Miss," Thomas said in a kind voice. "We're only visitors. Perhaps if you ask at the house."

She hesitated, glanced at both of them, then the manse. Madeleine noticed her hands moving nervously at her sides. "I heard there was a baby and that he needed help with it."

"Yes," Madeleine said softly. "There is an infant."

Dipping her head, she thanked them both and walked on past. So as not to appear they were shadowing her,

Madeleine and her father dawdled a few moments before continuing up the path.

"She is no ordinary servant," her father commented.

Madeleine agreed, trying not to sound overly interested; but her suspicions were on full alert. Something in the way the woman talked and carried herself bespoke an elegant upbringing. Obviously, she had fallen on hard times.

Giving birth to a child out of wedlock could do that to a woman.

Her imagination flew. How tragic the woman looked, and how sad her situation if she could only be with her baby by pretending to be her servant. It reminded her of the story of Moses, whose mother had set him adrift to be found by the daughter of the Pharoah. That mother, too, had been hired to care for her own child.

Well, goodness. Now that she suspected Ethan of trying to find his baby's mother, she was seeing potential candidates behind every bush. Next she would be accusing Betsy.

She stumbled. Her father murmured in concern and offered his arm.

"I'm fine, Papa," she said, laughing a little, shuddering at the hysteria she heard in her voice. "I believe I was thinking of elves."

Ethan awoke to tearing pain and the feel of cold wetness on his cheeks. A soft rain was falling through the canopy of leaves above him. He tried to rise, then groaned. The back of his skull pounded like thunder. His entire body ached, but his leg concerned him most. He leaned sideways and saw a long, bloodied gash in his pantaloons running from thigh to mid-calf. He must have scraped his limb against the knobby tree at his back as he fell. Carefully he bent his leg at the knee, then rotated his ankle. The pain was excruciating, but he didn't believe he'd broken anything.

It was then he saw Viking lying motionlessly a few feet away. All thought of his own hurts vanished. He dragged himself across the undergrowth and laid his hand on the horse's flank, not releasing his breath until he saw the gentle rise and fall of Viking's side.

Not dead. Not dead.

He struggled closer to the beast's head. "Viking!" he called, rubbing the black's mane. "Come on, old fellow, wake up!" Desperation seized him. "Viking!" He draped his arm around the horse's neck. "You are not going to leave me, do you hear? Open your eyes, you—useless animal!"

He breathed heavily, waiting, his gaze fixed on the noble profile of his finest friend. When he could bear the silence no longer, he lay beside him, his upper torso and head resting against the horse's neck, cradling him as best he could. His eyes watered suspiciously, and he felt glad there was no one here to see.

He was not sure how long he stayed thus before he sensed a small movement beneath him. So desperate was his grief that at first he thought he'd imagined it, but then he heard a snort and felt the jerk of Viking's head.

"Thank God!" he cried, crouching painfully to his feet. "This is more the thing." He circled to stand in front of the horse. "Now you must get up, my beauty."

Viking raised his head and looked about him as if wondering how he came to be on the ground. Ethan laughed. "Yes, I know; we took a spill. Naturally that's humiliating, but there are worse things. We'll keep it between ourselves, what do you say? Now, up you go." He put his hand to Viking's raised neck, guiding him upward.

The horse gamely struggled, snorting and panting, then collapsed back.

Ethan refused to give up. "Come on, old boy, you can do it!" He clapped his hands encouragingly, flinching at how the sound hurt his head. Viking whinnied and eyed him with desperation, a piercing look. But the black had to get up; he *must* no matter what the cost. And he was trying; how valiantly he tried! He lunged upward, his neck and shoulder arching with effort, then back. Again he surged, again and again, each time cracking Ethan's heart a little wider.

And then, just as the viscount's hopes were crumbling, the horse rolled to his feet. Ethan shouted and threw his arms around the proud neck; but Viking, having no patience for sentiment, tossed his mane haughtily, gave an arrogant snort, and started to walk forward. The pitiful neigh that followed tore at his master.

"Hold, fellow; easy, now. Let's see what damage we have." He ran his gaze along the horse's flanks and legs, his hands seeking what his eyes might miss. Other than a few scratches that didn't look serious, Viking seemed all right except for his right front leg. Ethan smoothed his fingers along it. The leg felt hot and was beginning to swell, but he couldn't detect a break; pray God it wasn't broken. His groom, Rathbone, would be able to say with more authority. Getting to him was another matter.

The Redding estate was closer than his own but not by much; and the thought of Alice and George's irritable father had no appeal. He had much rather go home. Taking Viking's reins, he led him forward for a few trial steps. The steed favored his leg but, after he learned not to put weight on it, seemed able to move without terrible anguish. He wished the same could be said for himself; it was going to be a long walk home.

At that moment he saw what had caused them to fall. Viking had not tripped because of clumsiness or inattention. A thick rope was stretched tautly between two stout oaks on either side of the path, positioned at the height of his stallion's knees, well out of the line of vision of either horse or rider.

"Here, here! Come back, woman, you have no right!" Burns's voice echoed through the viscount's library. Madeleine, who had stationed herself next to the window, looked away from the empty landscape to the figure rushing through the doorway. The woman she and her father had met outside before luncheon came to stand before Thomas wringing her hands, a desperate expression on her face.

"I beg your pardon, sir," she said, casting a dismayed look over her shoulder at the approaching butler. "But this one won't give me a chance for the position—"

"A thousand pardons," Burns tolled, seizing her arm. "She ran past me before I guessed what she was doing. I'll see she's put on her way."

The woman struggled against the pull of the butler's strength. "His master is not here to say whether he'll hire me or not, and this creature will not allow me to wait. You seem like kind people; I appeal to you to help me."

Madeleine's father laid aside his book and, over the crescent of his reading spectacles, looked from the woman to the butler. "Hold a moment, Mr. Burns—"

"Don't trouble yourself, sir; I happen to know Lord Ambrose's requirements don't include hiring another servant."

Antonia swung her feet to the side of the chaise lounge. "Perhaps we should give him the opportunity to decide for himself, though; do you not agree, Mr. Burns? Surely it would do no harm to allow this lady to wait."

The butler's face smoothed over, and he relaxed his grip. "As you wish, madam."

"Thank you," the woman whispered, lowering her eyes.

Antonia waved her nearer to her seat. "What is your name, dear? Do you live in the village?"

"I'm Rose McDaniel, ma'am, and I come from Cornwall."

"All the way from there? That's quite a long distance, if you walked. What brings you to Brillham, if I may make so bold to ask?"

The woman raised her lashes, looking slightly surprised at her interest. Madeleine smiled to herself. Her parents often scolded her for her curiosity, but in truth, her mother could be worse.

"I've been looking for work for a while," she said.

Antonia gazed at her with pity. "And you've not found anything closer to home?"

"Nothing permanent, ma'am," Rose McDaniel answered. "I—I've been hoping to find something with children. I love little ones but don't have references because I've never done this kind of work for hire. I recently lost my husband and find I must earn my own way. Children bring me comfort."

"You poor dear," Antonia sympathized.

Madeleine saw Burns raise his eyes ceilingward. No doubt he thought the woman was lying in order to play upon their sympathies, and she might be; but Madeleine believed she heard the ring of sincerity in Mrs. McDaniel's voice. Besides, her mother had a way of drawing the truth from people.

Antonia continued, "I'm afraid the infant will only be here a little while; her mother is expected to return any day now."

"That doesn't matter," Mrs. McDaniel said quickly. "If I could only work long enough to receive a reference, that would be a help."

"I understand. Well, surely Lord Ambrose will return soon. Burns, please see that this young woman is fed luncheon while she tarries."

"Thank you for your kindness," the woman said, her sad eyes sweeping from Antonia to Thomas and Madeleine.

When Burns, his back stiffened in outrage, led her from the room, Antonia turned to her husband. "We must do something for that poor woman if the viscount does not. Perhaps we could use another servant at home?"

Thomas went to help her lie back among her pillows, then kissed her hand. "Your heart is as tender as ever. Of course I shall hire her, if that is what you wish."

Madeleine, her nervousness pushing aside further thoughts of Mrs. McDaniel, pulled back the drapes and scanned the horizon. "I cannot imagine what is taking Lord Ambrose so long."

Thomas's doting expression faded to sternness. "Mayhap he searches for his elusive cousin."

"Papa," she said scoldingly. "I'm worried. Could we not send someone to look for him?"

"And where would we begin, child?"

"I believe he normally rides the boundaries of his estate . . ."

"Normally. Today he could be anywhere."

Madeleine gnawed at her lower lip and pulled back the drape again. "I'm feeling the need for a ride myself."

"In this rain? I think not." He regarded her for a moment, then softened. "Listen, child. If we don't hear anything by mid-afternoon, I'll go myself."

"Hold a moment, Papa; I think I see—" She made an impatient noise and dashed to the window on the other side of the bookcase. "There's a man leading a black horse—it's Ethan! He's hurt!"

She ran from the room and out the front door. The steps were slippery in the drizzle, but she didn't slow her pace. She raced across a portion of the graveled drive, then around the side of the house and onward, her shoes flinging mud across her dress. The rain plastered her hair to her forehead; her gown became heavy with water. She could hear shouts behind her, but she ran on. When she reached Ethan at last, she hesitated only an instant before flinging her arms around him. As he slowly returned her embrace, she felt as if she had come home.

Ten

"You ought to go inside and get something done with your leg," Rathbone said to the viscount later that afternoon in Viking's stall. "I tell you, the black's going to be all right. My poultice is already beginning to work. You can see for yourself the swelling is going down."

Ethan wasn't so sure. He stared at his groom, then eyed the messy mixture of clay and herbs distrustfully. Viking *did* seem calmer; he'd finally taken a little nourishment, and the wild look in his eye was gone. Shadows were gathering in the corners of the stable, and the thought of a bath and clean clothes was appealing. He still couldn't dismiss the notion that his horse needed him, though, or that something would go wrong if he left.

"I wish you *would* come inside," Madeleine said behind him, almost making him jump. She held a tray containing a large bowl and towel.

"Oh, is that more food? I haven't been able to finish the sandwiches you brought earlier."

"No, this is hot water to clean your leg. Has it stopped bleeding?"

With his cheeks warming, Ethan glanced down at his makeshift bandage, a towel tied in a knot. "Yes, I believe so. But I don't expect you to, uh, do the honors. Nasty business, that." Not to mention almost his entire leg was exposed beneath his tattered pantaloons, a fact that had not escaped her lively attention. Uncanny how she could make him feel like a maid on her wedding night.

"I don't fade at the sight of blood, my lord, but if you won't let me or anyone else help you, then you should do it yourself before infection sets in."

"I will."

They stood silently regarding one another. When Rathbone coughed, Ethan glanced down and took the bowl. "Thank you, Madeleine, how thoughtful you are; but I'm going inside for a bath in a matter of moments."

She gave him a skeptical look. "Are you? Then I'll stay and walk back to the house with you."

"That's not necessary." He set the tray on the floor in the corner.

"I think it may be."

He studied her, feeling irritation and pleasure all at once. She believed she knew what was best for him, when assuring himself of Viking's safety was what gave him the most peace. He grinned suddenly. She would see who could outlast whom.

"Very well," he said. "Stay as long as you like."

Rathbone rubbed his nose and shuffled past them, mumbling about seeing to his supper. The horses in the other stalls snorted as he walked by.

"Viking is looking much better than earlier," she said.

"Do you think so? I was just going to brush him."

"It appears as though someone has already done that."

He felt a tinge of irritation; she noticed everything. Limping to the shelf where supplies were stored, he took a brush, hobbled back to the horse, and slowly pulled the bristles down Viking's coat.

"It gives him comfort," he said.

"Yes, I can see that."

She was laughing at him. He sent her an annoyed glance. "Viking is the last of what once was a very fine stable."

The light died from her eyes. "I'm sorry, Ethan; I don't mean to tease. I know how much this horse means to you; I'm afraid my relief at finding both of you safe is making me giddy."

He smiled. "Then I forgive you." His brush stilled for a moment. "I gather that's why I received that unexpected yet delightful embrace in the full sight of God and everyone, including your father?"

Now it was her turn to blush. "Naturally I forgot myself in my relief."

"Your father didn't look pleased. You were turned away from him, but I could see his face."

"He has not said a word to me about it," she said loyally. "I'm certain he understood my emotions of the moment."

"I see." He resumed his brushing. "So I'm not to take it these *emotions of the moment* mean you've come to a decision regarding my suit."

"Not . . . yet."

His frustration was so sharp he could not find it within himself to look at her, and an uncomfortable silence stretched between them. Madeleine, who had been leaning against one of the divider walls between Viking's stall and the next, scuffed through the hay to stand closer to him. She stared at him so intently that Ethan had little choice but to cease his work and return her gaze.

"There can be no doubting my affection for you," she said slowly. "When I knew you to be late from your ride, I could think of nothing except your safety and that horrible curse. I don't believe I'm normally a superstitious person, but . . . well, perhaps I shouldn't say this to you, but I shall. Papa believes there is a power of the mind to cause things we expect to happen to come to pass. He can be most convincing. I beg you to be careful, Ethan. Try not to do anything dangerous that might cause an accident, especially until you reach your thirty-first birthday."

Her entreaty warmed him, for it indicated an encouraging depth of feeling. "You may ease your mind on that score. What happened today had nothing to do with the curse, for it was no accident."

She regarded him worriedly. "I don't understand."

He nodded toward a long piece of rope draped across the stall. "That's the reason Viking fell this morning. I found it stretched between two trees on our path."

With rounded eyes, she went to touch the frayed ends where he had cut the rope from the trees. "Who—who would do such a malicious thing?"

"An excellent question. I've thought of little else all day."

"The rope was set at a height where you could not see it?" The query seemed to be rhetorical, for she did not give him time to answer. "But anyone could have fallen . . . could possibly have been killed."

"Not anyone, I think." He spoke lightly, not allowing his outrage to enter his voice. "Since it's widely known I make that circuit alone every day, the trap was clearly intended for me."

"Surely not! Someone—a bored child, perhaps—merely intended a prank, I'll warrant. Or even more likely, a group of children were playing with the rope—perhaps it formed the boundary for some game—a race, no doubt—and simply forgot to untie it!"

He smiled grimly at how hard she was trying. She didn't want to believe anyone hated him so much that they wished him dead. Neither did he, but the fact must be faced.

"No child tied those knots. I cut the rope free with difficulty."

"But, Ethan, you don't have such enemies . . . do you?"

"I didn't think so, until now."

She abandoned the rope and returned to him. Despite her nearness, she seemed far away, her eyes brimming with thoughts. He could almost hear them. She made him feel both affection and exasperation. On the one side, he appreciated her intelligence. On the other, he sometimes wished she would simply accept his words without questioning or trying to find solutions. Most women would. But if she did that, she would not be Madeleine; and it was Madeleine he loved.

"Do you think," she said slowly, "it could possibly have anything to do with the baby?"

"The baby?" he repeated blankly.

"Yes. I have may questions about her, and now it occurs to me those questions may be more important than I thought. When you went missing today, all my suspicions retreated to a murmur in my mind. But now they have come back, this time with darker import. Oh, if only you would be truthful with me, Ethan, it could make all the difference."

His heart began to race. "Truthful?" Mindlessly, he turned back to Viking and drew the brush downward. "What makes you think I'm not being truthful?"

Madeleine stretched her hand over his, stilling his movements. "Ethan. There is no cousin, is there?"

A defensive protest rose to his lips. He stopped himself, catching the untruth only in time. After a moment, he leaned his forehead against Viking.

"No," he said, and felt as if his heart had been yanked out by the roots.

He heard the little intake of breath that signified her shock. Next she would tell him goodbye; he knew it.

"Whose child is she?" she asked, her voice quivering.

Carefully keeping his gaze away from Madeleine, he gave Viking a gentle slap on the rump, then limped back to the shelf, and replaced the brush.

"I don't know," he said softly.

"You don't know who the mother is, you mean."

"No, I mean I don't know who her parents are."

Her eyebrows raised in surprise. After an instant's hesitation, he began to explain. He told her everything, or almost everything, starting with the baby's arrival in his bedroom and finishing with his doubts about Leah. He did not voice his suspicions about his twin; to do so without proof would be an act of supreme disloyalty, he believed.

When he had done, she nodded and walked a few paces

away, leaving Viking's stall. He followed her. "So. You may be the father, but you're not certain."

"It's highly unlikely that I am. Despite what you may think, I haven't been careless. I—"

"Please!" She held up a restraining hand. "Don't give me details; I'll trust your word on this."

"No, I only meant the circle of possible mothers is very narrow."

"How you comfort me." She wandered further from him. Again he followed, limping quickly past to block her way.

"You asked me to be truthful," he reminded.

"Yes, I did. I hadn't realized how much it would hurt."

This made him smile. "You would hold me accountable for my behavior before I met you? You're very hard, Miss Murrow."

"I'm trying not to be," she whispered. "Why is it that women are expected to be virtuous, yet men are allowed to . . ." She turned on him suddenly. "How would you feel if the situation was reversed?"

"Interesting you should ask," he said, and told her of his previous day's imaginings.

"You thought I might be Dorrie's mother?" she repeated incredulously. "I cannot believe it! You've claimed to have deep feelings for me. Does your affection not hold any trust?"

"Desperation can make anyone do unexpected things. Even an angel, I imagine."

She appeared slightly mollified. "Well, in the event any doubts remain in your mind, let me assure you that I am not the mother. But yesterday, what did you think? Were you ready to send me packing?"

"To be honest, I was wondering if I could bear it. I came to the conclusion it would depend on the circumstances."

She frowned. "The circumstances."

"A woman does not always have a choice in these mat-

ters. If you had been seduced by a man you loved who promised marriage, for an example . . ."

"You would have been able to forgive that?" she asked doubtfully.

"I believe so." Actually, he was uncertain, but in this matter he could surely be pardoned for stretching. He knew he dare not give any other answer, not with her eyes so firmly alight. With greater surety, he added, "I wouldn't have forgiven *him.*"

Looking skeptical, she turned her face forward. They moved toward the stable doors, pain radiating from Ethan's head and leg at every step. Earlier, he'd found a bump at the back of his scalp. The thought of a bath and bed grew more pleasant at each breath, but there were things that must be settled first.

"And what of you, Madeleine. If it happens that I am Dorrie's father . . . would that finish things between us?"

"As far as my father is concerned, it would."

"I'm not concerned with your father, only you. Could you forgive me?"

"I think it would depend on the circumstances," she answered pertly.

"Madeleine . . ."

"Yes, I believe I would."

She said the words so rapidly and quietly that he could not be sure he heard correctly. But his heart must have; it was singing like a thousand birds taking flight. Painfully, he hobbled after her into the garden stretching between house and stable. Only one more thing need be said.

"If it does happen that Dorrie is my child . . . I want to keep her."

She stopped. "Yes, I suppose you would." The sun was low in the sky, casting a golden light across her face. "What if it came to a choice between us? Who would you choose?"

"You," he said without hesitation, although he felt a knot form at his throat.

"Correct answer," she said with a tiny smile. "But I would not ask you to choose."

"Correct answer," he threw back, his relief profound.

Her grin widened briefly, to be replaced by a look of determination. "We cannot breathe a word of this to my parents, especially Papa. It seems to me we must make it our business to find who Dorrie's parents truly are. It may be that your life depends upon it, if some jealous suitor has discovered the truth."

"Or *thinks* he has. I'm not convinced that what happened today has anything to do with Dorrie."

"If not the baby, then what? Have you made anyone angry?"

He thought for a moment. "I can't imagine who. I've hardly had contact with anyone since Lucan died."

"What of your list of possible mothers?" Her expression darkened. "Have you . . . had contact with any one of them? Maybe an irate father means to punish you."

"I've been nearly a recluse for the past half year. Before that . . ." He closed his mouth, deciding to think to himself. A litany of lovers could hardly endear himself to his intended.

They had come to a halt beside a backless bench placed among the weeds. Chilly, sore, and tired, Ethan sat, and Madeleine joined him, her spine stiffly straight.

His gaze wandered across the stone walls of his home as he recalled his past sins. There had been Sylvia Sharpe, a widow. But she could not be the mother; she married shortly after their affair and moved to America; she would hardly have shipped her baby across the Atlantic. He'd kept an actress for a brief time, flame-haired Amethyst Subarro, but they had ended nearly a year ago; certainly longer than Dorrie was old. Had there been another? He could not think of anyone. After many lost years, Lucan's entreaties had started to take effect; Ethan was beginning to settle down.

Lucan, whose life may have been more deceitful than his own.

"I don't believe I'm the father." Highly aware of Madeleine's steady gaze, he said, "One thing is certain. If Leah Abbott is the mother, I *know* I'm not the father."

"It's good you can be sure of something." This heavy irony did not go past him unnoticed, and he winced. "Well, it's very hard to imagine a woman would accuse an innocent man without reason, and that's what you're asking me to believe—that someone would abandon her child to a third party."

"Perhaps she made the mistake of thinking a title means wealth. Or her situation could have been so appalling that mine looked infinitely better."

Her expression turned pensive. Glancing downward, she inhaled sharply at the sight of his leg. "We'd best go in; your wound needs tending." He agreed and started to rise. "Oh! I had almost forgotten. There's a woman inside who has been waiting for you all day, a Mrs. McDaniel. She's seeking a position and hopes especially to care for the infant."

"I'm sorry I'm not able to accommodate her, but—"

"No, you don't understand!" She grabbed his arm. "You *must* hire her because it's too peculiar that she has shown up just now, don't you think? What if *she* is the baby's mother!"

He could not follow her logic. "And has changed her mind, you mean?"

"Yes, or she could intend to be close to Dorrie by working here. There is only one way to find out."

"Very well," he said, and set his teeth against the pain as he struggled toward the house. "This will only work if she's willing to labor for food and shelter."

"Oh, bosh; as to her wages, I can pay them from my pin money."

How the mighty have fallen, Ethan thought, one corner of his mouth lifting in a sad smile. In more ways than one.

* * *

During the next hour, Madeleine dressed for dinner, exchanging her day dress for a more formal gown of the palest green silk, hoping its long-sleeved velvet bodice would keep her warm in the viscount's drafty house. With Zinnia's help, she swept her hair upward into a crown of curls, twining an emerald bandeau among them.

Although it wasn't quite time for dinner, she was anxious to see how the viscount fared and so hurried downstairs. She wasn't in such a rush that she failed to gaze at the grand barrenness of the hall around her. She still did not know how to think of this residence, whether manse or castle or abbey.

With what she hoped was an objective eye, she studied the ceiling vaulting above her, the faded tapestries, the suit of armor, and the central table with its marble statue of Diana, bow and arrows gripped in one hand, standing companionably beside a reclining lion. There were several public rooms not in use because of economy; should she become mistress here, her first order of business would be to make them hospitable. Being restricted to the library, dining room, and her bedroom was beginning to make her feel like a prisoner. And color—how the house hungered for color! Now that she thought upon it, the lack of a warm palette was no doubt more responsible for her constant feeling of coolness than the temperature.

A trifle early for schemes of redecoration, she counseled herself wryly as she entered the library. There were more important things to think about. Somehow the viscount and she must discover the baby's parents—or mother— and quickly. She was certain Ethan's safety lay in that direction; and despite his denials, she was not entirely ready to dismiss the possibility of his fathering Dorrie. The viscount might wish to spare her feelings in denying parentage, but the rope across the path screamed hate and revenge.

She wished he would not be so reluctant to take responsibility. As he implied, she could hardly condemn him for past acts (although a woman would be, the thought stubbornly persisted). As Bettina's sister, she had reason to understand indiscretions of the heart.

Her parents and Mr. Brandt were already waiting in the library. After greeting them, she asked about Lord Ambrose.

"I checked on him less than a half hour ago," Mr. Brandt said, looking well in dark evening wear, his cravat crisp and white as a summer cloud. "Against his wishes, I fetched the surgeon to stitch up his leg. Afterwards, he had a good soak and was dressing when I left. I expect him down any moment."

"Such an awful thing, his falling," Antonia said. "I'm so glad he's all right"

"How's his stallion?" Thomas asked.

"I just talked to Burns, and the groom says Viking should be right as rain in a few days."

"That's good news."

Madeleine thought so, too, but wished Ethan would hurry. Although she conversed with civility during the next few moments, she fidgeted inside, growing wild to see him again. She could not stopping thinking about his safety. When he finally appeared, coming not from the stairs as she expected, but from the back of the house, she beamed.

His eyes met hers and softened. "Sorry I'm late," he said, raising the cane he used demonstratively. "Grandfather's walking stick; Betsy insisted on finding it for me in the attic. And I confess I looked in on Viking. Then I interviewed a new servant briefly; she caught me as I passed through the kitchen."

"Oh, did you hire poor Mrs. McDaniel?" Antonia asked, her expression eager.

Daring a playful look at Madeleine, he said, "In a manner of speaking."

"I'm delighted you did, for I suspect there is more to her story than she's telling. I see tragedy in her eyes."

"You have too kind a heart," Thomas said. "You see stories in everyone."

She tilted her head to the side. "But does not every person have an intriguing history?"

"Indeed they do, Mrs. Murrow," Ethan said, limping toward her.

"Some are more believable than others," Thomas added with a pointed glance at the viscount.

Mr. Brandt rose. "Have you decided about tomorrow, my lord?"

Ethan paused, leaning on his cane as he pulled a bench closer to the older lady. As he sat beside her, extending his leg awkwardly to do so, he echoed, "Tomorrow?"

"You and Miss Murrow were scheduled to ride with the Reddings, I believe."

"Scott, you're better than a calendar. Thank you for reminding me; with today's events it slipped my mind."

Madeleine felt as surprised as the viscount looked. She, too, had forgotten their Friday engagement, although on her part she believed the loss of memory was spawned by an eagerness to forget.

"It's obvious you're not able to ride," Brandt said. "Shall I send the groom to cancel? Unless Miss Murrow would like to go, of course; in which case I'd be pleased to offer my escort."

"How kind of you to sacrifice yourself." Ethan sent him a dark look, then rested his eyes on Madeleine. "Well, Miss Murrow, do you wish to accept Scott's invitation?"

Madeleine had little desire to spend time with the charming, but untrustworthy, Alice. She thanked Mr. Brandt as prettily as she could, but declined, straining to keep relief from her voice.

The viscount appeared satisfied with her answer. "It seems neither of us can go, so we had better let them know as soon as possible. Thank you for volunteering to tell them we can't be there. I'll have Cook keep your dinner warm."

Mr. Brandt gave a short laugh. "I'd thought to send the groom."

"But how impersonal that would be, especially when a

man of your elegant manners is available to soothe any
ruffled feelings."

"Ethan," he said, coloring, "it's raining, and I'm
dressed for dinner."

"I'm sure the Reddings will be even more appreciative
of your message because of that."

Brandt sent Madeleine a scalded look, but he said nothing, only bowed stiffly and left the room.

She studied Ethan with worry and more than a trace of
ire. It was not the first time she'd noticed his unkindness
to his friend, but this was the worst.

"Are you in pain, my lord?" she asked.

"Careful how you answer," Thomas said grimly, his lips
tight. "Only a headache the size of a volcano could justify
such a display, and I'm not certain even that qualifies."

"Scott is used to my ways," Ethan said dismissively, and
stood, offering one arm to Madeleine's mother. "May I
escort you to dinner, dear lady? You are looking uncommonly fine tonight."

It was so, Madeleine realized in spite of her irritation. All
day her mother's voice had sounded stronger, her breath-
lessness hardly noticeable. Her cheeks, while not blooming
with color, glowed faintly; and when she rose from the
chaise lounge, she did so with less difficulty than usual.

As Madeleine took her father's arm, she tried not to let
hope run rampant. Her mother had rallied before, and
she must not become overly optimistic. Still, she would
have smiled as she went in to dinner, if she were not so
appalled at the viscount's behavior.

Dinner proceeded with an awkwardness that gradually
diminished, although Ethan's actions were not forgotten
by anyone, Madeleine felt sure. Certainly Mr. Brandt had
not, for when he joined them afterward in the library,
dripping without apology on the viscount's Persian rug,
his smile was as cold as it was wide.

"The Reddings were very let down that you can't ride
tomorrow," he said after greeting them briefly. "When I
told them of your accident, Ethan, Alice extended an in-

vitation for you and Miss Murrow to join them for tea instead. Since you were not there to advise me, I accepted on your behalf."

"How good of you," Lord Ambrose said, his mouth twisting dryly. "And you'll be joining us, of course?"

Scott's lashes veiled his eyes. "Sorry, my lord. The shipment of wheat seeds, remember? Someone should be here to receive them."

Ethan smiled slowly. "Ah. Such a pity. You'll be missed."

Eleven

Word of the viscount's accident spread quickly, and by eleven o'clock on the following day, Lord Ambrose had entertained several unexpected visitors. "Curiosity-seekers," he told Madeleine after Mr. Tanberry, a gentleman farmer who lived nearby, departed. "All they want are the grisly details so they can spread rumors and feel important in doing so."

For the moment, they were alone in the library. Mr. Brandt was outdoors. Antonia, walking slowly but unaided, had gone upstairs to change for luncheon, with Thomas accompanying her. Madeleine sat alone on the settee, and Lord Ambrose sprawled in the chair opposite, his leg stretched upon an ottoman. She knew his limb pained him, for he walked very stiffly today, but one could make allowances for only so much.

"You're very cynical, Ethan. Sometimes I despair of you."

"Don't, fair lady; you're my only hope." His smile faltered as he plucked a piece of lint from his cuff. "I've not seen even one of today's guests since Lucan's funeral. They are like vultures, only around when the scent of disaster is in the air. Although why that should surprise me when the majority still suspect me of doing in my brother, I don't know."

"Have you visited any of *them*?" she challenged.

His eyes narrowed dangerously, making her heart accelerate even though she knew he was playing. "How boldly

you strike, Miss Murrow. I stand before you guilty as
charged. What sentence do you decree?"

She dared not answer what she was thinking, that she
would favor a kiss above everything. Even his bad-
temperedness could not put her off, because the delicious
spark in his eyes showed he did not mean half of what he
said. Besides, he had a right to be vexed; he could have
lost his life yesterday, and from all appearances, someone
wanted to kill or at least hurt him. And he still mourned
his brother; she often caught the bleak look in his eyes
when he forgot himself.

He was a complex man, the viscount, and not an easy
one. But he excited her, and she could think of nothing
more pleasing than kissing him at this very moment.

A fine idea, that. All her father needed was to return
and find them so occupied; he could hardly maintain civility to Ethan as it was. Best to change the subject, she
decided.

"I've noticed you haven't mentioned the rope to anyone."

"There's no use in that. If someone intended harm, he
would hardly confess."

"But if the rope was left there unintentionally, perhaps
someone would step forward and solve the mystery."

"Oh, certainly, just as they did for my brother's accident."

His eyes grew distant and troubled. She decided to stir
him from further morbid reveries about his twin.

"Have you devised a plan for finding Dorrie's mother?"

"I thought you decided she belongs to that woman I
hired yesterday."

"You are too quick to doubt, Ethan."

"My pardon, but it seems too much the melodrama to
me—the fallen mother hired to serve her child. Too trite
by far."

"Very well," she said, irked at his criticism of her de-
ductive powers. "Then how will you proceed?"

"My first plan is to recover full use of my leg." He bent

his knee slightly and pulled a face. Today he wore loose trousers rather than pantaloons; nevertheless, Madeleine could see the outline of bandages inside the cloth. "Or maybe I'll send Scott in my stead, since he's so worried I'll lose respect in your father's eyes. Surely he won't object to knocking on all the doors in the district and asking the householders if they've lost an infant. Yes, a brilliant plan; I amaze myself sometimes."

You amaze me, too, she thought. "Why do you dislike Mr. Brandt?"

This appeared to surprise him. "Beg pardon?"

"It's apparent in how you address him."

"Surely you exaggerate."

"You were very unkind to him last evening, sending him out into the rain."

"Someone had to go," he said in a reasonable tone of voice. "Why not him?"

"Oh, Ethan, really."

His grin transformed his face. Looking at him, she felt a wave of pleasant helplessness. He was maddening, a complete rascal, and utterly compelling. How could he think anyone preferred Lucan to himself? His brother must have been insipid in comparison.

Oh, she was lost, so lost.

"All right, Miss Murrow," he said. "I'll admit to having mixed feelings about Scott, but I don't dislike him."

He appeared to be done, and Madeleine's curiosity was far from satisfied. "I've wondered about him since we came. Sometimes he seems to be your servant, other times your friend."

"That's a fair summation, I believe."

"But if he's a servant, why does he live like a guest?" Seeing the amused look in Ethan's eyes, she hesitated. "Or am I being too inquisitive?"

"If you were not, I wouldn't recognize you."

Madeleine's eyebrows pulled together. "I beg your pardon; I didn't mean to offend." She extracted the ever-present copy of *Rob Roy* from her reticule and opened it to the embroidered bookmark on page five. "I shan't trouble you anymore," she added in injured tones. "I'm certain you are in pain, and that causes you to be . . ." She mumbled a word under her breath.

Ethan stretched forward and tapped her book with his cane. "Causes me to be what?"

"Difficult," she said quietly, not raising her eyes from her volume.

He laughed and tapped her book a second time. "Put that away; you hate it or you'd have made more progress by now." She continued to read, or made a pretense of it; she couldn't comprehend a word with him sitting across from her. "If you don't set it aside, you'll miss the complete story of Scott Brandt as I know it," he added tantalizingly.

She settled her bookmark in place, slowly closed the tome, and replaced it in her bag. Only after she folded her hands did she look at him. "As you wish," she said.

"You minx; you've been manipulating me." He dropped his cane to the floor beside him and shifted position carefully. "It's a peculiar relationship, I suppose. We grew up together, Scott, Lucan and I. Scott's father, Gordon, was older than mine and served as valet to both my father and grandfather.

"The year before my father's death, my parents journeyed to the Cotswolds for a holiday. During a hike in the hills, Father slipped and fell partway down a cliff. Gordon rescued him at great risk to himself. As a reward for saving his life, Father promised the valet that his children would be educated with Father's own. As it turned out, Gordon had only the one child, Scott, who was a babe in arms at the time.

"As you already know, my father died soon after; but he'd written his wishes into his will, and my mother honored them. Scott shared our tutor and later our house when his parents died."

"So he is almost like a brother."

"In a way, although there was always that difference.

Lucan and I received an allowance from the estate, but Scott's portion was regarded as wages. He has evolved into a kind of steward, but more; sometimes I think he worries to a greater degree than I about our future. And there's worse. Since Lucan's death, he's come to think of himself as my keeper, I believe. If I did not remind him of his place occasionally, he would slip the reins from my control." Ethan rested his head on the back of the chair. "Or he would *try.*"

"You resent him."

"To say truth, I wish he would leave. He's educated in the law; he could establish a decent living for himself somewhere. Instead he remains, as if bound to Westhall. I can't think it healthy."

"Westhall is his home," Madeleine said, feeling surprise that Ethan didn't understand. "Doubtless he *does* feel bound here."

"Too much so. I realize it's difficult for him, living as he does between two worlds, serving the estate but knowing he can never own it, never be viscount. There have been enough incidents over the years to give me a sense of his resentment. Even Lucan felt it, and he was more friend to Scott than I ever was. To give you an example: Scott's invitation to ride with you in my place today. I'm surprised he hasn't done such a thing before now. Lucan and I used to laugh at how he'd try to steal our ladies from us."

"That may be true, but I feel certain he was only being kind in my case. Mr. Brandt has been very proper to me. In point of fact, he has spoken highly of you on numerous occasions."

"His fears for the estate are the source of that. Once we marry"—He stared at her beneath lowered lids—"or perhaps I'd better say, *should* we marry, he will consider you fair game, I warn you."

"Good heavens; I can't imagine he's like that." She wanted to think jealousy caused Ethan to speak so, but she had known women who behaved as he described Mr.

Brandt. Their desire had little to do with the object of their attentions, but had everything to do with winning. She despised such people.

"You should have seen him pursuing Alice last year. She found his attentions so embarrassing she doesn't enjoy his company any longer."

She considered his words for a moment. "If you feel this way, why don't you ask him to leave?"

"Impossible. It was my father's wish he be provided for, and I can't ruin a man's dream. If the idea to leave came from him, it would be much better."

She tried to hide her smile. "Another example of your cruel nature at work, I see."

The look he gave her was so sensuous she could hardly breathe. Goodness, but he was dangerous. She almost wished her papa would enter the library and rescue her— not from Ethan, but herself. How easy it was to imagine curling into milord's lap and feeling his beautiful hands moving across her shoulders as they had that night . . .

"Oh!" she squeaked, realizing of a sudden that Burns was ushering yet more visitors into the library. She hadn't heard a carriage or the front door. Had she been asleep?

To her astonishment, Reverend Abbott and his wife and daughter stood on the threshold, all of them dressed in black. The clergyman held an old round hat in his hands, nervously turning the brim around and around.

"Welcome," Ethan said, flickering an intrigued glance at Madeleine. "Pardon me for not rising."

"Oh, no, please don't get up, Lord Ambrose, not for us," the reverend said. "We heard of your accident and wanted to tell you how very sorry we are."

The viscount thanked him and bid them to be seated. When Mrs. Abbott sat in the wing chair and her husband took the bench, Madeleine pointedly moved aside to make room for Leah on the settee. With her eyes cast down, the young woman reluctantly joined her.

"You look well," Elizabeth Abbott said to the viscount, fanning herself with her hand. She wore a high-necked mourning dress of thick wool, and evidently the fire or the activity of visiting was making her overheated. "What a relief! We'd heard—well, you don't want to know what we heard."

"That I was on my deathbed, probably," Ethan said.

"You can't believe all you hear," Reverend Abbott said heartily. "Take Mrs. O'Tooley. How many times have I gone to *her* deathbed for nothing!"

"Dear, that didn't sound good," his wife said with a forbidding look.

A chagrined expression crossed the clergyman's face. "You're so right, so right. What I meant to say is, I'm happy for her recovery, but I think she'll be the one to bury me!"

"She'll probably bury us all," Ethan said pleasantly, watching Leah.

As if taking her cue, Elizabeth said, "As soon as we heard about your accident, my lord, Leah couldn't rest until we came to visit this morning." When the girl made no response, the older woman lowered her head, her squinted eyes fixing on her daughter, reminding Madeleine of a bull about to charge. "Leah!"

"I'm sorry about your accident," Leah said without raising her head.

Ethan steepled his fingers as he gazed at her. "Thank you."

Mrs. Abbott nodded briskly. "Yes, our girl was devastated, especially after those silly things she said when you visited us day before last." Her voice grew louder. "Weren't you, Leah?"

"Yes," she mumbled. "Sorry."

"She wasn't feeling well," Elizabeth expanded. "You understand how these things are. Sometimes we women fly into the boughs over the least little thing, don't we?" She cast a conspirator's look at Madeleine, forcing her to agree or appear ungracious.

Reverend Abbott laughed companionably. "Yes, you should see how my wife gets at times, especially when she jumps on a certain subject—dare I say phaetons? Only imagine her hoping to have a carriage named after the unfortunate son of Apollo and that nymph, Clymene. When you recall what happened to Phaeton when he tried to drive the chariot of the sun, it makes you think twice, doesn't it?"

Mrs. Abbott glared daggers at him. His laughter choked into a cough and died.

"I want to see that baby," Leah said loudly into the sudden silence.

Ethan moved so quickly he winced. "You want to see the baby?"

"That's what I said, isn't it?"

Madeleine's hopes whirled. "But I thought you didn't like babies."

"I'm to get over it," she said through clenched teeth, her lovely but lifeless eyes leveled at her mother.

"Oh, what a delightful surprise!" Mrs. Abbott said. "You want to hold that sweet, precious baby!" She turned to Ethan. "Shall you send for it, or should I go after it myself?"

The viscount blinked once, slowly. He turned his head toward the hall and called Burns. Within moments the disgruntled butler returned with Mrs. McDaniel trailing him, the baby cradled lovingly in her arms.

As requested, the servant went to stand before Leah. She lowered the infant with the care of one handling a costly glass figurine. Leah accepted the bundle with wooden arms, holding Dorrie at a distance that precluded looking into her eyes or even Leah's own comfort.

"Oh, Leah," Elizabeth said, giggling with embarrassment. "Put her in your lap, or hold her closely to your br—er, chest. Your arms will tire in seconds like that, and you might drop her."

Leah's mouth drew downward. "Don't want her any closer. She might vomit or wet me."

Mrs. Abbott shrieked, then turned her reflexive response into shrill laughter. "Oh, let me show you, girl!"

She bustled to the settee, stared hard at Madeleine until she gave up her seat, then took the baby. "Snuggle her like this, see? Then speak sweetly to her. Heed me, Leah!" She turned her frenzied gaze on the child. "Look at de widdle dinkums, her is such a doll, dare never was such a sweetie, never in all de world." Her head swerved back to her daughter. "See? Babies love that. Now you try."

She lifted the infant toward her scowling offspring. Leah shrank backward.

Dorrie began to cry.

Mrs. McDaniel walked between them and took the child. "She is not a plaything," she said quietly, and, holding the babe against her heart and speaking soft words of comfort, she walked from the room.

"Well!" Mrs. Abbott burst. "Did you see that, Lord Ambrose?"

"I did indeed," he said thoughtfully, his eyes lingering on the empty threshold.

If I were King Solomon looking for potential mothers, Madeleine thought, I know whom I'd choose.

Twelve

Shortly before four that afternoon, the viscount drew his gig to a halt in front of Redding House and viewed the sprawling Tudor with affection and dread. So many hours of his life and Lucan's had been spent here. There was not an angle of roof, a jutting of chimney, or a mullioned window that seemed unfamiliar. The mold bleeding through the freshly painted walls, the fresh growth of ivy climbing the trellis, the splintering timbers framing the windows, the sculpted shrubbery and neat beds of spring flowers—all these were alive with memories of youth and dreams and, most of all, his brother. Inside, the images would be even more intense: the staircase leading to a large nursery packed with books and toys, and three attics where the five of them had played endless games; the baize door at the end of the hall sheltering an enormous kitchen and its cooks—a forbidden zone to the children, but one which they haunted constantly for bits of dough, tastes of beef, and bread warm from the oven, sprinkled with sugar and cinnamon and almond, oozing with butter.

The memories were vividly painful and bittersweet. He could hardly bear coming here anymore. There was a time, back when lovely Mrs. Redding was alive, that this house had seemed more like home than his own.

Even as Legacy proudly tossed her mane at achieving her destination, a groom came running from the stable, and two footmen descended the steps from the house.

Ethan could not help making comparisons with his own estate, where guests were fortunate to have the butler open the door for them, and the overworked stable staff *might* notice someone had arrived and tend to the horses when they found time.

No wonder old Redding had taken a dislike to Lucan and himself during the last year, when Alice became engaged to Lucan. Only two things seemed to matter to the former soldier: money and land. He knew the Ambrose estate was nearly penniless; the sole point in Lucan's favor was the Ambrose acres, which, when joined to the Reddings' two thousand, would make a formidable landholding. Nevertheless, Alice's father insisted she could do better for herself, and only when she threatened to run away did he capitulate. Before that he'd shown little interest in either of the twins. After the betrothal, because he'd never learned to tell them apart, Redding's distaste fell on them both.

Ethan understood Redding's objections to his brother and himself, but he could not forgive him. The old fellow caused Lucan trouble and discomfort, belittling him at every turn. The most scorching occasion came to him now, and the very memory stirred rage.

On one of the final days of his life, Lucan had appealed to Redding to hire some of the servants he had been forced to release for economy's sake. Redding responded by humiliating him in front of a small crowd of visitors, telling him loudly he would care for his own as any proper man would, but that he had no taste for mending the results of another's improvidence.

Every moment of Redding's cruelty had been unnecessary. If his twin's life must be so short, it should at least have been as pleasant as possible.

Beside him, Madeleine murmured with appreciation at sight of the house, and he forced himself to lighten his mood. On the drive over, she had spoken of nothing except her suspicions regarding Mrs. McDaniel. He'd argued that Leah could as easily—easier, since she lived in

Brillham—given birth to Dorrie; awkwardness in holding
a baby and dislike for an infant's bodily functions did not
exempt her from motherhood. Madeleine and he had
come to no conclusions, and he was glad she could think
of something else for at least a moment.

"The house is unpretentious, yet elegant," she said.

"And old," he added agreeably. "Not so old as the Tudor Dynasty, of course, as it was built around seventy-five
years ago. You'll find the interior is harmonious with the
façade; the furnishings were chosen for comfort as well
as durability. When things wear out, the Reddings tend to
replace them with something that looks the same. Nothing has changed since I was a boy."

He waved aside the footman's offer of assistance as he
slowly descended from the gig. On the opposite side, the
other servant helped Madeleine to the ground. Ethan offered her his arm, and the two of them walked inside.
The butler took Madeleine's pelisse and ushered them to
the withdrawing room where Alice and George were waiting. Ethan was surprised to find Jarrod MacAllister with
them.

"I'm sorry Father isn't here," Alice said, after greetings
were made. "He's in the village attending to some business, but he may join us later."

Ethan sincerely hoped he and Madeleine would be
gone by then, but he made the proper sounds of regret.

"Glad you made it, Ethan," George said. "Didn't see
how you could after what I heard. The second footman
said the surgeon was thinking about cutting your leg off.
Well, don't just stand there! Come in and sit, both of you!
What a fine cane. What is that, a dragon's head? Makes
you distinguished; you should use it always."

The withdrawing room was one of the most formal at
Redding House. Two blue sofas sat opposite each other
in front of an intricately carved fireplace trimmed in white
marble. Above the mantel was an oil portrait of Alice's
mother, her sweet eyes set in a pensive look, as if she knew
her life would end too soon. A low, circular table with

four curving legs extending from a pedestal squatted between the couches. Lightweight chairs were scattered in
groupings around the chamber. As Ethan limped forward,
MacAllister abandoned his seat opposite the Redding sib-
lings, pulled one of the chairs between the two sofas, and
stood beside it, inviting the viscount and Madeleine to
take his place on the couch. After they did so, he sat in
the chair and smiled genially.

"You are looking so well," Alice said to Madeleine, leaning forward as if she wished to touch her. She was always
touching people, Ethan noted with a measure of fondness.
Her warmth knew no bounds. It was unfortunate she had
overextended that warmth to him in her grief for his
brother. He had never felt the old level of comfort with
her since and wondered if he ever would. Every time they
were together she deferred to him and cast long, hungry
looks that made him squirm inside. She was doing so now.
"Doesn't she look pretty, Ethan? What a lovely shade of
peach; it sets off the duskiness of her skin beautifully. I
have always thought fashion silly for claiming fair skin as
the ideal. Why, I feel utterly pale and colorless in comparison."

Madeleine shot him an inquiring look beneath her dark
lashes. She didn't know how to react to this backwards
compliment, and neither did he. MacAllister answered for
both of them.

"Miss Redding, you shouldn't apologize for your fairness. There is room for both types of beauty, and the two
ladies in this chamber are the finest examples of each."

"Well said!" George declared. "Ring for tea, Alice. I'm
famished."

The next few moments were absorbed in the serving of
tea. Alice performed her office beautifully, and somehow,
in the midst of seeing each one of them had the requisite
beverage and his or her desired selection of toasted
French bread, cheese crumpets, cranberry muffins, and
delicate ham sandwiches cut in heart shapes on rolls so
light they seemed to float into one's mouth, she had a

padded stool brought to elevate Ethan's leg and pulled a chair next to him on the pretext of hearing every detail of his accident. He told her no more than he had his other visitors, trying to include Madeleine in his conversation; but the angle at which Alice had placed her chair made it impossible to speak with both at once unless he swung his head like a pendulum. Therefore, he felt grateful to hear Madeleine talking with George and MacAllister behind him.

"But how did you come to fall?" Alice asked. "You never fall, Ethan. You were always the finest rider of all of us."

"Lucan was the best," he reminded her gently.

"Ethan, my dear, in your mind, Lucan was the best at everything; but that's simply not true. He wouldn't be pleased that you idealize him so."

"As if you didn't. You adored him from childhood."

Her face lengthened, and she turned her eyes downward. "He *was* an unusually fine man. Did I ever tell you of the time we found a small child wandering along the lane close to the chapel?" When Ethan shook his head, she continued, "I was for leaving the little boy with the Abbotts, for we were riding to Anya Merriweather's and would be late if we didn't hurry. He wouldn't have it. Lucan retraced our route, asking at every cottage along the way until he found the boy's parents, who had so many children they hadn't even noticed he was missing! I can't think of many men who would be so patient."

She turned her eyes full on Ethan, and he saw with sadness they were filled with tears. She blinked, then dashed the moisture away, brightening suddenly. "But you are no different; your heart has always been kind, too. I recall the day you saved the baby hawk that had fallen from its nest."

"I have always been different from Lucan," he said quietly, leaning toward her, hoping the intensity of his voice would lend his words more impact. "We are not the same, Alice. You must remember that."

Alice scanned his face, her expression revealing gentle amusement, almost as if she were looking at a recalcitrant child. She had not heard him, not at all. "How is that delightful baby?" she asked. "I wish you'd brought her. I seem to recall nursery clothes stuffed into a dresser in one of the guest rooms; surely a number of my own infant outfits are there. We could play dress-up."

"Not if her new nursemaid was present," Ethan said, glad of a change of subject. "She would tell you Dorrie is not a toy."

Alice looked very interested. "Who is her new nursemaid? Do I know her? Is she a termagant?"

"What are you two discussing over there?" MacAllister said, raising his voice in a friendly fashion. "You're both very absorbed."

Ethan could not help feeling a trifle put out at the man's intrusiveness. He was, after all, a servant—an educated one, but a servant nevertheless, and his question bordered on overfamiliarity. Apparently, Alice felt the same.

"We're speaking of the baby's new nursemaid," she answered in annoyed tones. "Ethan says she is a shrewish woman who rules everyone."

"No, I didn't," he said, irritated, and turned to face the others. "She's marvelous with the child."

"Yes, she's a very kind woman," Madeleine added. "She puts the infant's needs first." She shifted her gaze in his direction. "Dorrie's own mother could not be kinder to her. Mrs. McDaniel is a very . . . *motherly* woman."

Imp, his eyes told her. Never missed a chance, did she? How he would love to kiss that teasing smile off her face.

"What did you say her name was?" George asked.

"Mrs. McDaniel," Madeleine answered. "Rose McDaniel."

George appeared to search his memory. "Don't believe I've heard the name before. Well, now, wait a minute . . ."

"Oh, everyone sounds familiar to you." Alice rejoined her brother on the sofa, her silk gown rustling like leaves in a gentle wind. Behind her, the scent of lavender lingered, reminding Ethan suddenly of her mother. "Have you heard the name, Jarrod?"

The tutor looked pleased to be included. "No, Miss Redding."

"She comes from Cornwall, I believe," Madeleine said.

George chuckled. "Well, that explains why nobody knows her."

Alice rang for fresh tea. "Why have you taken on another nursery maid, Ethan? Surely your cousin will return any day now."

Feeling Madeleine's eyes upon him, he studiously avoided glancing in her direction. "Oh, as to that I've not heard from Connie since she first came, and now I fear the worst. James was always irresponsible. I'm beginning to think they've taken off somewhere, that the story about his mother dying was a ruse. Connie and James knew the baby would be safe with me. Evidently they want to be free of responsibility while leaving open the possibility of returning at any time to reclaim their child."

The maid entered carrying a silver pitcher. "How horrid of them!" Alice said, then thanked the servant and began to freshen cups. "But how can you be certain they haven't had an accident, Ethan?"

"I'm sure I would have heard something by now if that were the case," he said uncomfortably, accepting a cup of tea he didn't want.

"Heard something about what?" said William Redding from the doorway.

Ethan's spirits dived as he regarded the elderly man. Redding had not removed his greatcoat, and he was rubbing his hands briskly as if cold. Judging by the flushed condition of his nose and cheeks, he was. Ethan thought that odd; on the ride over, he'd found the outdoors comfortable for the first days of May. Perhaps the iciness of Redding's spirit lowered his body temperature.

"Father!" Alice said gladly. "Come and have refreshment."

"No, my girl; Links gave me something in his office. I'll not stay; just wanted to give the viscount and Miss Murrow my greetings. What was it you were talking about?"

"We were discussing Ethan's cousin," Alice said, aligning the tea service as she spoke. "He believes she has run off and expects him to keep the babe indefinitely."

Ethan did not care for the knowing glint that appeared in Redding's eyes. "Haven't heard from her, is that it?"

The viscount lowered his tea to the table and broke one of the crumpets on his plate in half. "Not a word." He popped the morsel into his mouth without looking at Redding again.

"Hard to believe people could act like that," George said. "Unnatural."

Redding humphed. "Unbelievable is the word I'd choose."

"I've seen worse behavior," Ethan said, carefully keeping his gaze on the delicacies on his plate, "by people old enough to know better."

Redding could not have missed the meaning of this reference, and perhaps he felt a measure of shame, for he only cleared his throat and said, "How fares your mother, young lady?"

"She is improving, thank you," Madeleine replied.

"A fine woman, that. Puts me in mind of my own dear wife." With obvious reluctance, he returned his attention to Ethan. "And you, Ambrose; heard you took a spill. Best to look where you're going, what? How's your animal?"

"Doing well." He cut a wry look at Madeleine. "Viking should make a complete recovery."

"Father, aren't you going to ask how *Ethan* is?" Alice scolded.

"There's no need; I can see he's fine! Have you had a change of heart yet about your stallion, boy? I'll give you a good return on your investment."

"Viking's more than an investment," Ethan replied, struggling to keep his tone even. "He's not for sale now, nor shall he ever be."

"Careful what you say, Ambrose. No one knows what he'll do when the wolves are at the door. At least your beast would be safe here; we're not careless with our stock—haven't had an accident in years. Your black's bloodline is excellent and should be preserved."

"It will be," Ethan said softly, anger pounding at his throat. "At Westhall."

The butler had moved timidly near his master, and Redding shrugged off his cost and handed it to him. "Have it your own way, Lord Willfulness; but don't expect me to rescue you when your horse breaks his leg the next time you make him fall." He straightened his jacket and marched away.

"I will never go there again," Ethan said when he and Madeleine were once more in the gig, heading home.

"Of course you will," she said, her voice consoling. "Mr. Redding *is* difficult, but you handled yourself well, considering your temper."

He was silent for a moment, then said, "What do you mean, *considering my temper?*"

"Nothing, only that I knew you were close to losing all control."

"And how did you ascertain that? I was perfectly civil to him."

"I've learned to read the little clues you send out. You become very still, as if waiting for a lion to pounce; your fingers tremble oh-so-slightly, and the rate of your breathing increases. Also, your skin flushes and pales alternately, sometimes becoming mottled."

"How attractive you make me sound," he said with a cool stare. "Sometime I'll recite a list of his sins against my brother for you, and then you'll see why I'd rather be flayed alive than sit in the same room with him."

"Oh, I think that's a trifle extreme. At least he was kind enough to ask about my mother, unlike Alice, who seemed to have forgotten everyone except you."

She could always make him smile. "Jealous, are you?"

"No, merely surprised that she forgot to be her charming self. I thought she had that quality down to perfection."

His grin widened, and he made a sound like a cat hissing.

"Oh, please don't do that! I can't bear for women to be compared to felines, much as I like them."

Dismay seized him. "You don't own cats, do you?" His life was becoming too complicated: first a baby, hopefully a wife—*this* wife—but surely, surely not this.

"Not currently," she said sadly. "Tricksy died in her sleep last fall, and I haven't had the heart to replace her."

"In that case, will you marry me?"

She laughed merrily. "Oh, Ethan, you are priceless."

I'm not trying to be amusing, he wanted to tell her, but caution warned him not to pursue the subject. He knew what she would say: "Too soon!" or "We don't know who the baby's parents are." All her father needed was an excuse of that nature. Should her parents decide against him, he feared Madeleine would not go against their wishes. She had her own strong mind, but how could he compete against a lifetime of familial devotion? He was beginning to despair of a happy resolution.

"I shall keep asking until you accept me," he warned good-naturedly, although his hopes were plummeting.

Her eyes softened upon him. "Good," she said.

Shortly after dinner that evening, Ethan claimed his leg hurt and bid his guests an early good night. Truth was, he would like nothing more than to spend the evening with Madeleine by the fire; but his leg *was* throbbing, and he had plans other than sleep. His prime occupation now was to unravel the mystery that threatened his future and Madeleine's.

Stiffly, he climbed the back stairway to the nursery and encountered Betsy in the corridor carrying a tray of empty dinner utensils. "Well, well," she said, eyeing him up and down. "You're hobbling better than I reckoned you would. Nice of you to put the scare into everybody. Have you found out who strung the rope across your way?"

"How did you know about the rope?"

"Don't shout at me; I work for you out of the milk and kindness of me heart. Besides which, the whole household's talking about it."

He groaned. "I'll wager Rathbone started it. I told him not to spread tales."

"It weren't Rathbone that did the yammering—it were Lindon, the Murrows' groom. What are you doing up here, anyway—come to see your baby?"

"Hush, woman," he whispered fiercely. "All I need is for Janice or Mrs. McDaniel to hear you call that child mine."

"They wouldn't know what we was talking about if they did." She balanced the tray on one hip and smoothed a strand of brittle hair from her eyes. "Although that Rose is sharper than most. She tends your baby like it was her own—you don't think it is, do you?" She cackled while he prayed she wouldn't notice his silence. Apparently she didn't, for she went on, "Then, while the baby sleeps, she cleans the nursery almost as good as I would."

"High praise indeed."

She huffed. "Listen to me, milord; I do the best I can with all I've got to do. Here I try to give you a pretty word for finally hiring somebody worth paying, if it was ever to come to that, and all you do is talk down to me like I was a lowly slattern."

Ethan apologized and hastened around her into the nursery. Janice, who was sitting in one of the rocking chairs and knitting, glanced up, colored, then stood. Curtseying shyly, she slipped into the adjoining bedroom where he assumed her own child was resting.

Mrs. McDaniel was leaning over Dorrie's cradle, her back turned to him. From the look of things, she was changing the babe's napkin, and the viscount swiftly averted his gaze. When she finished and nestled Dorrie against her shoulder, Ethan joined them.

"Lord Ambrose! You startled me," she said. When he begged her pardon, a sweet expression lightened her face. "You've come to visit the baby, haven't you?" She gently placed Dorrie in his arms. As he could see nothing to be gained in refusing to hold the mite, he walked to a rocker and eased himself downward, staring into the infant's startling blue eyes while the maid continued to speak: "I've seen how good you are with her. Look how she smiles; she likes you."

Although her praise pleased him, he forced himself to move forward in his queries. "Join me, won't you, Mrs. McDaniel? And be careful to whom you say that. Some would suggest there's a reason for her preference."

"And what would that be, my lord?"

"That I'm her father."

In the process of drawing a chair near him, she paused. "Why would anyone repeat such lies? Dorrie belongs to your cousin and her husband; at least, that's what I've heard."

He studied the refined shock in her eyes as she sat opposite him. She looked much better than she had yesterday. Her moonsilver hair was drawn into a tidy chignon, and her Westhall livery, while not new, was an improvement over the ancient gown she wore at her arrival.

"That's the story which is circulating, yes," he said carefully.

Dorrie waved tiny fists in the air and thrust her tongue forward, then arched her back and squealed. Even at this age she did not like to be ignored, he thought, setting the chair into motion. Womanhood must be bred into the bones.

"Do you mean it's not true, my lord?"

He lifted his gaze from the infant and watched the maid closely. "As a stranger here, I'd be interested in knowing what you think."

"What could my opinion possibly matter?"

She seemed unduly upset by his question, and he felt a measure of satisfaction. "Because of your objectivity, naturally. You see, it's the question of timing that gives everyone concern." She sat very still, waiting, her features expressionless except for the anxiety he happily spotted in her eyes. "You met the Murrow family yesterday. Their visit is no ordinary one."

"I know, my lord. Betsy told me there's a possibility of marriage between you and Miss Murrow."

"How like Betsy," he said, annoyed. "At any rate, Dorrie arrived the same evening the Murrows did, but the Murrows never met Connie."

She appeared baffled. "That your cousin brought the infant on the same night seems a happy coincidence to me."

"But if someone wanted to discredit me in the eyes of my intended and her family, he or she could not have chosen a better time. Since there has been no public appearance of my cousin, people are beginning to gossip. As Mr. Murrow is also voicing suspicions, the chances of an alliance between his daughter and myself grow more slim every day."

Her forehead creased deeply. "But the timing of a baby's birth is not controllable," she reminded.

"No, but the delivery of it on my doorstep *is,*" he said.

She moved as if to rise, propping her hands on the wooden rocker arms, then sat again. "Lord Ambrose . . . I'm still not sure why you are telling me this, but . . . do you think your cousin is trying to prevent your marriage?"

How tempted he was to divulge everything, but she already knew the truth, didn't she? If not, telling her could only put himself at greater risk; for although she projected an air of dependability, one could never be certain.

Dorrie had fallen into a light sleep, her lids opening to a slit now and then as if she didn't want to miss a word.

"I can't speculate on what my cousin is trying to do," he said. "What I'm asking is, do you find it believable that she is the mother of this child, given the evidence I've presented?"

She gestured helplessly. "What evidence, my lord? You've mentioned only your word." Quickly she added, "Which is well respected, I'm sure."

"Not as well as you might think," he said, leaning his head against the rocker's high back. "Now you see my dilemma." You can confess now, he thought. Please.

Her gaze skittered from his. "Then . . . I'm very sorry for you, Lord Ambrose."

He stayed only a few moments after that. She was either innocent or a more formidable adversary than he thought.

Thirteen

The following day dawned so beautiful that Ethan, while filling his breakfast plate from the sideboard in the dining room, suggested they take a picnic lunch to the seashore. Mr. Brandt could not join them as he'd gone to Gloucester to visit a friend, he told them.

Madeleine was glad to hear her mother accept the invitation, for it meant she felt well; and naturally Papa could not gracefully deny to accompany them; but her spirits sank nonetheless. A picnic could hardly further their investigation into Dorrie's parentage, and she told Ethan so the first moment they were alone, directly after breakfast as they took a turn around the grounds.

"I suggested the picnic for several reasons, Madeleine," he said. "First, I'm half-mad trying to think of ways of finding Dorrie's mother. But consider: if you're correct about Mrs. McDaniel, perhaps some hours away from the baby will drive her to a rash declaration; what do you think?"

He seemed to be jesting, so she did not trouble herself to answer his question, but asked one of her own: "So you mean to bring the baby?"

"Yes, did I forget to mention that?"

She walked a few steps in silence, contemplating him. He looked uncommonly well in his buff pantaloons and bottle-green jacket, a hue that set off his fair coloring handsomely. Just looking at him made her ache inside.

"I think leaving the nursemaid is merely an excuse,"

she said, hearing her voice tremble. "You want to be with that infant yourself."

"Madeleine, Madeleine," he said, laughing incredulously. "I have better things to do with my time."

In spite of the shadow of fear darkening her heart, she smiled bravely. "I've seen how often you take her in your arms; I've noticed the fond gleam in your eye when you look at her. If you had not convinced me of your innocence, I'd begin to suspect there's more than a passing acquaintance between the two of you. Almost I fear you *are* her papa."

"I can hardly tolerate the brat," he protested. "The reason I want to bring her is that I've sent an invitation to the Abbotts to meet us, since there's not room enough in your father's carriage. This will give another opportunity for Leah to confess. You see how devious I am."

"The Abbotts again," she said, sighing. "I'm beginning to feel sorry for Leah." But she could not object to his scheme since she had no better ones; and at least they would be together. Ethan couldn't be hurt by anyone if they were together. He was a strong man; one could see that by how rapidly his leg was healing. But even the strongest specimen—even a *Hercules*—was vulnerable to an unknown assailant.

If anything happened to him, life would not be worth the living.

Her hand was crooked in his arm as they walked, and she moved her fingers reflexively, clasping his sleeve a trifle firmer. She gazed at the landscape around her, scenting the fresh growth of wildflowers, shrubbery, and hedges, now grown high and undisciplined. Although a portion of the viscount's property consisted of an infertile field, she knew some of his land was tillable and had already been planted with wheat and barley. She couldn't deny there was a dismal aspect to his estate, but she saw nothing that funds would fail to remedy.

Even if the disadvantages could not be made more pleasing, she didn't want to live anywhere else, not if it meant leaving him. The knowledge of it nearly shattered her. She, Madeleine Murrow, to whom order and beauty meant everything, especially since the loss of Bettina, would be willing to live with Ethan Ambrose in a thatched cottage with one room and a hole in the ceiling.

Well. She hoped it wouldn't come to *that;* but she loved him; there was no use in denying it. She wondered that he could not sense the riot of affection blooming inside her breast. Perhaps he did; his eyes were gentle and speculative when he looked at her.

Later that morning, as they traveled in her parents' coach toward a spot the viscount knew near Kingsweston, she grew stronger in her belief she could be happy here, deciding that the wildness of this part of England was entirely pleasing with its striking hills, rich vales, and romantic views. How gothic it all was; how Sir Walter Scott! The very air trembled with promises of castles and knights and chivalry. Even little Dorrie, snuggled in Antonia's arms, seemed to sense it; she chortled and cooed like an angel.

When they arrived at the designated area, a hillside off the Bristol Channel, the beauty of the prospect almost overwhelmed her. The grassy site overlooked miles of rolling countryside as well as a striking expanse of water glittering beneath the sun. Even now a ship sailed past them, bound for the port of Bristol, she imagined, and seagulls called in their high, brash voices as they flew toward it. As her parents enthused appreciative comments, she felt happiness radiate through her, a happiness that seemed to go beyond her newly discovered love, although perhaps it was caused by it; she simply overflowed with the pleasure of *being*.

"This land belongs to a friend of my brother's and mine we met at Oxford," Ethan told them as they walked a little way from the coach. Betsy and Zinnia had followed with the picnic supplies in the gig and, with the help of the viscount's driver, were in the process of setting up chairs and the table that had been carried on top of the carriage. "He told us long ago that we could visit anytime we liked, and we've taken advantage of that invitation on numerous occasions. This public road unfortunately came to divide his property, the majority of which is over that rise. Someday I'd like you to meet him and see his house; it's quite grand."

"I should love to," Madeleine said without hesitation. She felt her father's glance on her but avoided his eyes, turning instead to her mother, who still held the baby. Determined that Antonia not become overtired, she scooped Dorrie into her arms.

Rathbone, who was serving as their driver, finished attaching the legs to the table and tilted it upright. As he did, an argument ensued between Betsy and Zinnia about the best place to set it; Betsy declaring a little slope did not matter so long as there was a view; Zinnia, her mop of red corkscrew curls shaking indignantly, asserting they take the most level spot, else the dishes would slide off the table. Both possessed bold, high-pitched voices, reminding Madeleine of the gulls cawing overhead.

"Do you suppose the Abbotts are lost?" Thomas asked after a moment. He sounded hopeful.

"My brother often included them in our outings here," Ethan said. "They know the spot well."

Thomas appeared to deflate. "You seem uncommonly fond of that family."

Before Ethan could comment, a battered gig drawn by a dappled gray appeared over the horizon, going very fast down the sloping road. Madeleine recognized Mrs. Abbott and Leah as they drew closer; the older lady was driving, her hands drawn almost to her chin as she pulled back on the reins, and Leah had braced both arms on her seat, her face dark with terror.

"Stop, stop, *stop*, you foolish animal!" Elizabeth screamed, casting a wild look at her observers as she passed by. Just before the road curved out of sight, the horse slowed to a trot and finally halted in a patch of lush grass. While Ethan and her father hurried forward, Madeleine and her mother following at a slower pace,

Elizabeth slid from the carriage, pressed a hand to her bosom, and propped herself against the wheel. By the time they reached her, she had recovered enough composure to pull her bonnet back on her head and thrust her windblown hair inside it.

"Oh, you cannot know what a drive it has been!" she declared, sweeping harried eyes from one to the other of them. "Lord Ambrose, when Leah and I got your message this morning, Joseph had already gone on his visitations; but I couldn't send regrets, not with Leah wanting an outing so badly." The name appeared to jog her memory. She swerved, looking upward at the empty seat. "Leah? *Leah, where are you?*"

"Here," the young woman said as she circled the back of the gig. She wore a cotton day dress woven with small yellow checks; double frills of lace decorated the neck and wrists of the garment. Although the gown suggested cheerfulness, Leah looked glum and overheated.

"Thank goodness," her mother cried. "I thought I'd lost you around that last curve."

Leah's small brown eyes dismissed her mother, then widened as they came to rest on the babe in Madeleine's arms. "Oh, no."

Mrs. Abbott's gaze followed Leah's. Even she appeared to struggle for a moment, and Madeleine imagined the memories of her daughter's last interaction with Dorrie playing through her mind. In spite of it, her nervous grimace widened to a smile.

"Well, Lord Ambrose, you are full of surprises! Who'd have thought you would bring the baby along."

"I'm not holding it," Leah announced. "I don't care what anybody says."

The vicar's wife laughed wildly. "Nobody expects you to, child." And then, as if she could resist no longer, Elizabeth approached Madeleine, her features brightening at every step. "Well, look at de leedle dumpling, all so pretty in her white dress. Would Miss Murrow give her to me, do her believe her would?"

Madeleine obliged the lady, then melted away with the rest of the party, who seemed no more able to bear Mrs. Abbott's adoration of babyhood than she. They fragmented into groups: Mrs. Abbott, clasping Dorrie to one shoulder, pulled a blanket from her gig and spread it on the grass to sit with her charge; and Madeleine, seeing the pointed way in which Ethan walked off with Leah, remained with her parents. After a few paces, her father excused himself to see how the preparations were going for the picnic, and she and her mother walked on toward a rocky outcropping that promised a comfortable view of the channel.

She felt glad of the chance to be alone with Antonia, even if it was only for a few moments. Since Bettina's death, her father had become so much a part of her mother's life that sometimes she imagined them as one being, incapable of existing without the other—a thing that had added to her fears for Antonia's health. To lose one would be to lose both, she felt certain. In order to lend her mother strength, she linked arms with her and set a slow pace.

"You look well, Mother." An understatement, she thought, gazing fondly at her parent. During the past days, Antonia's skin had lost its pasty look, and her cheeks were faintly tinged with pink. Of late she had been eating more, and her face had filled out a little, the tiny lines at her eyes becoming less noticeable. Even the wisps of hair escaping her bonnet shone more lively beneath the bright sunlight.

"I feel better than I have in years." Antonia stated the words simply, but with such conviction that joy rushed through Madeleine. *Careful,* she cautioned herself. There had been other near-recoveries, all followed by relapses into a lower state of health.

"You don't know how it pleases me to hear you say so," Madeleine said at last, as if stepping among eggshells.

"Seeing you happy has helped me; I cannot tell you how much."

Sick though her mother might be, she missed very little. Madeleine smiled at her, thinking they were more alike than not, even though Bettina had been the one who favored her physically.

Antonia added, "At first I feared you only expressed interest in Lord Ambrose to please me. I could not live with myself if that were the case; not after neglecting you so much during the last years. Oh, my dear, I apologize for it. I know I've wallowed in self-pity at times."

"Oh, no, Mother! You've suffered a horrible loss. No one could blame you for your tremendous sorrow."

"But you and you father have suffered the same tragedy and managed to go on with your lives."

"It's different for mothers," Madeleine protested, although she'd had the same scorching thought at times, weeping into her pillow in the early hours of the morning, despairing that Antonia would ever return to her former self.

"Bettina and I had a special relationship," the older lady continued, trying to explain.

"Yes, it was apparent to everyone." Why did that fact still have the power to slice at her emotions? She was grown-up now, not a child. Perhaps in some areas, it was impossible to be adult. "You loved each other very much," she forced herself to add.

"I wish she had trusted me enough to come to me in her trouble. I would've forgiven her, and I know somehow we would have found a way to make things right. Oh, Madeleine, imagine how beautiful her child would have been. Perhaps we could have said a cousin dropped off the babe at our house, as the viscount has."

"Don't, Mother." How that beloved voice could tear at her heart! "You will only make yourself more ill."

Antonia gave her a slow smile. "I don't have to remind you the physicians have never been able to find anything physically wrong with me."

"I know," Madeleine said softly. "Their knowledge is limited."

Dr. Forthswaite had called Antonia's long illness a sickness of the mind, brought on by grief. Nonetheless, he told her father and herself that sorrow could kill. And, no later than last month, he'd said that if Antonia continued on her present course, she would not survive the year. Madeleine had trembled that the mind might hold such power, had even argued with the doctor that her mother's disease *must* be physical; otherwise, if people could will themselves to die, why could they not wish to fly as well?

She remembered vividly the physician's florid, pouchy face and sad eyes as he answered: "Because, Miss Murrow, all people die even without wishing for it, but no one has ever grown wings."

Madeleine and Antonia had reached their destination. One large, gray boulder squatted at the crest of the hill with a number of smaller rocks spreading before it like ducklings nesting around their mother. From here the land dipped steeply until it ended at a cliff. With only a small amount of assistance, Antonia stepped over the smaller boulders and sat on the indented surface of the bigger one, her skirt hiking above her ankles, her feet dangling a few inches above the ground. There was room enough for Madeleine to lean her weight against the rock, and she did so, drinking in the panorama as if her body hungered for it. The sight of the ship's sails holding the wind, the smell of salt, the probing breeze lifting tendrils of hair from her bonnet—on such a day, anything seemed possible: Antonia could recover, Dorrie's mother would be found, and Ethan and she might find happiness together.

Dreaming of it, Madeleine lifted her face to the wind's caress, shuttered her lashes, and smiled. After a moment, she felt her mother's regard and opened her eyes. Antonia's look was so tender she found it hard to breathe.

"You are in love," the older lady said.

A denial sprang to Madeleine's lips, but she swallowed

it. She could not lie to her mother. "I believe so," she said.

"It's even better than I thought, then. I'm so pleased."

"Are you, Mother? I know Papa doesn't approve of Lord Ambrose as much as he did at first." To put it mildly, she added to herself.

"He has a father's imagination, full of fears, hoping to save you from all hurt. I've spoken with him, reminded him that no one's life is free from trouble—not once the heart is open to love, for with love comes vulnerability. In losing your sister, you already know this."

"Yes," she said, feeling her heart dip a little. Everything always came back to Bettina.

"But Thomas fears you will suffer at the viscount's hands; he suspects him of the sins of a rake. If only he realized how much like Lord Ambrose he was at that age!"

"Was he?" She tried to imagine this and could not.

"Before we married, your father broke more hearts than I care to list; so many that *my* father warned me against *him.*"

Madeleine found this so hard to visualize that she laughed.

"I know it seems amusing to you, dear, because you're his daughter; but it's true. Since he is a man, Thomas cannot understand this parallel, either. He wants to throw every despicable deed imaginable at that young man's door."

"Such as fathering Dorrie," Madeleine said in dismal tones.

Antonia tilted her head to the side as she studied her daughter. "Do you think he is her father?"

"No," she said, her eyes searching for Ethan worriedly. She spotted him walking with Leah a few hundred feet away, along a finger of land that projected toward the sea. She hoped his conversation with her was going well, that he was finding out something important. "No, I don't."

The thought brought her former exuberance back to earth. If she learned differently—if it turned out he *had* sired Dorrie—she would forgive him; but she could not trust her instincts, or him again. Such did not seem the stuff of happily-ever-after endings to her.

Standing beside the mute Leah, Ethan gazed across the way at Madeleine with longing. Dressed in pink and talking with animation to her mother, she looked so lovely he could hardly stand his ground with the black-spirited young woman before him; but he had business with her, and here he must stay.

"Now, what do you think, Miss Abbott?" he asked with forced cheerfulness. "Was I wrong when I told you this spot commanded the best view?"

"No." Her brown-marble eyes surveyed the shore with all the excitement of a piece of wood.

He tried again. "You've come here with us a few times before, I recall." Truth was, he hardly remembered her presence. "What did you like to do—play croquet? Or are you one of the ones who enjoyed walking down the steps to the shore?"

"Didn't like any of it."

"Oh." *That* fairly well put death to a conversation, and he struggled to find another means of bridging to the subject he needed. He thought a man tied to a stake, covered in honey, and surrounded by fire ants would have an easier task. Perhaps the best plan lay in a direct siege. "The other day at the vicarage, you spoke of my brother's kindness to you. Do you have any memories of him at this place?"

She squinted up at him. "He talked to me sometimes. The only one who did. *You* don't remember. I saw *you*. Too busy with your friends and the ladies."

Guilty as condemned, he thought, and felt no remorse at all, not if he had avoided her in the doing. Talking with Leah was like hitting himself in the head with a brick.

"What did you speak about?" he asked as pleasantly as he could.

"Things."

Exasperated, he lifted his arms and let them fall, startling a snipe into flight that had landed nearby. "What things?"

"Why do you care?" she barked.

He grew very still, his gravity unfeigned, and she stepped back a pace as if afraid. "This may surprise you, but all of my brother's activities interest me. He means— meant everything to me."

Her eyes narrowed. After a moment, she rubbed her shoulders and shifted her glance to the sea. "Yes. All right." She puffed her lips, pulling air in and out, whistling softly. "We talked about death."

"Death!" This was so far from what he expected that the word was torn from him.

"Things die. Rats die different from rabbits. Their screams are different. People die different, too. I go with my father sometimes to see dying people. Some fight. Some go peaceful, like death is their friend."

Ethan could scarcely hide his distaste. What was wrong with this woman?

"When you spoke about these things, what did Lucan say?"

"He said I shouldn't think about it too much. He told me not to catch butterflies anymore, saying they had feelings. I know they don't because they never scream, but I didn't tell him that. His eyes would go sad when I said those kinds of things, so I learned not to."

His stomach rolled. "You must have felt very safe with him." She gave a single nod, and he went on, feeling as if the very question was a betrayal of his twin's integrity, "Did he ever"—the thought seemed so repugnant to him he almost shivered—"kiss you?"

Flat eyes skewered him coldly. "Had he touched me, I would have killed him."

He believed her. A sudden flash of the rope across the pathway skittered through his mind; but he'd known from childhood that she never rode horseback, and surely someone would have seen the Abbott gig crossing his land. Moreover, it had taken a man's strength to tie those knots. And though she resented him for being alive when his brother was not, was that reason enough to kill him— even for her, demented woman that she was?

Shakily, he asked, "Have you never had a beau, Miss Abbott? Never wanted to be married?"

"No. Never!"

He tried to disguise his astonishment. If she spoke truth, she was the first woman he'd known to hold that opinion. Such vehemence seemed unnatural. A sudden, horrendous thought struck him. If she had been taken by force, terror of men could be at the root of her feelings; even more so if a violent act had resulted in pregnancy.

But why in hades would she deliver her child to him? There was no logic in it; therefore, she must not be Dorrie's mother. *I'm sorry, Lucan,* he told his brother. *It was wrong of me to suspect you, even for a moment.*

Leah had been watching him closely, and now she said in forbidding tones, "You're not thinking of making an offer for me, are you?"

"What? No! I mean . . . no. My heart is engaged elsewhere, I'm afraid; not that such a prospect lacks appeal—"

"Because my mother would like it if you did."

"You surprise me," he said, beginning to retrace his steps along the promontory as quickly as politeness allowed. She followed, and he increased his strides, hoping she wouldn't notice he failed to offer his arm. He didn't want to offend her; she might cut his throat while he slept. "By that I mean, most mothers disapprove of me."

"She's a silly cow."

"Hah—hah! Well, I'm sure you don't mean that."

"I do. My father's not as bad, but he's like a boy. He knows nothing and acts like he knows all. I've found that to be true of every man except Lucan. I don't want to marry."

Thank God! "Yes, well, I'm sure you know best." Would she never stop yapping? Was this how it went with the quiet ones, once the floodgates were opened? He didn't know how Lucan had stood it.

"I belong to me," Leah continued. "Men expect you to do things you don't want to do."

"Yes, we're beasts; every one of us." He had almost reached Madeleine and Antonia; he could not be happier had they been the Holy Grail.

"Men don't want to know about important things like death."

"I would not dream of arguing the point, Miss Abbott." He covered the few remaining steps to Madeleine without a trace of a limp and with a gladness far out of proportion for their short separation. "Well, and who are these beautiful sea nymphs sunning on a rock?"

As he spoke, the vicar's daughter veered and headed off alone. Madeleine, her face glowing with beauty, goodness, and light—or so thought Ethan, who devoured her features thirstily—watched Leah's departure with a puzzled air. "Where's she going, I wonder?"

"To pull the wings off flies, I shouldn't doubt," Ethan answered, much to the Murrow women's surprise.

"Food's ready!" screamed Betsy above them, irritating the viscount. Long ago, Lucan had told her to use a particular silver bell for the purpose of bringing everyone together at picnics, but she could never remember to bring it. Nevertheless, he offered an arm to each lady, and they ambled toward the table.

Not until after the meal did Ethan have a few moments alone with Madeleine. Dorrie had begun to fuss, continuing even after Betsy changed her napkin, and the viscount feared it might be because she was hungry; although he knew the wet nurse had fed her moments before they departed, and they had brought sugar water for the infant to suckle. Madeleine disagreed, declaring that she sounded tired to her. As the servants put away the picnic supplies and the others wandered in various directions to view the sea, she sat upon Mrs. Abbott's blanket and sang to Dorrie while rocking her in her arms. Ethan joined her, leaning on one elbow and stretching out his game leg, which had begun to itch where the stitches were healing.

Madeleine had a tuneful, breathy voice that pleased his ear, and he smiled lazily as he watched her. She tried not to look at him but at the baby, and the glances that flickered his way alternated between resentment and mischief. Finally, Dorrie fell asleep, and Madeleine carefully placed her in the basket and draped one of the blankets halfway across the handle to guard her from the sun.

"How fortunate your children will be," he said, plucking a long stalk of grass from the ground and beginning to trace it along her bare arm.

A playful look entered her eyes as she moved out of reach. "Thank you, but I don't believe singing a baby to sleep one time is proof of anything."

"At least it proves you don't dwell in the valley of the shadow of death."

"I beg your pardon?" she asked, bewildered.

"Someday perhaps I'll tell you. Suffice it to say, spending a few moments with Leah Abbott has made me appreciate you even more. And you were correct about her. She can't be Dorrie's mother."

An innocent look swept across her face. "I'm sorry—what did you say? A bug of some sort was buzzing past my ear."

"I said, you were correct about—oh, you vixen, you only wanted me to admit I was wrong."

"There's nothing a woman likes better than to know her gentleman possesses humility."

"Is that so?" He stared at her through his lashes, and she met his eyes without flinching. His pulse began to race. "So I'm your gentleman, am I?" he asked softly.

She glanced away, suddenly appearing shy. She looked so adorable, he wanted to pull her on the blanket beside him and cover her face with kisses. Had her parents not been sitting on a rock a hundred feet from them, he might have done so.

"Do you have any further ideas?" she asked, startling him into thinking she had read his mind.

"You mean about finding the baby's mother." He gave an embarrassed laugh. "Yes, I think so. With the elimination of Miss Abbott, I'm left with only one contender, and I've thought of a way to force her hand, I hope."

"Ethan, it occurs to me we should widen our list of suspects, for if Dorrie's mother turns out not to be Mrs. McDaniel, what shall we do?"

"That's the beauty of my plan, Madeleine." He sat straight, growing more excited as his idea unfolded. "You see, my cousin is returning." Eagerly, he waited for her reaction.

"Your . . . mythical cousin."

"Yes. When word is spread abroad that she's returning to take her baby home on . . . let us say . . . the day after tomorrow, the mother will be forced to act."

She regarded him for a moment. "Dorrie's mother will know there's no cousin, and she'll think you mean to get rid of the child."

"Precisely!" He felt unaccountably let down when she failed to become as enthused as he. "You don't think it will work. Why?"

"No, it's not that. Perhaps your scheme *will* prove successful. But if it doesn't . . ." Her dark eyes probed his. "If no one claims the baby before your cousin is due to appear, what will you tell my father then?"

He had thought of that contingency. Growing very somber, he said, "I'm afraid in that case, a tragedy will have occurred. Nothing could prevent Connie from fetching her infant except death." He wondered briefly if talking to Miss Abbott had made him bloodthirsty; the plan hadn't occurred to him until after their conversation. "It will be a broken wheel on her carriage, I think. In that manner, both she and James can die together. Perfection!"

Madeleine shook her head. "Too perfect. Papa won't believe a word."

Ethan's eyes became glassy as he considered this. After a few seconds, he heaved a sigh. The scheme would work, that was all. It simply must.

Fourteen

Breakfast on Sundays at Westhall was served later than on other days, in part to allow the servants a half hour's extra sleep, but chiefly to meet the convenience of the viscount and any guests he might have, most of whom needed additional time to dress for chapel before arriving downstairs. At the appointed time, Madeleine, experiencing very mixed feelings, descended the stairs in her white muslin trimmed in blue ribbon. She could not wait to see how Ethan's proposed solution played itself out, but she quaked inwardly as she tried to imagine what they would do if his plot didn't produce results.

Entering the dining room, she discovered she was the first to arrive. Hunger could not wait, however, and she moved to the sideboard and proceeded to raise one silver lid after the other without finding food within a single platter. This perplexing dilemma resolved itself when Betsy pushed through the door dividing the butler's pantry and dining room holding aloft a tray.

"Morning!" Betsy said, bobbing, giving Madeleine no time to answer before she added, "I reckon you thought we'd run out of food. Well, not yet. Not for you folks, anyway. Here's the kippers and sausages." As the maid spoke, she filled the trays. "Eggs is up next, and I'll bring you some toast directly."

Moving her head from left to right conspiratorially, she walked very closely to Madeleine and whispered, "What do you think about what milord's up to, eh? He told me all last night and made me promise to keep my trap shut, except to you, o'course, because we're the only ones what know there's truly no cousin. Well, and Mr. Brandt, naturally; maybe he spilled all to him." She wrinkled her nose in disgust. "I don't think milord told His Highness the butler, for he seldom troubles to include that one in anything, so the least said in his direction, the better."

Madeleine recalled now that the maid had stood beside Ethan when he brought the babe downstairs that first morning. Of course, Betsy had known about the mystery from the very beginning, and Madeleine's first qualms settled. The servant had kept the secret thus far; surely she would continue.

"Where *is* Mr. Burns?" Madeleine asked, lowering her voice to match the maid's. "I didn't see him in the hall."

"On Sundays he gets a half day off, unlike the rest of us more deserving slaves."

The young lady was spared the necessity of making an answer by the arrival of her parents. "Thank you, Betsy," she said loudly and with such enthusiasm that her father cocked an eyebrow, "the kippers look *delicious.*"

Antonia waited until the maid exited before saying, "But, Madeleine, you don't like kippers."

"I didn't want to hurt her feelings."

Mr. Brandt walked in at that instant, and she greeted him effusively, happy to be off the subject of fish. Was there a secretive spark in the young man's eye? His glance lingered fractionally on hers, and she was certain the viscount had told him. He would have had to, she supposed.

Thomas pulled out a chair for Antonia, but the rest of them stood, waiting. No one wanted to begin serving his or her plate, since the buffet was not yet complete.

"How are you faring, Scott?" Thomas asked, his hand resting on the back of his wife's chair. "We don't see much of you."

"This is a busy time of year for the estate. The crops must be managed, and the need for repairs is constant.

I've also been consulting with an agricultural specialist who has some promising ideas for us to implement."

Madeleine studied him covertly. She had learned very little about Mr. Brandt during her sojourn here, but he impressed her as a mild-tempered man who seemed highly organized. His appearance today, as on all days, was impeccable; not a hair or thread dared fall out of place. He wore shades of brown that contrasted strikingly with his ivory shirt, and he looked quite attractive.

"The viscount doesn't help you much with management, does he?" Thomas continued.

Brandt leaned his weight against the sideboard and crinkled his eyes thoughtfully. "He's more involved than you might imagine, particularly since Lucan's death. Don't judge him by what you've seen during your visit. Naturally, when he has guests, they become his first priority."

"Yes, of course." Thomas waved a hand as if to say how little that mattered. "You know, Scott, I find myself wondering why a young gentleman like yourself buries himself so far in the country. From all I've observed, yours seems to be thankless work—or underappreciated at the very least. A man of your abilities could make much of himself in the city."

Madeleine stared hard at her father. He was not normally so inquisitive, and she suspected his purpose was to lead Brandt to say something negative about Ethan.

Scott did not rise to the bait, a thing which made him grow more worthy in her eyes. "I've lived at Westhall most of my life, Mr. Murrow," he said. "My loyalties lie here. There's great satisfaction in keeping the work of more than a century alive and ongoing."

Her father shrugged his disbelief. "If you say you're satisfied, who am I to debate it?"

He wanted to, though, Madeleine saw. Although she itched to scold her sire for prying, she had to admit Scott Brandt truly did *not* seem happy here. She'd been so absorbed with Ethan, she hadn't reflected upon the steward's frequent absences, his polite but detached conversation, the somber looks broken only occasionally with dutiful smiles. Now she recalled his actions in force, and wondered if they had significance for Ethan's safety. In the light of his near-tragedy, she dare not ignore any warning signs. If Mr. Brandt resented him, would he try to kill him? But wouldn't Ethan's death mean the end of this position, which he claimed to enjoy so much?

None of it made any sense. Her arrival at Westhall had been very like entering a confusing land where nothing was as it seemed. She would hardly be surprised to find people walking backwards next, or walking on ceilings.

Except for the danger to Ethan, she loved the confusion and the mystery that had been part and parcel of her brief sojourn here. Although her emotions rose and fell daily like a spring tide, she had not felt so alive since Bettina's death. No. She had *never* felt so alive. And the reason for that was the striking young lord entering the dining room, his hair tousled from the wind, his cravat slightly disarrayed beneath a blue jacket that echoed the brilliance of his eyes.

"I apologize for my tardiness," he said, and slid his palms together as if to calm his excitement "I've been spreading the word at the stables to prepare for my cousin's return tomorrow."

"And not a minute too soon," Betsy said as she burst through the door carrying the remaining items of food. "The way some people talk—my, my, my. *Now* they'll have to shut their traps, eh?"

"Your cousin is returning?" Thomas asked, disbelief throbbing in his voice.

Antonia, too, appeared surprised. "But I thought . . ."

"That Connie and James had run off?" Ethan finished. "So did I, but this morning I received a note by special messenger. James's mother died, sad to say, and they've been too grief-stricken to communicate; and there were all the details of the burial and estate to be seen to as well. But tomorrow morning they're finally coming for their daughter."

Antonia, sending Madeleine such a look of relief that the young lady glanced away guiltily, said, "We'll miss Dorrie awfully, but it's best she's with her parents."

"I'll believe it when I see it," Thomas grumbled beneath his breath.

Madeleine despaired of her father's skepticism as she and the others filled their plates and sat to eat, but the viscount's glowing enthusiasm gradually infected her, even if there was an aspect of desperation in it.

By the time they arrived at chapel, even Reverend Abbott's terrifying sermon could not deflate her.

As the vicar rumbled on—truly, she hadn't dreamed he could speak with so great an authority and fire! He seemed rather meek in person—her gaze roamed the simple, whitewashed structure with its long, slitted windows, dusty stone floor, and hard oak benches arranged in a U-shape around the pulpit. The building was filled with parishioners, and none of them looked shocked at his graphic listing of Job's troubles. From here she could plainly see Leah Abbott, and the young woman appeared so avidly absorbed in her father's sermon—she looked to be *enjoying it,*. actually—that Madeleine averted her gaze. She suffered gamely through the loss of Job's children and property, but when the vicar reached the part about boils covering the poor man from head to foot, she shut off her mind.

Afterwards, as they made their way outside through the crowd, their progress hampered by the curious who wanted to make Madeleine's acquaintance, she grew amused at the variety of ways Ethan worked his cousin's return into their conversations. Introducing her parents and herself to a prominent maker of muslin cloth and his family, he added affably, "Yes, I've enjoyed the Murrows' visit immensely and am now to see my cousin Connie and her husband tomorrow. They're coming for their infant daughter; perhaps you've heard they left her with us for a while?" He went on in the same vein, each time speaking loudly and jovially, until they reached the sloping grass in front of the church.

Madeleine became certain the viscount had never lingered so long after service, for the looks they received were colored with curiosity. She recalled what he'd said about his acquaintances: that many of them believed he slayed his own brother to steal the title. Now she came to wonder if that was true, or only a misinterpretation on Ethan's part. She had no sense of being shunned; she detected only a slight wariness on the part of the villagers, as if they were hesitant to approach. For years after Bettina's death, her family had been treated in a similar fashion. People tended to flee those who had experienced great grief, she believed. Perhaps they feared misfortune was contagious.

She felt a measure of relief when the Reddings and Jarrod MacAllister joined their circle, for at least they brought the advantage of familiarity. Her pleasure waned, however, as Alice sought a place on the other side of Ethan, her stark beauty drawing every eye, even Madeleine's. Miss Redding wore a blue gown nearly the same shade as the viscount's jacket, and to look at the two of them was to be pierced by azure eyes; hair sparkling with golden highlights, although Alice's was darker than Ethan's; and tall, slender bodies brimming with youthful health. Madeleine could not help finding them daunting, and wanted to slink away and disappear into the throng. Certainly *she* could fade into anonymity, but neither Ethan or Alice ever would.

"What have I been hearing about your cousin?" Alice asked, sounding intrigued. "Is she taking her baby away?"

"Yes, she's coming tomorrow," Ethan half-shouted, and flashed a brilliant smile at a passing trio of young women, rapidly adding at the same volume while turning his head after them, "Connie's missed her child dreadfully and can hardly wait to take her home. She and her husband live near the Scottish border, you know; quite a long journey."

MacAllister, who was wearing his black velvet jacket and looking warm in the noonday sun, said, "You must be relieved. Last time we spoke, you thought they had absconded."

"Yes, and I'm ashamed for it." He faced an elderly man walking past with a young lady clinging to his arm and called, "All this time, my cousin was enduring heartbreak, but tomorrow she's coming to reclaim her child and take her away."

"So you've said, Ethan," George commented in a complaining voice. "No need to go on and on about it. What think you of my cane? After seeing yours, I decided to get one. Makes me look mysterious, don't it?"

"As mysterious as a pie-eyed dog," said Mr. Redding, causing his son to frown and shrink a little. "Be certain to bring your cousin to see us when she comes, Ambrose. I'm curious to meet her."

"As am I," Madeleine's father said, exchanging a meaningful look with William Redding.

"Certainly, if there is time," Ethan replied. "Connie wrote of many things left undone at their home; they'll be in a rush."

"Then send word to me," Redding said. "I'll come to Westhall. This is one branch of the family I don't want to miss."

Ethan smiled faintly and inclined his head. As he looked up, his eyes hooked Madeleine's and darkened with exaggerated sorrow, confirming her thought that, did some nervous mother not come forth, poor Connie and James had only one fate in store for them.

On the journey back to Westhall, it became difficult for Madeleine to avoid Ethan's glances; every time she looked at his cheerful, self-satisfied face, she wanted to smile. She knew he was proud of how well it went at chapel; had even one person missed his announcement, she would be astounded. How she prayed he was not building his hopes for a disappointment.

When the coach pulled into the driveway, the viscount

and his guests unboarded and repaired to their rooms to freshen themselves for luncheon. Less than a quarter-hour later, she joined her parents and Mr. Brandt in the library. Ethan was nowhere to be seen, and she felt a sharp tug of frustration. She had hurried in order to spend more time with him, but it appeared his attraction for her was not quite so strong.

Mr. Brandt seemed to guess the reason for her offended look. "Ethan rushed through the hall and went outside just a moment before you came down. He didn't stop to say where he was going. Mayhaps he forgot something in the coach."

Soothed, Madeleine smiled her thanks and was moving toward the settee when Betsy tore through the hall, the ribbons on her cap flying as she cried, "Saints preserve us, saints *preserve* us!"

The inhabitants of the library gazed at one another in astonishment, and then, as one, hastened toward the hall, Madeleine's heart beating like thunder in her chest.

"What's wrong, Betsy?" Scott demanded.

The maid, her hand on the doorknob, swerved. "She's gone! Rose McDaniel has gone with the baby and I've got to search for her! It ain't my fault—Burns goes to his mother's on Sundays, and I had my hands too full with all I had to do!" She snatched open the door and moved forward.

Madeleine stifled a groan. This was not how it was supposed to go. Rose McDaniel had reacted far too fast. Ethan had planned to watch the nursery all day, but he hadn't expected any untoward actions until nightfall. Oh, the brazenness of her!

"Wait!" Thomas called after Betsy. "Are you saying the nursemaid has *stolen* the infant?"

"I don't know," the maid moaned. "She's just *gone*. Janice don't know nothing, she was bathing Clyde when Rose left with the child. I've got to find her!"

Antonia looked so pale that she frightened Madeleine. "Oh, I hope she hasn't kidnapped Dorrie! Do you think she became so attached that the arrival of Lord Ambrose's cousin drove her mad?"

"What cousin?" screeched Betsy, her words barely audible through the open door as she ran headlong down the steps. "It ain't no pretend cousin I'm worried about. That's *milord's* baby; any fool can see that by how he loves her!"

Ethan's pulse drummed in his ears and pain roared through his leg as he ran down the drive of his house, checked the lane in both directions, then raced to the stables. No one had seen Rose McDaniel. He gave Viking a distracted pat and ordered Rathbone to saddle Legacy. *Fool, fool, fool,* thumped his heart. Start a rumor and expect the results to fall at your own convenience. Had a greater idiot ever been born?

If anything happened to Dorrie, he would never forgive himself.

But how could he know whether she was safe or not if he never saw her again?

He mounted Legacy and rejoiced at the punishing ache in his thigh. He deserved that discomfort and more. Guiding the horse from the stable, he clicked her forward.

In the next instant, he pulled the steed to a halt.

Rose McDaniel appeared around the back corner of the house, the baby's basket swinging over her arm. Spotting him, she smiled. Grimly, Ethan dismounted and patted Legacy toward the stable, then walked forward to meet the nursemaid.

"Where have you been?" he demanded after seeing the baby appeared safe and happy within her basket.

She shrank from his anger, her smile dissolving. "In the back garden, my lord."

"What can you mean, taking the infant outside without telling anyone?"

"I often bring her outside at this time of day. The fresh air makes her sleepy."

He glared into her eyes, his rage and fear too strong

to fade all at once, even in the face of her obvious innocence.

"No one seemed to notice or care until now," she added worriedly. "Is something wrong? Would you rather I not do this again?"

"No, no, of course not."

Betsy, who had been running toward them, ground to a halt beside him, her hands cradling her cheeks. "You—you! I thought you'd stolen the baby!"

The nursemaid's fair skin became more pale. "Why would you think that?" Her gaze returned to the viscount. "Is that why you're upset, Lord Ambrose? You believed I ran off with Dorrie?"

Ethan sliced a burning look at Betsy. "Never mind, Mrs. McDaniel; forgive us for overreacting. Since the infant's leaving tomorrow, we've become a bit overprotective."

"Dorrie's leaving?"

"Yes; hasn't anyone told you my cousin is coming for her?" Evidently not, for the woman appeared dumbfounded. Ethan felt hope rising again; in the past seconds, he'd been to the point of believing Rose McDaniel could not be Dorrie's mother, given her reaction to their fears for the infant's whereabouts. But since the nursemaid had been unaware she might lose the baby, she still might stir to action, thereby making her motherhood plain. And this time, he'd be there to stop her.

His gaze dropped to the babe, who was dressed in pink ruffles and looked fragile and perfectly beautiful. Her eyes were open wide, and her fingers grasped outward as if she meant to grab the entire world and stuff it into her basket.

His heart twisted at the necessity of putting her at risk, but he knew of no other way to persuade her mother to expose herself. Not that he believed Dorrie was in *danger;* even if her mother made off with her, she would doubtless take good care of the child. It was the *not knowing* that would haunt him if he failed. He imagined himself ten years hence, then twenty, still wondering what happened to the baby girl who came to rest on his doorstep.

"No one told me," Mrs. McDaniel said, her voice hesitant and worried, her eyes shifting back and forth without setting on any one object, magnifying his suspicions tenfold. And then she added, as if in afterthought, "I suppose you won't need my help after tomorrow."

"Your place is secure for a while yet; Betsy is in great need of assistance," he said, patting Mrs. McDaniel's elbow. Was that all there was to it, then—she was merely worried about losing her position? He felt foolish for exaggerating the importance of everything, but she had not entirely put him off his guard. "Why don't you take Dorrie inside; she looks ready for her nap."

The servant ducked her head and walked rapidly toward the front door, the basket held stiffly in front of her body. Ethan followed at a more leisurely pace as he struggled to contrive what to tell Madeleine's parents about his behavior during the past minutes; he distinctly remembered ignoring Mr. Murrow's, "Is there a problem?" as he ran through the hall.

To his irritation, Betsy matched him stride for stride, her nervous energy driving him to distraction as she kept wringing her hands and drawing in deep breaths. Finally, he planted his feet and demanded she tell him what was the matter.

Looking everywhere except at him, she said, "Milord, ah . . . . when I came out to help you look for Dorrie, I . . ."

"Say what you intend to say, Betsy. I've never known you to be speechless."

Her pale, scanty lashes turned downward. "It's just—have you ever said something you didn't mean, when you wasn't listening to yourself?"

"No," he answered unhelpfully.

Her eyes flashed. "Well, that's what I just did, and if you mean to get vexed at me or summat, when I was only trying to help, then—then, a pox on you!" She turned and ran into the house, slamming the door behind her, leaving him with a sense of foreboding along with his irritation.

Seconds later, he entered the building and immediately knew he was in very deep trouble. A thick silence had fallen over his home, broken only by the sound of persistent, soft weeping. Ethan inhaled a swift, steadying breath and strode into the library.

Madeleine and her mother were ensconced side by side on the settee. Thomas stood behind them, his hands braced on the wooden back of the seat. Scott, his head turned downward, sat across from them in the armchair.

At the viscount's entrance, four pairs of eyes met his with daunting intensity. As he feared, it was Madeleine who wept, and her mother looked to be on the verge of joining her.

"There you are, finally," Mr. Murrow said. When Ethan moved toward Madeleine, her father commanded, "Leave her be, Lord Ambrose; she only remains in this room because I'm not heartless, and she begged me to allow it. Truth is, I'd rather be alone to hear your explanation, for I fear it's not decent for female ears; therefore, I counsel you to speak carefully."

Ethan swung his gaze to Scott; hoping for what, he could not say. There was sympathy in that corner, but no help; after a fleeting, wounded look, Brandt dropped his gaze to the carpet.

"What is this about?" Ethan asked, although he feared he knew what Murrow meant.

The older gentleman straightened and crossed his arms over his chest. "You lied to us about Dorrie. Your maid let it slip that the child is yours, and though I've tried to get a sensible answer from Mr. Brandt and my daughter, neither one is cooperating. My first inclination was to pack our bags immediately and leave; but since Madeleine has obviously formed an attachment to you and beseeched me to allow you the opportunity to explain, I decided to do so, if only to hear your apology. I give you fair warning, though; nothing you say is likely to change my mind."

So this was how it ended, he thought, darkness settling around him. He might blame Betsy for her loose tongue and wish to strangle her slowly, but the betrayal could have come from any quarter. Maybe one day he would discover Dorrie's true parentage, but it would do him no good now.

He deserved no better than this, to face the future alone without the woman he loved.

At least he lived. Lucan did not have even that.

His head began to throb. Without thinking, he lifted a hand to one temple and massaged for an instant, then dropped his arm as Mr. Murrow's eyes grilled him without sympathy.

"I did lie to you," Ethan said in a low, unfaltering voice, and flinched when Antonia gasped. "I do apologize for it, even though the lie was meant to be temporary."

"There, you see, Thomas; he planned to tell us the truth eventually." Antonia's voice shook, but she sent Ethan an encouraging look. Had his heart been less heavy, he would have smiled at her.

"It sounds to me as if he makes excuses," Thomas said.

Scott moved forward in his chair and entreated, "Please hear him out, Mr. Murrow. I think you'll understand why he acted as he did. Lord Ambrose is not normally an untruthful person."

Ethan had not the heart to comment on this mixed praise, and he went on as if he'd not heard Brandt's comment. He began by telling the Murrows of the baby's arrival and concluded with the events of only a few moments ago, leaving nothing out, not even the note with its ambiguous insinuation.

When he finished, a silence fell for a brief space of time, and he felt compelled to add, "I feel certain I'm not Dorrie's father—"

"But you're not one-hundred-percent sure," Thomas interjected.

After a brief pause, Ethan slowly admitted that this was so.

"Well, I believe your story, and that surprises me probably more than it does you, given the amount and scope of your lies. I'll go even further: I hope you discover the truth about Dorrie, or whatever her true name may be, though more for her sake than yours. However, whether you do or not has little bearing on my daughter's future, because her future does not include you."

Madeleine flew to her feet and swerved to face her father. As she did, Ethan said quickly, "But if I could prove to you the infant's not mine—"

Thomas grunted. "Impossible!"

"—if you would only give me a little more time—"

"A true gentleman doesn't need to research his behavior; he's certain of it, every moment of the day. But perhaps noblemen don't fall into that category; you would know more about that than I. Whatever the case, we're leaving as soon as my wife's maid packs the valises."

"Oh, Papa!" Madeleine cried, "you cannot do this. I love him!"

Despite the weight on his shoulders, Ethan could not fail to draw strength from her declaration, although he was not sure he could believe it. She was in the frame of mind to say anything right now. Nevertheless, his eyes locked with hers as he said softly, "And I love you."

"Very tender, Ambrose," Thomas said coldly. "Why not tell *her* the truth, at least? It's my money you love."

Antonia clutched her handkerchief to her mouth. "Thomas, think what you are saying!"

"I mean no disrespect to my daughter, for she is attractive and charming enough to capture the heart of a far better man than he!"

Ethan said, "I can't deny the truth of that, but I will challenge your former statement. I'd love Madeleine if she were a pauper."

"Hah! If she had no funds, you wouldn't have considered her."

"That may have been true at the beginning, but not now."

"Save your pretty words for the next heiress, Ambrose." Thomas circled the settee and offered his assistance to his wife. Reluctantly, her features downturned in sorrow, she took his hand and rose. He then offered his other arm to Madeleine. "Come, child."

She shook her head and stepped back a pace. "I'm not going with you, Papa." The air suddenly shot through with magnified tension; so much so that Ethan felt the hairs on the back of his neck rise. "I'm staying with Ethan . . . if he'll have me."

Drawn by the fierce look of loyalty Madeleine swept his way, he went to her without hesitation, seized her hand, and brought it to his lips. "There could never be the slightest question."

"Daughter," Thomas said, "you don't know what you're saying; you're letting your emotions sway you. Allow me to remind you that I'm your father and have only your happiness in mind."

"I know you do," she said in agonized tones. "I know you love me, Papa, just as I love you. But you're asking too much. You're asking me to give up my future. If I leave the man I love, I shall never be happy!"

"The man you love?" Thomas repeated, sounding amazed. "What can you know of love in the fraction of time you've known Ethan Ambrose? And where is the loyalty of a lifetime as my daughter?"

"She's my daughter, too," Antonia said quietly. No one seemed to notice except Ethan, who pressed his lips into a smile as he met her troubled eyes.

Madeleine said entreatingly, "I can't fight my feelings, Papa. The last thing I ever intend is to hurt you, but I cannot obey you in this!"

Thomas's body grew rigid, and he appeared so angry that for a moment words escaped him; but at last he said, "If you insist on staying, I'll disown you. There will be no inheritance." Even while Antonia moaned softly at his side, he swerved on Ethan. "Do you hear me, Ambrose? There'll be nothing to improve your estate; and that was the point of the marriage, I believe; your great vision, you said—unless that was a lie, too, and you intended to throw it all away on one vice after another. I mean to cut her off without her dowry, without even an allowance. Marry my daughter, and you'll be as penniless as before; no, moreso, for you'll have another mouth to feed!"

In the silence that followed this speech, the room seemed to resonate with currents of wrath; yet Ethan felt himself grow remarkably calm. He stared downward into Madeleine's eyes and returned her timorous look with his most reassuring one. God bless her, she trembled on his arm thinking he would cut her loose at her father's decree. Did she have so little confidence in herself, then? Did she think he only pretended to love her to obtain gold?

He turned his smile upon Thomas, a thing that did little to calm the older man by the look of him. "The best thing for Madeleine's sake is for me to say that I think too highly of her to ask her to make such a sacrifice."

"Yes," Thomas agreed. "That would be the very best thing."

"But, as you've suggested before, I'm not much of a gentleman; I'm too selfish. If Madeleine is willing to have me among the rubble and disorder of this old house; if she's ready to settle for only one or two new gowns a year and a filling but inelegant cuisine, then she will make me the happiest man alive."

The smile that consumed his beloved's face almost made the pain disappear, the inevitable pain that came with the death of his strongest dream: to fulfill his brother's vision. *Lucan. I'm sorry. Forgive me.*

Some dreams were more important than others.

"Ethan," Scott said, rising hastily and coming to stand by the viscount, "perhaps you should consider before making your decision." His concerned gaze moved back and forth between them. "Don't misunderstand me, Miss Murrow; I mean you both the best, but we've made a commitment to the estate—"

"Any commitment to the estate is for *me* to make," said Ethan, having had enough of Scott's nagging reminders about his responsibilities.

"But Lucan wished—"

"I know what Lucan wished!" Ethan lashed, feeling his soul ripping apart. "He would wish me to be happy," he added in a softer voice.

Brandt, his face ashen, held Ethan's gaze for a long moment, then crumbled. He perched on the edge of the chair as if his legs had lost their strength, and his breaths came hard and fast, like a man nearing the end of a race.

The viscount could almost find it in his heart to feel sorry for him, if he weren't irritated beyond measure at his impertinence. He did not need to be reminded what Lucan desired.

"Very well, then," Thomas said, sounding old. "Let us go, Antonia. We've lost one daughter; now, it seems, we're to lose another." He moved forward, pulling his wife with him. She accompanied him slowly for several steps, then stopped abruptly. Groaning faintly, she sank against him. "Antonia?" he cried in alarm.

She turned a hollow, bewildered expression to him and whispered, "I . . . feel . . . odd . . ."

Ethan watched in horror as her eyes rolled backward and her face fell slack. Repeating Antonia's name desperately, Thomas lifted her and, amid the tearing cries of Madeleine and the concerned confusion of Ethan and Scott, he carried her upstairs.

Fifteen

During the next hour, the house flew into an uproar. Ethan sent Scott to bring the physician; Zinnia and Betsy flurried about burning feathers, fetching basins of both hot and cold water, hunting towels, and shouting orders at each other until Madeleine's father barked that they should leave them in peace. As they departed, both of them appearing highly offended, Madeleine pulled a chair to one side of Antonia's bed and rested her finger-tips upon her mother's shoulder, and Thomas, clutching his wife's fragile hands in his, sat on the opposite side. The door to the chamber stood open; beyond it in the hall, Ethan paced back and forth looking lost. Madeleine drew strength from simply knowing that he was there and concerned.

Antonia lay motionless, her chest barely moving as she breathed. Madeleine had never seen her lose conscious-ness completely, not even during her worst times of illness. She fought to keep her composure for her father's sake and her own. Should she let her emotions run free, she feared a complete loss of control. If this was the end the doctor had forecast, she didn't know how she could bear it. Quietly, she lowered her head to the sheets, cradled her head in her arms, and began to pray silently.

Hardly had she begun her petition when her mother stirred, blinked slowly, and turned her head from side to side to see both of her companions. A weak smile curved her lips, causing hope to blossom in Madeleine; and when she met her father's eyes, she saw an equal eagerness in his expression.

"What happened?" Antonia asked feebly.

Thomas leaned over and kissed her hands, then her forehead. "You passed out, beloved. Don't talk, now; conserve your strength. The physician is coming; he'll know what to do."

"Don't worry, dearest," she whispered. "I'm sure I'll be better soon."

"Of course you will," Thomas said, tears glittering in his eyes. "Of course you will."

Madeleine felt water springing to her own eyes. How like her mother to be concerned for their feelings, even in the midst of her suffering. She would never be the woman Antonia was, never. With the thought came a sob that she could not restrain, and her mother immediately turned to her, freeing one of her hands to search for Madeleine's. As the women laced their fingers together, Antonia once again looked at her husband.

"Darling." Her words were so faint, Thomas had to lean forward to hear. "Please allow me a moment alone with my daughter."

Thomas's stark, bleak gaze flew to Madeleine's. Did he suspect, as she did, that these might be the last words she would exchange with her mother on this side of the veil? He shook his head as if in denial.

"You mustn't strain yourself," he said.

"I won't." Her mother's voice sounded much stronger for an instant, and Madeleine cut her a surprised glance. But as quickly, her tone modulated to its former faded graciousness. "Just for a moment, dear."

Thomas nodded reluctantly. "Just for a moment, then." He moved to the door, saw Ethan, halted for an instant, then shouldered past him.

Antonia's voice lifted slightly. "Close the door, please."

Thomas leaned back into the room. "What, my dear?"

"Close the door," Madeleine and her mother said simultaneously, and it would have been hard to judge which voice rang the louder. This time, the young lady's wide eyes fastened on her elder.

As the door clicked shut, Antonia gave her daughter a very slow and mischievous wink.

After leaving Antonia's room a few moments later, Madeleine found her father waiting some distance down the hall from Ethan, as if he could not forget his hostility even in a moment like this. Recalling the gravity of her mother's situation, she cast her eyes downward as she approached Thomas and bit the inside of her cheek to keep from smiling.

"Mother wants to spend some time alone with you," she said glumly. "I think I'll go downstairs for a few moments . . . try to force a little nourishment if I can."

If her father did but know it, she was ravenous enough to devour the tapestries from the walls.

"Yes, my child. You do that." After nodding and pressing her into a quick embrace, Thomas hurried into Antonia's room. Madeleine felt a prickling of guilt at her father's worry, but the sight of Ethan's bereft face forged steel into her spine.

"Do you think we are so late for luncheon that Cook has despaired of us and thrown everything out?" she asked as she joined him.

Appearing slightly taken aback, Ethan said, "I'm certain there's something." Seeing she intended to keep on walking past him, he moved forward, too. "It's good you're trying to keep up your strength; that's the best attitude."

He was trying so valiantly to justify her lack of sensitivity that she caught her tongue between her teeth in perverse delight. "Well, surely no one expects me to become a skeleton simply because my mother fainted and took to her bed," she said in exaggerated, argumentative tones. His eyes widened. "Oh, Ethan," she laughed, and, taking pity on him as they approached the dining room, related what her mother had said to her:

"I love your father more than life itself," Antonia had explained, "and I would not distress him for the world. But truly, he can be stubborn at times. I would never dream of using illness as a tool in this way if he were not about to make the largest mistake of his life—cutting you off indeed, and without so much as asking my opinion! I have bought you time, my dear child—time in which to find Dorrie's mother if you can. At the very least, my collapse will give your father a period in which to cool his temper, and hopefully come to his senses. You'll have to be a good actress, mind, and so will I; for I've never felt so well, not in years!"

And they had laughed together, stifling giggles worthy of the silliest schoolgirls.

"How you relieve me," Ethan said as he seated her in the chair beside his at the head of the table in the dining room. "For a moment I thought I'd given my heart to a dragon."

"Perhaps I *am* a dragon." Feeling inexpressibly light since the events of the past hour had not resulted in a tragedy of one kind or another, she slanted a flirtatious look at him through her lashes. "Perhaps I only pretend to be a reasonably nice person in order to trap you, but once you are in my lair . . ."

To her shivering delight, his eyes began to radiate their seductive power, and she felt her knees go weak. Stealthily, he came to stand behind her chair, then slid his fingers down her arms, stooping to bring his cheek alongside hers as he whispered in her ear, "Once I am in your lair . . . *what?* Will you breathe fire and consume me, dangerous lady?"

She could feel his breaths upon her skin, and her own rate of breathing increased to match his. She leaned back her head and closed her eyes, her lips parting with the sheer pleasure of simple sensations, yet not so simple: the smooth touch of his hands tracing fire through her veins, the spicy scent of his cologne. Moving slowly, he circled the chair and slid his hands to her waist, a slow, leisurely slide that caused her heart to flutter like a mad humming-bird. When his lips closed over hers, she circled his neck with her arms, trailing her fingers through his beautiful golden hair.

"Well, very pretty *this* is," Betsy said as she barreled through the pantry door carrying a porcelain soup tureen. "Someone's mother is lying deathly sick upstairs, but *downstairs,* a *couple* of someones are playing like two o'erheated cats in a haystack. It's good I don't look to me betters for me morals or I'd be in a dandy fix, wouldn't I now?"

Ethan, sending Madeleine a wicked look that held no shame in it that she could see, retreated to his chair. For her part, she found herself unable to meet Betsy's eyes.

The viscount unfolded his napkin with a flourish. "You'd do well to spend less time counseling others on how to behave and more on serving luncheon, Betsy. Miss Murrow is in *uncommonly* fine appetite today, isn't that so, Madeleine?"

As she could make no answer to this without laughing, Madeleine kept her stare centered on the tablecloth.

"Hmph." Betsy's gaze seared through Madeleine's eyelids as she clattered soup bowls to the table, then ladled messy scoops of vichyssoise into them.

"One more, Betsy," said Scott as he rounded the entranceway and took the chair opposite Madeleine. After the maid served him and left, Brandt leaned toward them pointedly. "I must counsel you to keep your voices down. I've been in the library and heard more than I intended"—at this, Madeleine's cheeks brightened to crimson—"about your mother's act, I mean," he added charitably, making her feel worse, since it had to mean he heard *everything*. "While I'm happy she's well and is willing to do this for you, I believe her charade will only be effective if it remains a secret."

Regarding him with detached interest, Ethan took a cautious sip of his soup, then swallowed. "You surprise me, Scott. Less than an hour ago you were advising me

to proceed with caution in my pursuit of Madeleine. Have
you changed your mind?"

Brandt's face took on a pinched look. "I've been in
support of this match from the beginning, as you well
know, Ethan." As he spoke, he stirred his soup with his
spoon, keeping his eyes downcast. "I hope Miss Murrow
understands why I expressed my concerns for the estate
when her father spoke as he did, that what I said has
nothing to do with my sentiments for her. Truth, no one
could wish for a more charming or lovely viscountess, and
she will bring a long-needed feminine presence to Westhall. However, without funds there will be no house, or
not much of one—but you know that already. At any rate,
when I accidentally overheard your conversation about
Mrs. Murrow, my hopes revived. I'd like you both to know
I'm at your disposal if there's anything I can do to help
discover Dorrie's mother."

Madeleine, who had come quickly to the bottom of her
bowl although the soup was wholly lacking in taste,
thought the viscount's half-smile the friendliest look he
had given Mr. Brandt in her time here. Ethan thanked
him, adding, "If Dorrie's mother fails to confess but feels
pressured to act instead, she'll likely make her move under the cover of darkness, as she did when she brought
her baby in the first place. I plan to keep the child in
sight this afternoon, then secretly watch the nursery tonight. You could patrol the grounds outside in case I miss
something. Tell no one of our extra precautions, not even
your parents, Madeleine; the fewer people who know, the
less the chance of accidentally letting something slip to
the wrong ears. The last thing we want to happen is for
the mother to be warned off."

Madeleine and Scott agreed to this scheme, and the
meal proceeded with a certain warmth that Madeleine
could not help thinking boded well for the future, especially if the steward were to continue residing with them.
She didn't relish the prospect of living with friction, especially between two gentlemen who were supposed to be

lifelong friends. It was incomprehensible to her that such discord existed at all. Initially, the blame seemed to lie entirely on Ethan's side, for he often spoke curtly to Scott. Yet, as she had grown more used to Mr. Brandt, she'd begun to notice a certain quality of watchfulness and tension interwoven into his demeanor; sometimes it seemed as though he wasn't entirely present when he gave his polite, measured answers. He gave off vibrations of something; whether disapproval or condescension, she could not tell. She thought it might be this that brought forth Ethan's ire.

Perhaps she, too, was being unfair to poor Mr. Brandt, she thought as Betsy returned with a platter of rarebit and roasted potatoes that made her mouth water despite the servant's cross glances. The steward was probably only worried to distraction about his responsibilities.

After luncheon, Madeleine excused herself to sit with her mother awhile; to do otherwise would raise suspicion. As she ascended the stairs, however, she couldn't help reflecting that while Ethan had enlisted Mr. Brandt's aid in his scheme, he'd given *her* no assignment. Well, tonight she would help him whether he wished her to or not.

After a mostly enjoyable afternoon and evening playing guard to Dorrie, Ethan told Mr. Murrow, who left his wife's side for a few moments to eat a hurried dinner, that he meant to retire early. Of course, he did not go to his room at all, but climbed to the servants' quarters, stealthily entering one of the vacant bedrooms and narrowing the door to a slit behind him. Like the other workers' chambers, this room was small and contained a single bed, washstand, chiffonnier, and a wooden chair, which he pulled closely to the small opening of the door. From here he could observe the comings and goings in the hall with a modicum of comfort.

To his chagrin, Madeleine was the first person he saw less than a quarter-hour later; she had tiptoed as far as the nursery and was looking uncertainly from one end of the hall to the other. Both exasperated and warmed by her presence, he leaned from his hiding place and motioned her into the bedroom before she brought all the servants running. It was a mistake. Despite his best protests, she refused to leave.

"I dread the look in your papa's eye if he finds us here," Ethan said, warning her one last time. "This is a bedroom, in case you haven't noticed." He, for one, had; and with her standing near, it was all he could do to keep his mind off the bed. At least she was still dressed in the gown she wore to dinner. Had she slipped into her nightrail . . . the thought did not bear dwelling upon.

"He's with my mother and thinking only of her; but if by accident he happens to discover us, I'll simply tell him I was wandering and became lost."

"I had not anticipated a wife who tells lies."

"Hopefully that will be the first in a long series of surprises. I shouldn't like to be a boring spouse."

Her saucy comments and teasing eyes nearly undid him. "Don't tempt me into forgetting why we're here. I'll—"

"Who's there?" The wet nurse's voice rang down the hall. Ethan and Madeleine froze, redundantly signaling each other to be quiet. "Thought I heard something," Janice Marshall mumbled, returning to her room.

When the nursery door clicked shut, the viscount released his breath. Whispering, he and Madeleine agreed to maintain silence and, as there was only one chair, to take turns watching the hall. He allowed her to serve the first watch, while he lowered himself to the floor with the bed at his back. He continued to imagine Thomas storming the stairs and finding them here. If so, neither one of them would be caught lounging in bed, that was certain.

The time dragged by slowly. Every half hour they changed places. By ten o'clock, the house lay silent and still. Anticipating at least several more hours of this before anything happened—if anything happened at all—Ethan felt a surge of gratitude that Madeleine had joined him. He could not live with himself if he fell asleep on duty, and watching her fidget in the darkness was a delightful way to stay awake.

Not long after this observation, Madeleine straightened and waved frantically. He'd not expected activity so early and did not allow himself to hope as he drew close to peer into the hall. But to his unbridled joy, Rose McDaniel was softly entering the corridor, the baby in her arms. She took a long time closing the door behind her. Exchanging a gleeful grin with Madeleine, he waited until the nurse-maid passed down the stairs before opening the door wider than a crack.

"Aren't you going to stop her?" Madeleine whispered.

"Not yet," he said quietly, hurriedly, his hand on the doorknob. "If I follow, perhaps she'll lead me to the father of her child, or to someone who will tell us who he is."

"What if he doesn't live nearby?"

"I won't chase her forever, don't worry." He stepped into the hall and walked lightly toward the servant's stair. To his perturbation, he could hear Madeleine's footfalls close behind, and he turned. "What are you doing?"

"I'm going with you," she whispered.

"No." She looked so taken aback that he felt a chuckle rising. He seized her by the arms and kissed her quickly, causing her to look even more startled. "It could be dangerous, my love—"

"Dangerous? Oh, of course—if your accident is connected to the baby in some way." Her eyebrows turned downward. "Ethan, you shouldn't go, either! Tell Mr. Brandt to do it!"

His emotions were already on the ceiling, and she only made it worse, causing him amusement at every turn. "I don't have the heart to convey how little you care about *his* safety. Now, you must let me go, or she'll get away."

He moved forward once more. She trailed after. He sighed. The servant's stair began to seem as far away as a desert mirage.

"I'm going with you," she repeated stubbornly, when he stopped again.

"Madeleine. One person may be able to keep hidden, but she would surely notice two."

"I can stay as hidden as anyone, Ethan," she hissed. "Do you think I'm clumsy and will make a lot of noise?"

"You are the most graceful creature I've ever seen. Now, listen to me. If, for any reason, I'm unable to return before morning, I'm not willing to face your father after keeping his daughter out overnight. Are you?"

At last he had said something to cause her to stop dead in her slippers. When she slowly shook her head, he kissed her a final time, then crouched by the balustrade to listen. As soon as he heard the latch lifting on the back door downstairs, he lifted his fingers in farewell. Madeleine waved back pensively as he moved downward.

Sixteen

At the junction of the servants' hall and the kitchen, Ethan paused to peer past the doorway. Cook's pots were aligned neatly on the brick wall above the stove, and the long, scarred table upon which she prepared breads and vegetables was empty of debris and had been scoured clean; he could smell Cook's own pungent blend of cleaner. The shelves of the enormous hutch on the far wall drooped with their burden of everyday platters and plates, cups and saucers, the mixture of patterns and colors hardly discernible in the dimness. Of people, the kitchen was empty; Rose McDaniel had gone.

Her deviousness struck him as extraordinary. How innocent she'd looked that afternoon when acting as if taking Dorrie was the very last thing she would think of doing. He recalled their recent conversation concerning the timing of the baby's arrival; she had speculated about his fictional cousin's motivations as if she believed there *was* a cousin. From the day she arrived, every word she'd said to him or any of them had been false. For that reason, he dared not stop her and demand an explanation; she would only lie again.

Quickly, he went to the kitchen door and looked out the diamond-shaped pane of glass in its upper half. The woman had already moved from sight. With his heart pumping in his throat, he swiftly exited. If he'd lost her this soon, his only hope was Scott. He didn't relish the feeling of depending on someone to do his work for him.

He emerged into darkness and, taking a guess, moved to the right and skirted the corner of the house. Although he could not see her, he continued around front. Unless she intended to swim across the river in back, she must surely plan to use the lane.

When he reached the front of the house, he saw her walking steadily down his drive, brazen as brass, a pelisse covering the thinness of her body, her reticule dangling from her arm, and the baby, snug in her basket, held in front. She suddenly seemed a sinister figure to him, stealing Dorrie away in the night. She had no right to act this way, carrying off her bit of sunshine as if the loss would not matter to anyone. He didn't care if she was Dorrie's mother; she had no heart.

He scanned the front and side garden, looking for Scott; but he saw no sign of him. He was probably sleeping beneath some tree. There was no time to search for him and enlist his aid; Ethan would have to follow the woman himself, which was what he preferred to do in any case. He hesitated long enough to see the woman turn right into the lane, then followed.

The night was unusually thick and sticky for spring; not a star twinkled through the layer of clouds blotting the sky, not a sliver of moonlight illuminated his way. But Rose McDaniel struggled through the same darkness burdened with a reticule and a baby, and he had no trouble maintaining his distance, even though he kept to the thickets and shrubs and ditches in order to stay hidden. His worst difficulty was to stay far enough behind so she didn't hear him rustling through the undergrowth.

He planned to follow for a space of time. If nothing happened within a couple of hours, if it seemed she meant to travel all night as though she didn't have an immediate destination, he would stop her. By waiting until she walked some miles from the house, he would at least prove her intent was serious. She could not say she'd merely meant to take Dorrie for a moonlight stroll.

How he hoped she intended to meet her lover some-

where, for then he would obtain Thomas Murrow's for-
giveness—and apologies, too; he believed he deserved
that—and the accomplishment of both his dream and Lucan's. In his mind's eye, he saw Madeleine's sweet, pert
face melting into happiness. He could almost taste the
flavor of her lips, feel her satiny skin, so firm beneath his
hands, yet soft, yielding . . .

When he tripped over a root and fell face down into a
hedge of juniper, he bid his brain stop its cruel imaginings
and pay attention. Mumbling assorted words he would not
care for Madeleine to hear, he momentarily cast aside his
need to remain hidden and rolled and clawed his way to
the road. Fortunately, the runaway servant did not choose
that moment to glance behind her, and, after plucking
greenery from his sleeves and rubbing dirt from his jacket,
he returned to the underbrush and proceeded forward.
The fall had not helped the ache in his leg any, he was
sorry to discover.

The going became more difficult after that. He had
reached an area of cultivated fields, and the cover of wild
underbrush and trees at the edges of the road diminished
to small clumps spaced at unhelpful intervals. Ethan allowed Mrs. McDaniel to gain a greater lead, then
crouched as he ran from one island of vegetation to the
other. Increasingly, there was nothing to hide him at all,
and he felt grateful for the woman's determined pace.
Had she decided to look around for a place to rest, were
she of a more fearful frame of mind and inclined to keep
alert for possible assailants or followers, he would be
found.

He had been walking for a little more than an hour
when the first raindrops began to fall. After a few seconds
of accumulating wetness, Mrs. McDaniel stopped. Ethan
froze; there was not so much as a tall blade of grass to
hide behind, and he slowly, painfully eased downward,
making himself as small an object as possible. He needn't
have bothered. The woman tended to the baby in some
way, probably trying to protect Dorrie from the mist, then

set off at a more rapid pace without looking in any direction except the path before her.

She certainly gave the impression of having a destination in mind, Ethan thought, trying to keep hope alive. If not, surely she would seek shelter from the rain; the possibilities were growing for such hideaways. They were drawing nearer to the village of Brillham, and several cottages lined the way, some of them possessing small barns. She had almost reached the largest of them, Cotter's Cottage, which was something of a local curiosity.

Brushing damp hair from his eyes, he recalled the legend as he walked. Henry Cotter and his family had dwelled in the home he built for something like twenty years, farming the land and making a better living than most. One morning, a hired laborer arrived for work to find the entire family missing—husband, wife, and three grown children—as well as the livestock and much of the furnishings inside the house. No one ever discovered what had become of them.

In the decades since their disappearance, not a person had claimed the cottage or dared live in it. The building's inevitable deterioration had been slower than what might be expected, and Ethan remembered many gleeful, childhood excursions exploring its small rooms and strangely deep cabinets, racing up dusty, steep stairs to a loft in which no spiderwebs had laced into corners, no small animals nested in the rafters. All of the children expected to find apparitions at any moment, or at least a pile of bones, although Lucan and Scott pretended to be too sophisticated for such beliefs. For himself, he remembered taking particular joy in frightening Alice by feigning trances and jumping out at her when she least expected it. As for George, he could never be persuaded to enter the cottage at all.

The recollection was enough to make him smile despite the miserable, wet darkness. How he wished Mrs. McDaniel would turn her steps toward that unlucky cottage; although, as a stranger she might not be aware that it remained uninhabited. He watched tensely as she drew abreast of the abode, then passed it by.

Sharply disappointed, he decided he could not endure much more of this. Madeleine would be worried. Moreover, the further he walked from his stable, the less likely he would be able to apprehend the servant should she rendezvous with someone having transportation. The thought chilled him. Quickening his steps, he closed the distance between them.

Through the increasing patter of rain, he heard a sound to his left. He swerved, thinking perhaps someone followed *him*. Instants later, a shadowed flurry of wings broke skyward; an owl clutching a small, writhing form.

He returned his attention to the road ahead. Mrs. McDaniel had disappeared.

Two windows, both smeared with raindrops, flanked either side of the bed in Madeleine's chamber, and she had long ago pulled a chair beside the left one; although to what purpose she could not say. Her view encompassed only a portion of overgrown garden at the side of the house, then the field beyond; not the drive or the lane where Ethan would most likely appear first. She considered going downstairs to one of the front receiving rooms as she had done just after Ethan set out, but those chambers were considered off-limits; should someone find her mooning about the windows there, she'd face unwanted questions. The library offered no better prospect than her bedroom.

She was so tired of waiting. Ethan had been gone almost two hours. He had mentioned the possibility of staying away all night. She felt tempted to don her nightgown and go to bed, but sleep would not come if she did. She thought it best to remain dressed in case something happened. *Surely* something would happen soon.

She clenched and unclenched her fists to relieve the tension, wishing she'd accompanied Ethan no matter what he had said. It would not be dangerous, following a fallen woman; only sad. She could have stayed hidden as well as he. Why did men think only they deserved adventures? Staying at home and waiting was far more difficult. If Ethan expected to command her to do distasteful things like this after they were married, she needed to clarify his thinking.

At least they could be wed with Papa's blessing now, she thought for the hundredth time. She could hardly wait to see his expression when they told him. He would be happy for her, she knew, once he understood Ethan was not the rake, or not quite as *wicked* a rake as he feared. And her mother! Madeleine smiled, anticipating her joy. She could barely restrain herself from running to her bedroom and waking her.

Oh, if only Ethan would hurry!

A movement caught the corner of her eye, and she rose and stepped closer to the window. She saw a flash of white, then made out the figure of a man. For an instant she thought it might be Ethan, but it was only Scott Brandt. The viscount had ordered him to patrol the grounds, she recalled. Perhaps he knew something. At least she could talk to him instead of sitting here like a lump, and a little rain wouldn't melt her. She went to the wardrobe to search for her hooded cape.

It was as though Mrs. McDaniel had vanished into the mist. His heart dropping to his boots, Ethan raced forward. An unpaved trail branched off the main road a short distance beyond Cotter's Cottage; if the maid hadn't taken it, he didn't know where she could have gone. A vestige of superstition spiced his fears as he ran.

When he reached the turning and saw her treading resolutely through the grass and mud ahead, he breathed deeply in relief. She had narrowed her choice of destinations considerably by taking this trail. He knew of only a few possibilities of shelter back here: three one-room cottages—little more than huts, actually—all of them built by Cotter for his laborers. These, too, were abandoned and seemed ideal for hiding inside, now that he thought about it; although how Rose McDaniel came to know of them after dwelling here for so short a time puzzled him.

She passed by the first hut, her pace quickening. A short distance later, Ethan saw the reason for her hurry. A lamp shone in the window of the second cottage, and in the thicket beside it stood a horse tethered to a tree. Ethan proceeded more cautiously now, his hopes flying. But when Mrs. McDaniel entered the hut, placed the basket on the table, and handed the baby to her companion, who lifted Dorrie in a warm embrace, the three of them framed by the window like actors on a stage, his jaw tightened in shock and crushing dismay.

By the time Madeleine exited from the kitchen door and walked to the side of the house beneath her window, Mr. Brandt was no longer there. Knowing he must be nearby, she circled the house and found him striding toward the stable. She broke into a trot until she drew close enough to call his name softly. Hearing her, he pivoted with a look of surprise.

"Have you seen Ethan?" she asked without preamble, although she noted he appeared more disheveled than she had ever seen him. The rain had flattened his hair to dripping strands, and his countenance in the dim light seemed disconsolate and troubled. She felt a sudden stab of concern for him.

"No," he answered. "What are you doing outside in this downpour, Miss Murrow?" Before she could answer, the significance of her question appeared to strike him. "Has Ethan gone?"

"You don't know, then. Mrs. McDaniel went away with the baby."

"Then she *is* the mother," he said, and the gladness on his face renewed her own delight. Of course, he was not concerned for their happiness but the estate's well-being; nevertheless, her smile grew wider.

"Yes, and Ethan followed her, thinking she might be on her way to meet someone, maybe even Dorrie's father."

"I suppose that's possible. She had time to dispatch a message this afternoon." He moved as if to take her hands in his excitement, then, recollecting himself, drew back. A tense, faraway light came into his eyes. "There's no chance she could be . . ." He seemed to become aware again of Madeleine's presence. "No, of course not."

"What?" she asked anxiously. "What worries you, Scott?" She said his given name without thinking, and apparently he didn't notice or mind.

He hesitated, then said, "It couldn't be that she isn't the mother but intends to kidnap the child for ransom."

"Oh!" Her spirits plummeted. "Surely not!"

Looking contrite, he said, "Don't worry, Miss; please. I'm always thinking the worst thing. Everyone says so, especially Ethan. My imagination is ridiculous." But his worry was increasing, she saw it in his eyes.

Madeleine recalled how caring the nursemaid seemed with Dorrie, how protective. "She never struck me as the kind of woman who would do such a thing."

"No, naturally not."

But she was the kind of woman they wanted to believe could give birth out of wedlock, abandon her baby, and pretend she wasn't the mother. They stared at one another, the unspoken thought shimmering between them.

Madeleine spoke first. "If it is a kidnapping attempt, Ethan could be in danger."

Scott rubbed a hand across his chin. "How long has he been gone?"

"Two hours," she said in a voice of dread, thinking she should have sought Scott before this.

"Did you happen to see which direction he took?"

"I watched him from the window; he turned right at the lane."

"I don't know how I missed seeing them leave the house, although I was in the stable for a few moments . . ."

There was no time for his guilt. "Scott, shouldn't we search for him?"

"Yes. That is, *I* will. You'd best go inside where it's dry."

She glared at him. Every man in the world was the same, it seemed. "I will *not;* I'm coming with you."

"For myself, I'd be delighted; but Ethan will have my head if I allow such a thing."

"It will go even worse for you when he finds I've set off alone because you wouldn't take me."

Scott swallowed, staring miserably at her through the damp. "I'll fetch a pair of your father's horses," he said.

"Good." She watched him move away, then scurried after him lest he change his mind. With a little smile for her own assertiveness, she thought of Bettina. How her sister would have laughed to know she'd almost staged a tantrum to get her way, to help the man she loved.

For some length of time, Ethan simply watched the inhabitants of the cottage. The window was a generous one for so small a structure; he could see much of the roughly built interior from his hiding place behind a thornbush. It was impossible to hear the two adults within speak, however, especially with the steady drumming of rain deadening his ears. He needed to hear them. He had to understand this worst of betrayals.

And betrayal it was. There was no possibility that Rose McDaniel was the babe's mother; the presence of these two supposed strangers could spell only one meaning.

As he glared fixedly through the window, something moved in the undergrowth behind. He swerved, his eyes scanning the night. Only stillness answered him. He was frightening himself, as he had as a child.

No, he was delaying the inevitable. Abandoning the cover of the shrub, he stood, made an attempt to counsel himself to calmness as Lucan would have done, then strode toward the hut, his pulse racing. He didn't bother to knock, but swung the door open with a mere fraction of the rage he felt.

"Alice?" To say more was unnecessary; by his tone he invested her name with a volume's worth of meaning.

Alice Redding regarded him wordlessly, the pink rosiness of her skin fading to ashes, her mouth and eyes rounding in horror. She must have been waiting for some time, he observed, for her velvet riding habit was untouched by the rain, unlike himself and Mrs. McDaniel, whose sodden clothes and hair dripped miserably onto the wooden floor. As if reading his mind, Alice's gaze slid condemningly to her companion.

Mrs. McDaniel shrank away from that look. "I didn't tell him, Alice. He must have followed me. I didn't dream anyone would do that."

The younger woman tenderly placed the baby in the basket and closed her eyes, sighing deeply. "You should have been more careful," she said, and turned her back to the viscount, resting her fingers on the baby's basket. "Ethan can be cunning."

"I'm sorry," said the servant. "I did everything you told me."

The viscount stepped deeper into the room. "Is it Mrs. McDaniel you should be blaming, Alice?"

"Oh, dear God," Alice moaned, her voice as despairing as anything he'd ever heard, and he felt his resolve melting. She was his friend from childhood, the first girl who had revealed her thoughts to him. That had meant much to a lad inclined to think of females as a separate species. Even though Lucan won her greatest devotion, she had spent enough time with Ethan to become close, as close as a sister. It hurt to know the solution to his dilemma would spell disgrace for her.

But she had been willing to disgrace him, when he'd done nothing at all. She had treated his feelings cavalierly, had trampled across his hopes with the finesse of an elephant. He'd almost lost Madeleine because of her. Discovering the truth suddenly became easier.

"Tell me everything," he commanded, "starting with Dorrie's father. Who is he?"

She swerved, her hands clasping together, her eyes searching his face with desperation. "Is it possible you haven't guessed?"

To his left was a crudely built wooden chair, and Ethan reached for it and brought it closer, bracing his hands on its back. He did not mean to sit down, but he felt a sudden need for support.

"Lucan?" he whispered hoarsely.

Alice's eyes flared. "Dare you imagine anyone else?"

Dorrie whimpered, and although both women turned to the infant, it was Mrs. McDaniel who lifted her from the basket and soothed her, taking her to the far end of the room, giving them a measure of privacy. He might have to revise his opinion of that woman, he thought fleetingly; but that, too, remained to be seen.

There were weightier issues on his mind to be considered, such as the loss of his brother's unspotted reputation. Well, he'd imagined Lucan as Leah's lover, however briefly; how much greater sense it made for him to have been Alice's.

He had been naive to believe Lucan had no personal life, no secrets, that his existence was an open book for everyone, especially Ethan, to read. And as secrets went, this wasn't such a terrible one. Seduction wasn't *murder.*

But Lucan and Alice were going to be married; after nearly a lifetime, how difficult would it have been to wait a few weeks? Although, for all he knew, they might have been playing little games for years, reaping the penalty only at the last. How ironic, if that were the case.

The thought scalded him like acid. All that time, all those years, while his twin counseled him about his behavior, forever asking more of him, telling him he was a better man than he acted, Lucan lived a double life. Why, compared to him, *Ethan* was the finer gentleman. At least he'd restricted himself to women of experience.

No, to think such a thing smacked of sacrilege. And yet . . . Lucan, seducing his young neighbor . . . the viscount mulled the thought through his mind and found it not to his taste, and decidedly out of character for his brother. However, people could not be expected to act in the same way at all times. Could they?

He had no answers; therefore, he centered his vision on the woman who would destroy his life if she could. She returned his look without flinching, although he read the suffering in her eyes. *Guard against pity; she is deceptive.*

"Why did you bring Dorrie to me?" he challenged. "Or perhaps I shouldn't call her that—I'm certain you named her yourself."

"I did, but Dorrie seems more suitable now; I shall keep the name for her."

This brought only a splash of pleasure and did little to cool his wrath. "You knew Madeleine would arrive at almost the same time you brought your baby. It couldn't have escaped you what conclusions would be drawn, and to what effect. Why have you tried to ruin our chances?"

"If you would think a moment, you could guess."

"I don't want to guess. I want you to tell me."

"What would you have me say, Ethan? Do you want me to humiliate myself again as I did recently? You know how much I love you—"

"You don't love *me;* you loved *Lucan.*"

"Yes, I did—passionately." She gestured eloquently with her arms, entreating him to understand. "He was my life, and I'll never deny that. But you are a part of him. I've always loved you, too. You're the only proper father for Dorrie."

"I'm happy to be her uncle, but I'll not serve as her sire."

"I knew you would say that. All those long, lonely months, I knew I couldn't trust you to do the correct thing, to make the gesture your twin would have wanted you to make—"

"You don't know that," he interrupted angrily. "Don't tell me what my brother would have wanted."

"He certainly wouldn't wish me to suffer for what he did."

"What *he* did? Are you saying he raped you?"

She flinched at the starkness of his words. "No, of course not—"

"Then you must have been part of that decision, too, Alice. Correct me if I'm in error."

"Yes, yes, naturally, but neither of us dreamed Lucan would die! Can you guess how I felt—not only did I lose the love of my life, but I was alone in my condition! You don't know the sleepless nights I spent, wondering if I could keep my condition hidden from Father and everyone. And can you imagine his reaction, if he had known? I had no one to whom I could turn, Ethan—no one except Rosemary, who counseled me through her letters, and then later"—She turned to the woman he'd called Rose McDaniel—"personally, as you can see."

He peered around Alice. "Rosemary?"

The nursemaid, standing before a small window in the far wall with Dorrie resting against her shoulder, turned to face him. "I took a different name when I came here, Lord Ambrose, because Alice thought someone at her home might recognize my true name, Rosemary Danniver, from my correspondence to her. I'd never met her father or brother personally, of course; our contact was through Miss Bradshaw's, which is a school for young ladies in Warminster."

"He remembers where I went to school," Alice said softly, although Ethan did not. "Rosemary was my favorite teacher. She taught French and German lessons and became very close to many of the girls—probably because she was only a few years older than we were. She and I left the school at almost the same time; I had completed my studies, and she married."

Rosemary added, "I went to Cornwall with my husband, and after we'd only had a few years together, he died at sea. Not everything I told you was a lie. I'm sorry for the necessity of fabrication; I don't make a habit of it."

"She did it to help me. I begged her to come and be my eyes at Westhall. I trust you explicitly, but I couldn't leave Dorrie without some assurance that you would not send her away. And today my very worst fears came true— or so I thought. You spread it abroad that Dorrie was leaving tomorrow, but you only did that to frighten me into stepping forward; I understand that now." She broke off on a sob, then continued, "You were always one for playing tricks, Ethan!"

Ethan said, "With good cause, at least in this instance." He clenched the chair's back tighter, his knuckles whitening. "There were several days before your teacher arrived. Tell me: what would you have done had I removed your baby immediately?"

"I felt confident you wouldn't do that, but in the event you did, Rosemary *was* here, and between the two of us we managed to keep watch over Westhall. We delayed because we thought if she arrived on the same day as Dorrie, it would look suspicious."

Madeleine had been right in her instincts, Ethan remembered, although as wrong as he in choosing mothers. Had it not been for Madeleine, he wouldn't have hired the nursemaid. She would be proud to know how crucial her help had been in solving the mystery.

Ah, here was solace for his hurt: nothing stood in their way now. He and Madeleine could be happy. But before he allowed himself to fall into hazy dreams, he must first understand a few matters. Fortunately, now that she had begun, Alice appeared willing to tell him everything.

"I could have done nothing without Rosemary's assistance," Alice was saying. "I knew she would come to my aid. When I realized I was with child, I wrote her. She told me what to do to relieve my sickness during those beginning months; she sent receipts for herbs to help me sleep.

She even gave me suggestions for my wardrobe! Did you notice how often I wrapped myself in shawls this winter, Ethan? Do you recall how I complained about the cold all the time and wore my pelisse, even inside?"

He did have a vague recollection of this, it seemed to him now; but women were forever going on about being cold. When he made no response, only regarded her grimly, she gave him a hesitant look and continued:

"As my time drew near, Rosemary traveled here to help me. She has given birth twice herself, although both of her babies were born too soon and didn't survive, it grieves me to say. As soon as I felt the first pains, I told my father I meant to spend a couple of days with a friend in Thornbury and drove the gig here. I shall never cease to be grateful to Rosemary, for I couldn't have survived without her."

Mrs. Danniver responded to this remark with a faint smile. "You're giving me too much credit, Alice. You're very strong and courageous, and God was kind in giving you an easy delivery."

"If that was easy—!" exploded the young lady with a little laugh and a tilting of her eyes.

This kind of feminine bonding was not at all to Ethan's taste, and he said sternly, "Nevertheless, you put your child at great risk simply for the opportunity to tarnish my reputation in the Murrows' eyes."

Alice stepped closer to him, her face lengthening in sorrow. "Not for only that reason," she said beseechingly. "I thought if you spent time with my child, you would come to love her."

"And what then, Alice?" he clipped, staring down at her through slitted eyes. "If I loved the child, it would naturally follow I'd want to marry her mother? What's happened to your reasoning?"

Renewed hope swept into her face. "You do love her! I can see it in your face. Rosemary, I told you he would!"

Ethan looked at her in disbelief, wondering if the events of the past year had unhinged her mind. Of course he loved the child; who could not? But that was far from the point.

His gaze moved to the window beside them; it seemed the darkness beyond mirrored the growing gloom in his heart. Restlessly, his glance fell upon the eyes of her teacher, who watched him with an intelligent sadness that communicated sympathy for both of them. Mrs. Danniver broke the connection first, returning her attention to the babe nestled in her arms.

In the grips of desperate excitement, Alice went on, "I thought if you believed Dorrie was yours, you'd be less inclined to rid yourself of her. I was counting on the tenderness of your heart, Ethan, and you didn't disappoint me. From the way you spoke about Madeleine before she arrived, I believed you only wanted to marry her for her dowry. There was no intention to hurt you. Yes, of course I hoped the baby's presence would frighten her away. And then . . ."

"You would have stepped in."

"Yes."

"Gracious Alice, with her lovely dowry inherited from her mother."

Her laugh sounded brittle to his ears. "I'd rather you had said, *'lovely* Alice with her *gracious* dowry.' "

He stared at her. "If that had happened—"

"Oh, it still *can* happen," she assured him.

"No, it can't. But if it had, when did you plan to tell me you were Dorrie's mother—before or after the wedding?"

Smile fading, she lowered her eyes. "What does it matter?"

He grunted in disbelief. "This may surprise you, but I've yet to meet a bridegroom who wouldn't appreciate knowing his intended was already a mother. Wars have been fought for less, I imagine." As she remained silent, an unwelcome suspicion crept into his thoughts. "Alice. You *did* plan to tell me eventually, didn't you?"

"Of course," she said after a moment's pause.

No, she wouldn't have, he saw with a sense of wonder at her lack of honor. The certainty of her intentions shook him to the very center of his being. He had never truly known her.

"*When* would you have told me?" he lashed. "On our fiftieth anniversary, perhaps, but only if I was too deaf to hear you? Where is your conscience, Alice? Don't you think Dorrie deserves to know who her mother is?"

"But I would serve as her mother and love her with all my heart."

"Leaving Dorrie to endure the stigma of illegitimacy alone, while all of Brillham praises the Viscountess Alice Ambrose, who turns a blind eye to her husband's indiscretions and raises his bastard with the dignity of an angel. Oh, very good, Alice."

"You needn't speak to me with such scorn, Ethan. My intention was not to win praise for myself, but to save my family from shame—"

"To save *yourself* from shame," he cut in.

"Yes, that, too! Is such a thing not to be understood? What's to be gained by my humiliation? And recall your brother's part in this. Oh, don't become angry again, Ethan—you are like a bear when you do so! There's no need for either of us, *or Dorrie,* to be shamed. We can continue the brilliant story you concocted about your cousin—how I enjoyed listening to you build your castle of lies, by the by—we could say she gave her to us to raise or something like. Dorrie will not be damaged by it; we'll provide her with more love than any child needs!"

"Wonderful plan," Ethan said. "Except you've forgotten something."

Her shoulders tensed. "Madeleine—always Madeleine! But you will recover. I've lost someone, too, as you know. The scars will heal in time."

She ran to him, pressing her head against his chest, circling him with her arms. Surprised and dismayed, Ethan held his own arms away from her; then, moved by her plight in spite of his bitter disappointment in her character, lightly patted her shoulders.

"Listen to me, dear Ethan. If you cannot find it in your heart to do this, I shall have to leave Brillham and take Dorrie with me. That was what I planned to do sometime in the next few days, until you found us. Rosemary and I were going to think of a solution, but it wouldn't have been nearly as perfect as the one I've been hoping for. Do you want to lose your final link with Lucan? Can you travel through life without knowing what happens to your only niece?"

From the darkened end of the room, he heard Mrs. Danniver groan quietly.

Ethan grew very still, his wrath a terrible thing he dare not release until he brought it under a semblance of control. He breathed deeply and backed away from Alice's embrace.

"You sadden me," he said finally, although in truth she made him want to throw every stick of furniture against the wall. "If this—*threat*—was your best attempt at changing my mind, it's failed miserably." He paced in a circle, running his fingers through his hair. "Alice, marriage to me is not your only choice for dignity. Hire someone— perhaps Mrs. Danniver, if she's willing, since she's so excellent with Dorrie—to care for your child. The two of them might leave for a few months; babies change radically during the first years, or so I'm told. They could return using different names and live nearby; a widow and her child. Mrs. Danniver has met few people here who will recognize her after that length of time, except perhaps Betsy, and she will do as she's told, if I pay her. You could remain at home but still see your little girl."

"No. I won't be separated from Dorrie like that. It's been difficult enough already. I cannot."

He felt some relief; at least she had maternal sentiments and was not entirely a changeling from the girl he believed he knew. "Then I'm sorry, Alice. I can't help you. At least not in the way you wish."

Her eyes glassing with tears, she turned and went to take her baby. "Lucan would hate you for this," she whispered spitefully from the far end of the room.

"Alice," murmured Rosemary in censuring tones.

Ethan walked to the door. "I regret you feel that way." With his hand resting on the door latch, he added, "I won't say anything to your father or George; I leave that to you. But I will of necessity tell the Murrows. I know you can rely on their discretion, as you can on mine." He moved as if to leave, then hesitated. "I wish I could offer monetary assistance, but I'm comforted by knowing you have sufficient means. Don't leave Brillham, Alice. I do want to be part of Dorrie's life and will help you in any way I can—as a brother would, I mean."

"Go," she said seethingly.

He went.

Seventeen

It did not take more than one minute of traveling through the gloomy soup of this long, long night for Madeleine to hope she would never find it necessary to do so again. Riding, *yes;* traveling after dark, *perhaps;* being without shelter in the rain, *maybe;* but all three? Never. Seated sidesaddle atop Legacy, she could scarcely see past the horse's head, but she tried, her back wrenching as she twisted to peer into the dimness at either side of the lane that ran past the viscount's estate.

She feared she would be of little help in finding Ethan, but she was determined not to be a hindrance to Scott. Unfortunately, from the manner in which the steward forged ahead, then drew back to match the pace she'd set for Legacy, then pulled into the lead again, she believed that was exactly what she was: a hindrance. Well, if he thought riding a horse nearly twice one's height, sideways and on a slippery saddle, in a soggy gown and cape through utter blackness was easy, *he* should try it.

"If I'm slowing you, please go ahead," she snapped at him.

"Pardon?" he called through the drone of rain, and brought his horse closer to hers. When she repeated her words, he replied, "My apologies, Miss Murrow; I'm allowing my concern to overtake good sense. A walking pace is best for us to make a more thorough search."

"I despair of finding him in this," she admitted, forgiving him.

"As do I."

She glanced at his profile, wishing he had spoken more positively. He possessed none of Ethan's brash optimism, but perhaps that came from having to depend on the generosity of others who were not one's family. In spite of her anxiety for the viscount, she felt curiosity stirring about Scott.

For an uneasy space, she recalled her fears that the steward might have caused Ethan's accident. But if Scott did such a thing, would he be so eager to search for him now, so concerned for his safety?

Perhaps he intended to divert her suspicions. He had neglected to notice the viscount's leaving Westhall this evening, after all. Would someone truly loyal make that sort of mistake?

But no one could be watchful every moment, she argued to herself, studying Scott again. Only the best of actors could project what she saw in him now: tightly reined tension, determination, even dread. If she were not already afraid for Ethan, a look at Scott's demeanor alone would throw her into terror.

A hedgehog chose that instant to scuttle across the road. Legacy balked, stamping, tossing her mane and whinnying. Madeleine spoke sharply, and the horse snorted, but settled back to a walk.

"Nicely done, Miss Murrow," Scott commented.

She thanked him and begged he use her given name henceforth. They were no longer strangers, she said, not after sharing this drenching midnight ride.

Her words appeared to please him. Noticing she had fallen into silence again, he said, "I didn't mean to sound defeated a moment ago. I believe the most likely conclusion is that Ethan will arrive home before we do and have the house in turmoil searching for you. He'll find I'm gone as well, and either he or your father will be waiting for me with the dueling pistols—probably both."

Knowing he meant to brighten her spirits, she forced a smile. "When I tell them I gave you no choice but to take me, you will receive only their sympathy." Impulsively, she added, "Papa thinks you waste yourself at Westhall. Whether or not that is the case, I'm glad you're here." A brief pause stretched before she offered tentatively, hoping it was true, "Ethan could not wish for a better friend."

Rather than seeming flattered, Scott set his jaw grimly. "Oh, he could wish for better, Miss—Madeleine. I owe him much, just as I owed his brother; and I've not always been the kind of friend I should have." His lips clamped together for a moment, and she imagined him holding something back; but when he spoke, it was only to say, "I can never repay what the Ambrose family has done for me."

"I'm aware his mother practically raised you, but surely you've given more than you've received. No one expects you to remain indebted forever."

"You're wrong, Madeleine, if you'll forgive me for saying so. There are some debts that require a lifetime to repay."

This puzzled her greatly, and she stared at him, flicking Legacy's reins now and then, willing Scott to say more. Abruptly, the gentleman pointed out a small building on their right. "There's Cotter's Cottage," he added brightly. "Have you heard the legend?"

Changing the subject, she thought, twisting her mouth a little; but she decided to humor him and shook her head. With visible relief, he began to relate the tale of a disappearing farmer. It was a long story, and he told it well as they clopped down the muddy lane. In spite of herself, she became intrigued and asked questions long after the cottage had vanished in the distance behind them.

It had been a long walk to discovery, Ethan thought, and was bound to be a longer one back. Striding through the puddles and boggy mess of the track leading away from Alice and her secrets and treachery, his mind churned with anger, disillusionment, and a sharp, steadily growing conviction that he did not understand anyone. Perhaps Madeleine, too, hid a dark side that she'd keep concealed until they were securely leg-shackled.

The thought sickened him with guilt. He could not imagine her hiding anything from him; she was far too straightforward and honest. And who was he to cast judgments, anyway? No paragon of virtue, he.

Nevertheless, Alice had hurt him deeply. He doubted he could ever look at her again without thinking of this night.

He turned up his collar and hunched his shoulders against the driving rain. Reaching the lane, he angled left and proceeded a little faster, the pavement being less muddy than the trail leading to the laborers' cottages. His leg burned as if branded with a poker, but it was best not to think of that.

After some moments had passed, distance—or perhaps the cooling effect of the incessant water pounding on his head—eased his wrath to a degree. He began to wonder what Alice would do now. Surely she wouldn't take Dorrie away; he'd miss the child if she did. Tomorrow he would pay a visit to the Reddings and talk to Alice privately, when they both were calmer. He recalled her mentioning that she and Rosemary didn't plan to act for a few days; and he hoped his arrival wouldn't press them to do something desperate. Surely Alice needed time to make arrangements, gather her inheritance, and pack her clothes. She was too vain of her appearance to leave her expensive garments behind.

Through the drumming of the rain, he detected a more urgent noise behind. A man was approaching on horseback, riding at a canter; rather too quickly for the conditions of the road, he thought, but felt relief anyway. Perhaps he'd be willing to share his horse for a mile or two, given the pitiful conditions. Ethan stepped farther into the lane and held up one hand peremptorily. The rider, rather than slowing, increased his speed. Disbelieving of his rudeness, the viscount squinted, struggling to recognize the source of such inconsideration. He could not discern the rider's visage through the darkness, but he paced backward as he suddenly realized the stranger was headed directly for him; and, incredibly, he appeared to be raising a cane to strike. Outraged, Ethan leaped for safety, but too late; the blow exploded blinding pain across the side of his skull and shoulder.

Momentum rolled him to the edge of the road and into the ditch, where he lay motionless, facedown, his world spinning, blazing with agony. He tried to raise his head, to bring his arms and legs into motion, but the effort nauseated him and sent him into a brief period of darkness. When he returned to consciousness, he heard with horror the return of hoofbeats and forced himself to lean to his side, to look up and see the madman who could do this to him. His eyes failed to focus, and he saw only shapes; the heaving sides of the horse, the booted legs of the rider as he dismounted and stood over him. He was moving closer, bending over him, and again Ethan ordered his limbs to move, realizing that here stood greater danger than he'd known in his life, but his body would not respond.

When his assailant seized him roughly and pulled him from the ditch, Ethan clenched his teeth to prevent himself crying out. Inexplicably, the man propped him against his horse—perhaps to rest, for he was breathing hard—and the viscount feigned a slump, then launched his fist at the monster's jaw, making contact. The other grunted in surprise and anger, then lashed several blows at Ethan's face that folded his knees. He had only a remote, fiery awareness of being heaved across the saddle before his awareness edged into total darkness.

"Madeleine?"

Scott's voice vibrated with concern, and she meant to

reassure him when she was able. Just now, she found it hard to speak.

They had arrived at the village of Brillham, but it was not this which troubled her. Even in this flood it was easy to recognize the shops she and her parents had visited on one of the first days of their sojourn at Westhall. Under the proper conditions—sunshine and daylight, primarily—the village might be called picturesque.

No, there could be nothing frightening in this haphazard collection of business establishments. Rather, the source of her disquiet was a steadily growing conviction that something was terribly, horribly wrong. She tried to laugh it off, to tell herself that Scott's story about the farmer and his cottage had put her nerves on edge, but it was not working.

She had never been given to premonitions and the like. She knew of a lady in Kent who had made herself a laughingstock by constantly forecasting gloom for everyone, and Madeleine had thought her very foolish. Nevertheless, she could not deny the strength of her own foreboding now.

"We should have found Ethan by now," she said, finally. "He was on foot."

"Don't be worried that we haven't discovered him yet. I didn't expect to be successful this soon, because he could have turned off the main road a dozen times between Westhall and here. Do you wish to return home?"

She looked at him, not liking how eager he sounded. "I don't want to give up too quickly."

"He may have returned and be searching for *us*. If not, I could enlist the groom and the stable boy to help. Maybe Burns. We could cover more ground in that way."

And rid yourself of me, she thought dismally. Not a man alive, it seemed to her, no matter how gentlemanly they might act, wanted a woman along when they did things like this—even though there was not a whit of danger in them. Oh, they might mumble authoritatively about all the things that could happen on their excursions: highwaymen, horses going lame, tree limbs crashing down on heads, floods, fire, famine—she was growing angrier by the second—when in truth, no one was ever safe, not even sitting in their own parlors sewing. She had heard of one old lady who pricked her finger with a needle while embroidering altar cloths for church, contracted an infection, and died.

"Let's return, yes," she said heatedly, "but if Ethan isn't there, I'm going to continue searching with you—I don't care what you say!"

"Fine," Scott said, his eyes widening humorously. "I wouldn't have it any other way."

I would laugh, Madeleine thought as she reined Legacy around, if I didn't feel so much like weeping.

Someone was dragging him. Ethan forced open his eyes and saw a lacy network of trees overhead. Memory returned, and with it, excruciating pain. His assailant had wound his arms across his chest and was pulling him through a wood. Startled, he recognized the landscape as his own; they were moving through the small stand of trees banking the river, a tributary of the Bristol Avon, which marked the northwest boundary of his estate. Through the gloom he saw the villain's horse reined to a tree, steadily growing farther away. Whoever this madman was, he had brought him here on horseback and was now pulling him toward the river. A sudden, deadly conviction seized him concerning his assailant's intentions.

Ethan's head lolled backward. They were clear of the forest now. The rain had stopped. A soft wind was scattering the clouds into long wisps, and he could see the moon above him, almost perfectly round, coldly beautiful, and very far away. Beneath his boots he felt the drag of vegetation soften to the moist earth of the riverbank. Making an agonized effort, he pushed at the hands imprisoning him and was dropped to the ground, jarringly, for his attempt. While he fought the return of darkness and struggled to breathe, a boot settled firmly on his chest.

"We can do this in as civilized a manner as possible," said a pleasant voice, "or I can kick you into cooperation; your decision, Lord Ambrose."

Ethan lifted his gaze incredulously. "MacAllister?"

The tutor gave a short bow. "The same. I'm pleased you're alert enough to recognize me. It will make the next few moments more meaningful. I should think it would be frustrating for you to die without knowing the reason."

"What—why—"

MacAllister smiled coldly. "Why am I doing this? I can understand your confusion. A man of your social position never considers those beneath him—and I use the term *you* would use, because I do not consider myself beneath *anyone*—to have ambitions and desires of their own."

Encourage him to speak, Lucan whispered in his ear. *The longer he raves, the better the chances to recover your strength.*

Ethan shivered. Was that truly his brother's voice he'd heard, or had his injuries made him delusional? Either way, it didn't matter; Lucan was with him.

"I don't know what you're talking about," he said.

"No, I suppose you don't." MacAllister lifted his boot from Ethan's chest and went to stand at his feet, looking tall as a tree from the viscount's position. "I've sat in the same room with you on many occasions and listened to your thoughts on agriculture and females and horseflesh. I've heard you talk about your social life—dinners and picnics and balls and croquet. Never once did you ask *my* opinion on anything though, did you? No, you were too proud to even acknowledge my presence. Even though I have the advantage of greater age and wisdom, and my education puts yours to shame, you could not lower yourself to treat me as an equal."

"Is that what this is about?" Ethan rasped, his ribs sparking fire into each breath. "You want to kill me because I've hurt your feelings?"

MacAllister laughed. "No, not precisely." He sobered.

"I'm not an idiot. England's social system did not begin with you. But I intend to move through the ranks in the only way possible for such a one as myself, who was unlucky in birth. I plan to marry Alice Redding, and you are standing in my way."

"Marry Alice?" Under different circumstances, he would have been highly amused. "She'll never have you." Too late, it occurred to him he might be ill-advised to ridicule a madman's fondest wish. Quickly, he added, "Your jealousy is misplaced. I have no interest in Alice and intend to wed Madeleine."

Face darkening with disbelief, MacAllister said, "You're only saying that to obtain my mercy. I watched you tonight with Alice at the cottage. I saw you embrace her. I witnessed that she had won you over at last—not that anyone could resist her long."

So that explained the noise he'd heard. The tutor had followed Alice to the hut, doubtless arriving before Ethan had. He must have hidden his beast in the thicket. He could not have known the viscount was following her as well; MacAllister's actions smacked of the habit of long practice. This sign of obsession gave Ethan no comfort.

"You misread the situation. We were saying goodbye."

MacAllister appeared to consider this for a moment, flaring Ethan's hopes. "Even if you speak the truth, it doesn't matter," he said, and the viscount closed his eyes briefly as this last chance faded. "As long as you're alive, she won't consider me. I thought when your brother died, she'd turn to me, especially once I realized she carried his child. But it appears she's been enraptured with both of you for years. Once you're gone, though, who else will be willing to give her child a name? She's ruined in Society's eyes, but never in mine."

"You know about Dorrie?" Ethan asked dully, seizing on the last part of the tutor's conversation while he mulled over the rest. Something MacAllister had said nagged at the edges of his consciousness.

"I've known for months. Could I keep such close watch

over her and not know? Although no one else did, including you. That alone should prove how devoted I am to her."

Beneath Ethan, the damp earth seeped coldness through his bones. Overhead, the wind had blown all but a few cloud strands from the sky, and the stars were exposed in their brilliance. The treetops framing the back of MacAllister's head whispered secrets companionably in the breeze.

A beautiful night to die, Lucan, he told his twin.

You are not going to die, Lucan answered him firmly.

I'm tired, Lucan. So tired.

Think of Madeleine. Do you recall how her sister died? Can you leave her to mourn this double loss?

No, he groaned. He could not.

Play for time.

Ethan forced himself to speak: "Was Alice aware that you knew about her pregnancy?"

"I could not presume to tell her, although I've tried to make myself available and useful. She didn't take me into her confidence, and I blame myself for that; I should have been more assertive. I'm willing to admit I've hurt my case by such misjudgments. Imagine my distress when she brought her baby to you. I thought all had ended! But you didn't react the way she hoped, and now I have another opportunity to gain the love of the woman I adore more than life."

"The *heiress* you adore, you mean," Ethan said, sneering.

"Make no mistake; the money is only a pleasant addendum. I would do anything for Alice—certainly more than you or your brother would have."

"You're a fool. My brother loved her enough to marry her."

"Yes, he would have married her; but not for love. Surely as his twin you realize that. Even I, *a lowly servant* as you would call me, saw it."

Ethan struggled to raise himself on one elbow. Was the

tutor merely raving about what he hoped to be true, or did he know something Ethan did not?

Listen to him, Lucan whispered. *Learn the truth, and give us both rest.*

"My brother would never seduce a woman he didn't love."

"You're very idealistic."

Moving abruptly, the tutor circled Ethan, intent on dragging him into the water, he knew. The viscount set his teeth and rolled to the side, rising to his knees.

"There's no point in this, MacAllister. Even if I'm dead, Alice won't accept you."

"She will learn to love me in time," he said angrily, and moved forward.

Ethan weaved to his feet and stepped back, the world spinning slowly around. "What good will that do if you hang?"

With a condescending smile, MacAllister gestured expansively. "Why would I hang for your accidental drowning?"

"No one will believe this is an accident."

"When I scatter a few bottles on the shore, they will. And even without such evidence, everyone will account it to the Ambrose Curse." His eyes gleamed, and he lunged forward, his words nearly buried in movement: "It offered the perfect cover for your brother's demise, did it not?"

Stunned, Ethan, who had braced himself for the onslaught he knew was coming, dropped to the ground, and MacAllister fell with him. Crazed by fury, the viscount used their momentum to roll on top of him.

"Did you kill Lucan?" he shouted, his hands at the tutor's throat. "Did you kill my brother?"

MacAllister was a large, solidly built man, and a strong one. He clawed the viscount's hands away and scurried to his feet. Ethan quickly scrambled upward. The tutor had time to bare his teeth angrily and say, "How easy it was. He made a far better target than those ridiculous birds!"

before the viscount barreled into him, landing them both in the shallows.

It was now Ethan's turn to punish.

He felt no pain. His body was a machine with no sensations at all saving the white heat of his rage, his arm an avenging hammer as he pounded and pounded at MacAllister's face. The murderer's ineffectual, defensive blows phased him no more than the water splashing his cheeks. Finally, MacAllister made a desperate lunge, and both men rolled deeper into the river, their fists slowing with the weight of water. The viscount scrabbled his fingers around the tutor's throat and began to squeeze. MacAllister's eyes bulged as he fought, but nothing he did could stop him, nothing.

Ethan, he heard a voice saying. *I don't want this.*

"I do!" he cried to Lucan aloud. "This is justice!"

No, my brother.

He shook his head rebelliously and continued his grisly work. And thus did not hear Madeleine screaming his name until she plowed into the water beside him and pulled at his arm.

"No, Ethan, stop! What are you doing?"

He came close to turning his anger on her, so complete was his trance, and when she flinched backward he knew a moment's regret, but a moment only. He did not wonder how she came to be here, nor why. "He killed my brother!" he threw in, without relenting his hold on the tutor.

"Oh, dear God!" Madeleine's fingers covered her mouth, and she turned to Brandt, who was circling to the viscount's other side. Their eyes locked, and she saw all color had leached from the steward's skin. "Don't do this, Ethan—the law will deal with him!" When he paid her no heed, she begged, "Stop him, Scott!"

With hollow eyes, Scott clutched the viscount's shoulder with an iron hand. "Leave go, Ethan," he said close to the viscount's ear. "You'll break the heart of the woman you love if you kill him. Stop, now. He'll be punished."

Slowly, very slowly, Ethan relaxed his hold on the tutor's neck. MacAllister heaved a deep, agonized breath and caught his balance weakly, his eyes ravaged as he watched Ethan turn to trudge toward the shore.

Madeleine grasped his arm, evidently thinking he needed support, and he supposed he did. Now that it was over, his body began to betray him, his pain returning tenfold. He shivered like a new colt. They waded to the bank, and he sank to the earth, incapable of going further. Madeleine sat beside him, her eyes like two luminous moons in the darkness. Tentatively, she reached out and ran her hands along his arms to warm him. Her concern restored a touch of humanity to his bestial emotions, but he was not himself; not yet.

"He killed my brother," he said.

"I know, Ethan," she murmured.

"He killed Lucan."

"Hush, dearest." She moved closer and drew him to her, cradling his head on her shoulder, and he was lost. He wept without shame while she held him, murmuring comforts and stroking his hair as if he were a child.

Some time later, he became aware of Scott wading toward them. Shamed, Ethan dashed the tears from his eyes, then looked to either side of the steward, his heart seizing with panic.

"Where's MacAllister?" he demanded.

Brandt's colorless mouth barely moved as he said, "Gone." Before Ethan could misunderstand, he added, "The river took him."

As Madeleine gasped, Ethan's lips parted. "The river—" Using Brandt as a prop, he struggled to his feet and scanned the dark water. "Scott?"

"You didn't do it," Brandt said woodenly. "The river did." He glanced briefly at Madeleine, then away. "It was an accident."

Madeleine, lowering her lashes, stood and leaned against Ethan, linking her arm through his. With his free hand, the viscount clasped Scott's fingers.

"An accident," he confirmed, his eyes blazing with gratitude.

Eighteen

When they returned to Westhall, the time was nearing four in the morning. Madeleine could not believe it was not four in the afternoon; she had lived a lifetime during a single night.

She had lived a lifetime, and the tutor had lost his.

As the house gradually stirred to life at their arrival, she tried not to think of what Scott had done and what Ethan *would* have, had she not been present at the river. But perhaps she was wrong about the viscount; he might have returned to his senses in time. She clung to that hope.

She understood the power of the gentlemen's emotions, for she had longed to see Bettina's seducer destroyed; if not by death, at least by reputation. But nothing could bring her sister back, just as nothing would ever return Lucan to Ethan. She was only happy he would not have to live with the guilt of Jarrod MacAllister's death.

The question that troubled her mind most was, *why?* Why had the tutor hated the Ambrose brothers so much? Ethan, winded and emotionally spent, had promised to explain everything when they reached Westhall, and she was on pins and needles waiting.

Fresh from his half day off, Burns responded first to the summoning of the bell, although he did so clothed in an opulent brocade robe. When he spied the wet and bedraggled threesome in the library, he blanched.

Ethan, reclining on the settee with his head propped by cushions, commanded him to fetch hot water for baths and fresh towels. "Awaken Betsy and Cook," he added. "Betsy can assist me with my scratches, and we need sandwiches and hot tea."

"Make mine brandy," Scott said.

Burns, his face a study in refined curiosity, looked a question at the viscount.

"Only tea for me," he said, and glanced at Madeleine and smiled, then winced as the cut on his lip widened.

Madeleine scarcely noticed his restraint from strong spirits. "And send Rathbone or Lindon for the physician," she ordered the butler. When Ethan began a protest, she reminded him he'd required Scott's assistance to mount Jarrod MacAllister's horse, that he'd lapsed into a stupor for most of the journey home and had needed both their shoulders to climb the stairs into his house. "And it hurts me every time I look at you," she added, viewing his badly bruised face with a frown.

Ethan feigned an offended expression. "I promise I'll never say the same to you." He waved the butler on to his duties, then looked from Madeleine to Scott and back again. "One thing puzzles me; how did you manage to find me at the river?"

Scott explained how they had gone to Brillham and turned back to seek help. "About a half mile from Westhall, we saw MacAllister guiding his horse into the wood."

"Naturally, we didn't know it was he; not then," Madeleine added. "We couldn't see from that distance."

"To my eyes, MacAllister appeared to be an anonymous man on a horse with something draped over the saddle. I assumed he was a poacher who'd bagged a deer." Scott slouched lower in the leather chair, stretching his legs. "On a normal evening, I would have followed him as a matter of course. Tonight I felt returning to Westhall was the most important thing. Madeleine disagreed. Had it not been for her intuition, I would have kept going."

"A deer, you say? My antlers gave me away, I suppose." The camaraderie of Ethan's tone removed any sting from the words. "Thank God for Madeleine."

"Thank God," Scott agreed.

Madeleine felt a current of warmth flowing between the two men, and her heart lightened to sense their rift mending.

"As for Madeleine," Ethan added with a look that made her shiver with pleasure, "I think we'd both do well to heed her advice. Have I mentioned how grateful I am, my dear, for what you've done this night?"

"At least a hundred times," she said in a gentle voice. Were it not for the steward's presence, she would have the viscount's head nestled on her lap instead of those stiff-looking needlepoint pillows. For the time being, she had drawn a chair close to his knees so she could comfortably hold his hand.

"Good." Ethan cut narrowed eyes to Brandt. "Then I can safely tell Scott that I'll slice off his legs if he ever puts you in jeopardy again."

"I would have gone by myself if he hadn't permitted me to go with him," Madeleine said instantly.

The viscount stared. '*Would* you? Yes, I can see you mean it. My pardon, Scott. I believe we've met our match in Miss Murrow."

"She's a brave lady," Scott affirmed, causing Madeleine to glow.

"And why is that?" asked her father from the doorway. Like Burns, he wore a brocade dressing gown tied with a tasseled belt over his nightshift, only the butler's robe had appeared newer. "Madeleine? What goes on here?"

Coloring, the young lady started to rise, but the strong tug on her hand reminded her of a new allegiance. Her father dragged a chair near hers as she related the part of the night's adventure she had experienced. With anxiety, she watched his face move expressively as she spoke.

His scowl deepening, he directed a glare at Ethan. "I blame you for this."

Ethan started to speak, but his gaze moved suddenly to the doorway as Antonia entered, looking soft and frail in her emerald silk negligee.

"I don't understand why you blame him," she said. "I've been listening behind the wall, I'm ashamed to say, but I didn't want to interrupt our daughter's story. Nothing Ethan did was worthy of blame, Thomas; he was only trying to discover the baby's mother—for our sakes, I'll remind."

"Antonia, you shouldn't be up!" Thomas said, standing.

"I heard the commotion and couldn't rest." She walked gracefully to sit in the chair her husband immediately vacated, Thomas assisting her as if she were made of glass. "Besides, I'm feeling much better." As he drew another seat into the circle, she added, "Or I was until hearing this. Madeleine, you should not have taken such a risk, my child."

Ethan nodded. "Exactly what I told her."

Clearing his throat, Burns entered carrying a tray of tea and a platter stacked with sandwiches. Seeing more members had been added to the group, he glided regally from the room to bring additional cups and saucers.

"If those were your sentiments, you should have done better in keeping Madeleine home," Thomas said, causing Madeleine to squirm at his lack of logic. "Now my daughter has been witness to something she's too sensitive to forget: a murder."

"It was an accident," Ethan, Madeleine, and Scott said all at once.

Thomas looked from one face to another. "Why?" he asked simply, voicing the question burning uppermost in Madeleine's mind. "Why did the tutor do these reprehensible acts? Was he mad?"

Ethan moved slowly to a sitting position, and all eyes centered on him. Burns reentered with the additional tea accoutrements, then exited swiftly, the heavy silence speeding him along. Madeleine began to pour tea into white china cups so thin they were almost transparent. The viscount accepted his cup, drank deeply, and set it on the table beside the settee.

"He was jealous," Ethan said. "MacAllister had aspirations of marrying Alice Redding, and in the beginning, he saw Lucan as his sole obstacle. Perhaps he *was* mad."

"He wanted to marry Alice?" Scott exploded.

Ethan briefly lowered his lids. "What I'm going to say must remain within the walls of this room, as it would damage the reputation of a lady should it become widely known." He scanned the faces watching him. Seeming satisfied with what he observed in their expressions, he continued, "MacAllister thought if Lucan was removed, Alice would grow to love him. But when it became apparent she was with child—"

Madeleine's jaw dropped. Thomas jerked forward, as if intending to refute milord's statement, and Brandt shouted, "What?" and leapt from his chair, the cup and saucer balanced on his knee falling heedlessly to the floor. Fortunately, the porcelain did not break, but tea stains darkened his pantaloons and seeped into the carpet.

"I know it's unbelievable, the manner in which she kept her condition hidden from us," Ethan continued. "There was only one person she didn't deceive: Jarrod MacAllister. He thought she would rely on him when her infant was born, but instead, she turned to me. That's why he decided to kill me." Ethan directed a weighty look at Thomas. "Dorrie is Alice's child."

Aghast, Madeleine gazed at her father. He appeared as stunned as she, and for once, he remained speechless.

"I had wondered," Antonia said musingly. "There was an unusual spark in her eye when she looked upon the infant—the kind of prideful glow a first-time mother gets before she understands her child is a separate being from herself and not her own creation."

"I wish you had said!" Madeleine declared with feeling.

"Oh, no one listens to me," Antonia answered lightly, her eyes resting sweetly on her husband.

Thomas finally came to life. "And who do you claim is the father? Certainly not yourself. I know you will say you're innocent."

Ethan remained silent for a long moment. "I don't

claim anything. MacAllister accused my brother." Madeleine, comprehending his distress, stroked his hand consolingly. "From Alice's behavior, I would have to say he was correct."

"No," said Brandt in a strange voice. "No, he wasn't."

All eyes now turned to Scott, who had gone to stand beside the fireplace. He rippled a hand through his hair and patted his neckcloth distractedly. Madeleine thought she had never seen anyone appear so uncomfortable with himself.

"I—I'm the father," he said at last.

This brought the viscount to his feet. "And you have kept silent?" he lashed.

Madeleine, who in the past seconds had come to think she would never be surprised by anything again, grew weak with shock and sank back in her chair.

Brandt, rubbing his chin and gazing incredulously into the distance, appeared more struck than any of them. "I didn't know Dorrie was Alice's baby, Ethan. I never knew she was going to have a child—she never told me." He pressed his hands over his face in a washing motion. "This is like her—so like her to deceive everyone, probably even herself. Lucan, always Lucan. Oh, dear God."

The viscount limped to stand beside Scott, and Madeleine was relieved to see he no longer appeared angry, only eager. "Slow down, Scott. Speak so that we can understand you."

Brandt's eyes skimmed over the inhabitants of the room. "I don't know . . . ladies present . . ."

"These ladies are hardier than they appear." Ethan raised an ironic brow. "Or do I speak out of turn, Madeleine, Mrs. Murrow? Should the gentlemen leave you to finish this?"

"I'll have a relapse if you do," Antonia warned.

"And I shall die," Madeleine asserted.

Thomas looked disapprovingly from one to the other of them, but remained silent.

Scott, casting an anxious look at Ethan, said, "I'll try to

explain. I've loved Alice for years, but it was Lucan who held her heart. Yet Lucan . . . there was something that made it difficult for him to love a particular woman, and he had no interest in marriage or children. Please don't misunderstand; this was not a failing in him as it might be in some men. It was as though he . . . flew above the rest of us, dwelt somewhere higher. He loved everyone equally and would have given his last shirt if someone needed it, but he was . . . how can I explain this? There was an *impersonal* aspect to his caring. After five minutes with him, you felt as if he'd known you forever and was your best friend. But it might take years to realize you knew very little about *him*. I think I was closest to him save for his brother, yet I never really understood Lucan."

Madeleine looked to Ethan for confirmation, and his expression was so drawn with sorrow that she averted her eyes.

Brandt sighed. "Last summer, he told me he meant to reject the title and give it to you, Ethan. It was his dream to move to London and become a part of a charity serving the poverty-stricken. At the same time, Alice increased her efforts in his direction, nearly driving him to distraction because he detested hurting her. He thought of her as a sister; that's what he told me.

"When he didn't respond to her overtures, she pretended to become interested in me. I couldn't resist even the crumbs of her affection, especially since I knew Lucan didn't love her. Then I became confused. You see, I thought at first she pursued me to make Lucan jealous, but she was insistent that no one know we were meeting secretly."

He turned penitent eyes on the viscount. "I begged her to marry me, Ethan; I'm not a complete villain. I deluded myself into believing she truly loved me. When she refused my offer, I couldn't comprehend that she would"— He glanced guiltily at the ladies—"would act in the way she did, if it weren't for love. Finally, when I understood she had no deep feelings for me, I broke off our relationship. Less than a month later, she and Lucan were betrothed."

For the first time in a long while, Thomas stirred to attention. "If what you're saying is true, why did Lucan change his mind about her? How can you know the child wasn't his?"

"The timing, sir. The child could not be his, because around . . . that time Lucan went to Scotland for six weeks—do you recall it, Ethan? One of our mates at school fell from his horse and broke his back—Richard Anderson. Lucan received a letter from Anderson's sister begging him to come."

"That's true; I remember." Ethan bent slowly to sit on the hearth. Madeleine rushed to join him and slid her fingers within his, then cast a defiant look at her father, daring him to say anything.

"Then why did Lucan decide to marry her?" Thomas persisted.

Brandt said, "I don't know for certain, for he was extremely closemouthed about it when I asked him that question. Knowing his tender heart, Alice must have used her pregnancy to beg him to prevent her being disgraced. I can only imagine what she gave him as an explanation for her condition—probably said she was assaulted. If she'd accused me, I know he would have demanded I fulfill my own obligation." Scott paused, and for a space of time the library seemed to vibrate with silence. "I'm wondering now if this was her purpose all along—to become with child in order to coerce Lucan to marry her."

Ethan's skin had grown very white. "And by so doing, she inadvertently caused his death. Had they not become engaged, MacAllister wouldn't have killed Lucan."

Madeleine laid her other hand over their clasped fingers, her heart breaking with his. Once again, silence crowded the library.

After a long moment, Brandt said, "I beg you will forgive my part in his death. I have struggled every day with

my guilt. Although I'm certain he didn't love Alice, I feel
as if I betrayed him."

"You couldn't have known a madman waited in the
wings, Scott. I don't blame you. I can't even be angry with
Alice anymore. She loved him, and love can make you do
foolish things." Without looking at Madeleine, he kissed
her hand. "I understand that now."

"I wish she had felt one-tenth the love for me she had
for him," Scott said.

Surprised, Ethan tilted his head to meet his eyes. "After
all that has happened, your feelings for her haven't
changed?"

Brandt smiled wryly. "Did you not just say that love can
make you do foolish things?"

After a moment, Ethan said, "I can't guarantee love,
but Alice has never needed anyone more than she does
now. If you hurry, you might still find her behind Cotter's
Cottage."

For the space of a dozen heartbeats, Scott said nothing;
but a flicker of hope dawned in his eyes. "Perhaps I should
look in on her."

"It's worth a try," Ethan said, gesturing toward the
threshold.

Brandt smiled tentatively, took his leave, and hurried
away.

"Surely she will accept him now," Madeleine said,
dreading Scott's disappointment if it happened otherwise.

"If she doesn't, she's a greater idiot than I am,"
Thomas said, rising to extend his hand to the viscount.
Without hesitation, Ethan clasped it. "Forgive me, my
lord, for doubting. You and Madeleine have my blessing."

"And mine," Antonia sang from her chair, her smile
threatening to reach her ears.

Heart filled to bursting, Madeleine swept her arms
around Ethan. He returned her embrace with only the
slightest recoil of pain. Fearing she would hurt him further, she kissed him very gently.

In the midst of their joy, Burns entered to say the physician had arrived and would be awaiting the viscount in his room. Ethan groaned at the pain to come.

"Should you like a hot toddy afterward, my lord?" the butler inquired with what Madeleine supposed passed for a smile on the servant's stern face.

"Burns, you've never offered to make a toddy for me." The viscount's voice inflected with wonder.

"Haven't I? It's been my custom in the past to make a special blend for the viscount. I beg your pardon for my oversight, my lord."

Ethan, examining him curiously, nodded and told him he would look forward to it. The butler exited on soundless feet.

"He heard everything," Antonia said with conviction.

"This house is full of echoes," Madeleine remembered.

"It's full of big ears, you mean," Betsy said at the threshold. "Your hot water's ready for baths upstairs, milord and my almost lady; and I've got just one thing to say. The next person what speaks bad about Lord Ambrose is getting a fistful in their gullet."

The laughter which met this remark far outweighed its humor, but Madeleine knew their highly charged emotional state needed a release of some kind. Leaning her head on Ethan's shoulder, she reveled in the changes wrought during the past hours: the discovery of Dorrie's parents, her father's blessing, and overshadowing all: Ethan's safety. She laughed until the tears came, thinking, *how like a family we are.*

After sleeping all that morning, Ethan gathered his aching bones from bed, dressed, and hobbled downstairs using the accursed cane again. Pausing beside the newel post, he heard his guests clinking dishes in the dining room and talking. When he recognized Madeleine's laughter, he smiled. Instead of joining them, he turned and entered his study, his eyes fixating on the portrait as they always did.

"Justice at last, Lucan," he whispered. "Your murderer is dead." He waited, listening for his brother's response. When none came, he hurried on, "I've found a beautiful bride; the line will go on, just as you wished, God willing." He paused, his smile faltering. "Lucan?"

He discerned no answer, no soundless voice whispering inside his head. With torn feelings, he swept his gaze across the room, snagging on the chairless side of the desk, his brother's books, back to the portrait. Lucan no longer dwelled here. Had he ever done so since his death? Ethan wondered. Did he himself, in his overwhelming grief, only imagine his brother spoke to him from the grave, or had his twin finally found peace?

He would never know.

His eye caught movement at the doorway to the study, and he veered abruptly. Dressed in a white gown dotted with lilac flowers and looking utterly captivating, Madeleine stood hesitantly, her smile uncertain.

"I thought I heard you and your cane descending the stairs," she said. "What are you doing? Is anything the matter?"

"No," he said, smiling. "I was simply thinking . . . how happy I am."

After a leisurely kiss that he wished to prolong but could not, thanks to his ridiculous, growling stomach convulsing her into giggles, he placed his arm across her shoulders and walked her to the dining room.

The wedding took place on the following Sunday afternoon, the Murrows having agreed to remain a few extra days for the special event. The service, a small affair, was held in the great hall of the viscount's home. In addition to the Murrows, only Lord Ambrose, his servants, Rosemary Danniver, the Abbotts (Joseph, his good nature strained at this rather shady turn of events—but who kept assuring everyone the ceremony was better late than never—officiated), George Redding, the bride and bridegroom, and of course, the baby. The bride's father, unable to forgive, was conspicuous in his absence, but no one mentioned his name; and apparently, no one missed him.

Alice made a stunning bride descending the stairs in a gray taffeta gown that Ethan did not recall seeing before, making him wonder if she had found time to order a new one stitched up. He would not be surprised if she had; when Scott told him the size of her inheritance from her mother, the viscount's last misgivings for his old friend vanished. With such a beginning, with Brandt's talents and Alice's charm and beauty, they would do very well in London. The two had decided to make a new start there. Despite the viscount's best efforts, gossip had spread throughout Brillham, and neither Alice nor Scott wished to raise Dorrie beneath a cloud.

As Alice approached her bridegroom, she met Lord Ambrose's eyes for one heart-stopping second. Standing as Scott's best man, Ethan deliberately looked beyond her to fix his smiling attention on Madeleine. By the time the bride took her groom's hand, the awkward moment had passed, and afterward she kept her vision centered only on Brandt.

When Reverend Abbott pronounced the couple husband and wife, the viscount felt a great weight fall from his shoulders. Dorrie, who had remained placid in the arms of Rosemary, the matron-of-honor, for the duration of the service, gave a sudden, piercing squeal that caused the company to fall into relieved laughter.

Before the couple departed, a modest reception was held in the dining room. Ethan brought a plate of lacy sandwiches and sweets to Madeleine, who was sitting beside her parents on one of the side chairs lining the chamber.

"I keep thinking of next month, when it will be *our* wedding," he said, taking the seat beside her.

"As do I," she said, with a dark look of promise that heated his blood.

"You're not alone," Antonia said with a smile.

"Only it won't be quite so cozy as this, I warn you," Thomas leaned across his wife to say. "Your chapel here would fit nicely into the narthex of ours, and Antonia intends to invite half the shire."

Madeleine's eyebrows moved expressively. "You will frighten him off, Papa."

"Not a chance in ten thousand," Ethan said gamely. He would endure anything to achieve the hand of the woman he loved; and if truth be known, the thought of an overdone wedding was overshadowed by his jubilance that her relatives lived so far away. Although his future father-in-law had learned to tolerate him, and though the viscount had grown quite fond of Antonia, he could not wait to have his bride to *himself*.

He scanned the crowd, his eyes skipping over Leah Abbott, who kept looking at him in a pouting manner, and on to Alice. The portrait of respectability, she stood biting cake beside her besotted new husband, whose gaze lingered on her every move and word. Ethan's emotions tugged to see it. He hoped she would be a good wife to Scott, that she would truly love him.

There was one person he wanted to spend time with but couldn't find. He asked Madeleine to search with him, and she willingly gave her plate to her father and took the viscount's hand. Crossing the hall to the library, they discovered their quarry sitting in Rosemary Danniver's lap. Seeing the look in Ethan's eye, the former teacher smiled and handed him the infant, then slipped quietly from the room.

Snuggling Dorrie in the crook of his arm, Ethan drew Madeleine to the settee, then settled beside her and traced one finger down the babe's cheek. Such soft skin she had, such big eyes that stared trustingly into his.

"I'm going to miss this brat," he said.

Madeleine took one of the baby's tiny hands in hers. "She'll miss you, too."

He laughed. "Dorrie's too small to remember her own fingers."

"Well, you'll see her again; haven't they named us as godparents? Anyway, I think you're wrong about her forgetting. She responds to you in a special way; don't you see how happy she looks in your arms?"

"Do you really think so?"

"Well," she said in a considering tone of voice, "*I* find you special, and I know how wonderful it feels when your arms are around *me*."

He could not ignore so bold a hint and gladly swept his free arm around Madeleine's shoulders and pulled her close for a kiss. Dorrie grunted her objection at being inadvertently squeezed, and both adults chuckled.

"Put your hand on my chest," he ordered Madeleine suddenly. She looked startled, so he added, "Over my heart." Eyes rounded with curiosity, she complied, slipping her fingers beneath his jacket and waistcoat to lie warmly over the thin linen of his shirt. "Do you feel my heart beating?" She smiled, nodding slightly. "That's the rhythm of happiness. Because of you, I'm complete."

Madeleine closed her eyes for an instant and snuggled her head against his shoulder. "When I came to Westhall to satisfy my mother's dying wish, I didn't dream I'd find the love of my life, but that's what has happened. And not only that, but my mother seems to be making a complete recovery!" She faltered. "There is only one thing . . ."

He tipped her chin upward and prompted, "Only one thing . . ."

"That dampens my joy," she added in a small voice. "The—the legend . . ."

Comprehension came into his eyes. "Ah, yes. The curse." He pulled her closer to him. "I'm not afraid of that, my dear, nor should you be. I want you to put superstition from your mind and not think of it again." He glanced down at Dorrie for an instant. "One day, when we are old and have our own children gathered around us for some celebration or other, we will speak of this and laugh."

Her teeth edged over her lower lip. "I can't wait until you're thirty-one."

He gave a grunt of laughter. "Thank you for wishing my life away! The future is uncertain for everyone, my darling. There are no guarantees. That's why we must clutch every moment and savor every morsel life has to offer."

She eased the fingers of one hand around his neck and lay her cheek against his jacket. "I love you so much, Ethan."

He squeezed her to him, then freed his hand to caress her hair. "Do you understand how difficult it is for me not to see you in my arms every time I'm near you? When I approach a room, it's your voice I listen for; your eyes I hope to meet. You're the first woman I've desired to take not only to my bed, but into the secret places of my heart."

He gazed deeply into her eyes and saw something dark emerge: a look of wonder edged with an innocent wildness that made his heart pound more rapidly.

"I can't bear to be alone anymore, not as long as you're in the world," he said. "I want to be with you however long it may be, whether forever or a day."

"I'll take forever," Madeleine said, and guided his lips to hers.

BOOK YOUR PLACE ON OUR WEBSITE AND MAKE THE READING CONNECTION!

We've created a customized website just for our very special readers, where you can get the inside scoop on everything that's going on with Zebra, Pinnacle and Kensington books.

When you come online, you'll have the exciting opportunity to:

- View covers of upcoming books
- Read sample chapters
- Learn about our future publishing schedule (listed by publication month *and author*)
- Find out when your favorite authors will be visiting a city near you
- Search for and order backlist books from our online catalog
- Check out author bios and background information
- Send e-mail to your favorite authors
- Meet the Kensington staff online
- Join us in weekly chats with authors, readers and other guests
- Get writing guidelines
- AND MUCH MORE!

**Visit our website at
http://www.zebrabooks.com**

LOOK FOR THESE REGENCY ROMANCES

ROMANCE FROM JANELLE TAYLOR